OTHER MARC EDWARDS MYSTERIES
BY DON GUTTERIDGE

Turncoat
Solemn Vows
Vital Secrets

DUBIOUS
ALLEGIANCE

A MARC EDWARDS
MYSTERY

DON GUTTERIDGE

A TOUCHSTONE BOOK
Published by Simon & Schuster
New York   London   Toronto   Sydney   New Delhi

Touchstone
A Division of Simon & Schuster, Inc.
1230 Avenue of the Americas
New York, NY 10020

First Touchstone trade paper edition July 2012

TOUCHSTONE and colophon are registered trademarks of Simon & Schuster, Inc.

For information about special discounts for bulk purchases, please contact Simon & Schuster Special Sales at 1-800-268-3216 or CustomerService@simonandschuster.ca.

Manufactured in the United States of America

10 9 8 7 6 5 4 3 2 1

ISBN 978-1-4391-6372-6
ISBN 978-1-4391-7269-8 (ebook)

For Jean McKay, author and friend

ACKNOWLEDGEMENTS

I would like to thank Jan Walter, my editor for this edition, for her insights and tactful suggestions. Thanks also to my dedicated agent, Beverley Slopen, who has been a guiding force behind this series from the outset, and to Alison Clarke and Kevin Hanson of Simon & Schuster, for their continuing faith in the Marc Edwards mysteries.

AUTHOR'S NOTE

Dubious Allegiance is wholly a work of fiction, but the encounters between the rebels and loyalist forces during the rebellions in Upper and Lower Canada are based on the historical record, and the political and societal tensions that fomented the uprisings and fuelled their tragic aftermath—while fictionally represented here—are nonetheless true to the spirit of those difficult times. Particular actions and characterizations attributed to actual historical personages like Charles Gore, Allan MacNab, and Francis Bond Head are fictitious. All other characters are the invention of the author, and any resemblance to persons living or dead is purely coincidental. My rendition of the raids on St. Denis and the death of Captain Weir were materially aided by Joseph Schull's *Rebellion: The Rising in French Canada, 1837*. The serio-comic clash between Mackenzie's "army" and Sheriff Jarvis's pickets on Yonge Street is vividly recounted in Edwin C. Guillet's *The Lives and Times of the Patriots: An Account of the Rebellion in Upper Canada, 1837–38*. Also, in its Appendix of Select Documents can be found a contemporary description of the hanging of Peter Matthews and Samuel Lount. I have taken some imaginative liberties with it, including moving the date up from April to January 1838. In general, though, I have endeavoured throughout to convey the tenor of the period as faithfully as possible.

DUBIOUS
ALLEGIANCE

PROLOGUE

I t is the fall of 1837 and the colonial provinces of Upper Canada (later Ontario) and Lower Canada (Quebec) are on the eve of open revolt. The Reform Party of Upper Canada has tried for years to secure legislation that will alleviate the many grievances suffered under the stern and self-serving Family Compact. This small group of Tories holds control of the Executive Council and the Legislative Council and uses its power to block any such legislation forwarded by the democratically elected Legislative Assembly. Moreover, the new lieutenant-governor, Sir Francis Bond Head, secured a majority of Tories in the Assembly in the election of June 1836. The Reformers are left without hope for relief or justice from the governing institutions. A radical wing of the Reformers under the leadership of fiery William Lyon Mackenzie has begun to agitate in the hinterland, threatening insurrection.

In Lower Canada, the restless French population is suffering harsh oppression at the hands of the English minority and the land-owning French seigneurs. An economic depression brings many habitants in rural Quebec to the brink of starvation, while those in the cities see their numerical majority threatened by massive immigration from Britain. All that is needed is leadership, and the Reform-minded *patriotes* find two in former members of the Legislative Assembly of Lower Canada, Montreal lawyer Louis-Joseph Papineau and Wolfred Nelson, an English-speaking doctor and politician.

Sensing trouble in Lower Canada, Bond Head decides to send all of his regular troops, garrisoned at Toronto, to Montreal to reinforce the regiment there, leaving Upper Canada relatively defenceless. Mackenzie immediately lays plans for a rebel march on the provincial capital.

In Lower Canada, hostilities have already begun. The French rebels under Nelson occupy the town of St. Denis, south of Sorel. The British response is quick and decisive. A large force of regulars, including the Toronto regiment, advances from Montreal to join battle. Life in the Canadian provinces will never be the same.

ONE

I t may not be Waterloo, Marc, but by Christ, it's going to
be a bona fide battle!"

Ensign Rick Hilliard had to shout his enthusiasms
in order to be heard above the roar of the night-wind, even
though he was riding stride for stride beside his superior officer.
Lieutenant Marc Edwards made no reply, but Rick's excitement
could not be dampened.

"Don't you think it was a bold move of the colonel to
march the men down to St. Denis in the dark? The element of
surprise, eh?"

Marc gave him a non-committal grunt but kept his mind
on the business of manoeuvring his mount, a hackney-horse
commandeered at Sorel, through the muddy shoals of what
passed for a road along the east bank of the Richelieu River.

The cold rain had begun not a minute after the battle-group had cleared the outskirts of Sorel and aimed itself southwest towards its target, a fortified position of the rebels just above St. Denis. It comprised four companies of the 24th Regiment, one company of the 32nd, a motley collection of militia cavalry from Montreal, along with a twenty-four-pounder and its artillery crew.

Half an hour later, snow was added to the rain. It was late November in Quebec, and the weather showed no mercy. The wind-gusts were icy and keen as flails against the exposed flesh of face or finger. The chilling damp soon penetrated every crevice of clothing, every nook of body warmth. Uniforms stiffened. Boots grew slick. Footing became treacherous.

"There's something up there in the woods," Marc said.

"I can't even see the woods," Rick said, leaning across his saddle so that he was no more than a foot from Marc's shoulder.

"That shadow up there on your right, at two o'clock."

Shielding his eyes with his right hand, Rick could discern, between gusts of wet snow, the ragged profile of a line of evergreens that must border the nearby river itself. "Yes, I see it now."

"Something moved up there, animal or human. Do you want to have a look?"

Rick grinned and dug his heels into his mount.

"Take some men with you!" Marc called out after him. "If you can find any!"

Marc's squad was at the head of the column to reconnoitre and skirmish with any scouts or advance units of the rebel contingent, should that be necessary. At least that was

Colonel Gore's plan. But the quagmire of the road and the late-November storm, not to mention the pitch dark, reduced the infantryman to a staggering, lurching parody of the proud and fearless redcoat. Should the moon have been perverse enough to burst out and illuminate the scene below it, not a wink of military scarlet would have been visible. At the end of a single hour's march, three hundred of Queen Victoria's finest were caked with mud, boot to cap. Many sank up to their knees in the frigid gumbo, and in a desperate effort to free a boot from permanent lodgment tipped backwards into the mire and had to be helped erect by the nearest upright comrade. And since nothing could be seen in the darkness, the only means of communication was the disembodied shout. The curses and cries of the foot-soldiers could be heard but faintly. Only the roadway guided them, defined by its ribbon of mud between grassy verges, irregular hedgerows, or the ragged vestiges of the autumn's failed crops.

The mounted militia unit from Montreal fared no better than the men on foot. Assigned to protect the flanks of the straggling column, the cavalry floundered about, with more gusto than guile, on the periphery of the slogging riflemen, bumping into each other in the impenetrable murk and periodically stepping on a soldier unable to leap aside. Three of their horses broke a limb in such collisions and had to be shot, the report of the Brown Bess shuddering through the column and momentarily silencing all complaint—a sharp reminder that the mission they had embarked upon was much more than the minor inconvenience of a forced march over inhospitable ground.

But if man and horse had difficulty with the mud, the rain, and the absence of light, then the wagons carrying the supplies, the twenty-four-pounder and its sixty-eight round shot were bound to suffer an even worse journey. A mile above St. Ours, a village halfway between Sorel and their destination, the road had simply vanished into a swampy morass, and the wagons sank to their axles. The men in charge lashed the stalled horses—more in spite than hope—and then had to be themselves rescued by their mates: bootless, chilled to the bone, and too weary to curse God or their officers. Marc had ridden back to one such mêlée, barked orders at a squad of the Montreal cavalry who were milling about ineffectually on the grassy verge of the woods nearby, and soon the wagons and gun carriage had been hauled laterally onto firmer ground, where they proceeded cautiously forward until some semblance of the road reappeared.

"You were right, sir," Hilliard shouted as he rode up beside Marc. "I spotted three fellows, civilians, in that clump of bush over there, but they scampered off into the dark towards the river. I ordered the men to hold their fire and went after them. But they had a little dory of some kind waiting and were out into the river before I could draw my pistol."

"So much for the strategy of surprise," Marc said.

"Well, it was a decent idea in theory," Hilliard said, defending Colonel Gore's unpopular decision to attack St. Denis and the rebels by stealth in the pre-dawn mists. Nor was the mood of men and officers much cheered by the fact that Colonel Gore was deputy quartermaster-general of British forces in the Canadas, a man whose only battle experience to this point had been skirmishing for the high ground of magazine and commissary.

"We'd better keep this news from the rank and file," Marc said. "We can't be sure that those habitants weren't spies or scouts for the rebels."

"Quite right, sir. Although three hundred soldiers marching on a farm road at ten in the evening in a snowstorm is bound to occasion some notice," Rick responded.

As Marc's outriders entered the main street of St. Ours, a sudden peal of church bells rang out from the cathedral tower just ahead in the town square. It was no summons to the faithful, but a clanging cacophony of warning—or threat. When it paused for a minute, in the far distance to the south and east, several more such tocsins echoed ominously across the sombre countryside.

"Jesus," Hilliard said, "the whole damn province knows we're coming."

"Let's hope Colonel Gore has a backup plan," Marc said. "I'd better go and tell him what we've seen and what these bells mean. Have Sergeant Ogletree form up the troop here to wait for the main body of the column to move up."

When Hilliard looked skeptical, Marc said quickly, "Remember, Rick, we are in enemy territory."

Thirty minutes later, near midnight, the full brigade was ready to enter the village. The colonel had allowed the men to pause long enough to scrape the worst of the gumbo off their boots and weapons, and to reassemble into their double column. One of the draught horses died in its frozen harness and had to be extricated and dumped on the roadside. A drummer and two fifers were commanded to strike up their most flamboyant martial air, and the entire column then marched in glorious, daunting formation down the main thoroughfare of St. Ours. The mounted officers and cavalry pranced warily along both flanks. Colonel Gore, a small moustachioed gentleman more adept at whist than war, rode impassively before the gun carriage and its awesome intimidation.

No sniper opened fire from rooftop or belfry. No curtain shifted surreptitiously at its casement. The shrill bells had stopped abruptly. The only sounds were the tramp of boots in unison, the jangling of harness and scabbard, the padded thump of weary horses, and the strident disharmonies of the fife and drum. And while the silence of the town itself was welcomed, it was also eerie, unreadable, and just a little unnerving. So it was with some relief that the column moved out of the village and into the countryside again, to the relative safety of the quagmire.

"I don't suppose it matters all that much whether we surprise Nelson and Papineau at St. Denis," Hilliard said a few minutes later when wet snow and frozen fingers had put an end to the musical escort and the column had begun to unravel once more in the dark. "After all, General Colborne's orders are to move on St. Denis from the north while Lieutenant-Colonel Wetherall attacks from the south."

"In a pincer movement, you mean," Marc said dryly, behind a smile that his good friend could not see.

"Don't you find it exciting that in our first campaign we are going to execute one of the classic battle strategies, going all the way back to Caesar, Alexander, Hannibal—"

"Maybe we should have commandeered a few elephants."

Immune to Marc's ripostes, Hilliard carried on boldly. "And if it's true that Papineau, Nelson, O'Callaghan, and the other rebel leaders are all in St. Denis, then this tin-pot revolt will be put down by this time tomorrow night. If we don't get them, Wetherall will nab them from the south. Their only hope is the American border, and the Yankees are welcome to them!"

"I trust you're not putting Gore and Wetherall, fine gentlemen though they be, on the same rostrum as Caesar and Wellington."

"Well, no. But as unregimented as this rabble up ahead may be, they nonetheless threaten the stability and very future of British North America. The outcome of tomorrow's battle will surely be as significant as Wolfe's vanquishing of Montcalm."

The cry of a beleaguered cavalryman immured in the mud to their left recalled Hilliard to his duty, and he vanished into the swirling snow. That the coming clash of forces was not Waterloo was evident to everyone who had resided in Quebec for more than a month. Despite the rumours and frenetic news reports, no arms or cash had poured in from the republic to the south. Marc knew that Louis-Joseph Papineau, like William Lyon Mackenzie in Upper Canada, was principally a politician, a talker, a negotiator, and a high-stakes gambler. While his followers armed themselves with ageing muskets and pistols, and drilled in pastures in the dead of night, they were, though numerous, not a cohesive army. No man of military stature and experience had stepped forward to take command. So even if the hundreds or thousands who had gathered around the Liberty Pole at Nelson's distillery chose to fight, there would be no classic battle between uniformed, disciplined armies serving under their national flag. What, then, would there be? Shooting, mutual determination, and death. And with Colonel Gore's superior force already exhausted, hungry, and dispirited, who but God knew the outcome. Perhaps Lieutenant-Colonel Wetherall had arrived from Chambly in the south and settled the issue. Certainly, their own colonel's judgement was already suspect.

Everything had begun smartly and according to protocol. The three hundred men and their support units had been mustered with enthusiasm and precision on the wharf at Montreal. The band had stirred the modest crowd of well-wishers to cheers as Colonel Gore led his troops up the gangplank and aboard the *Hochelaga,* bound for Sorel at the mouth of the Richelieu River. Major Owen Jenkin, who had become Marc's friend and surrogate father in the past year, shook Marc's hand and wished him luck before returning to Montreal. Neither of them had been willing to speak of the indefinite postponement of the wedding of Marc and Beth Smallman that had been made necessary by the transfer of Marc's regiment to Quebec. But it was never far from their thoughts.

Then, as the afternoon of November 22 waned, the steamer moved steadily downstream to the occasional shout of encouragement (or otherwise) from the shoreline. By six o'clock, with the sun setting behind foreboding clouds, Sorel was reached. By seven, in a darkness unrelieved by streetlamps— the town could no longer afford such a luxury—fife and drum conducted the colourful brigade to the barracks. Here it was expected they would have their evening meal and rest until daybreak. Horses would be conscripted, extra wagons appropriated, scouts sent out to reconnoiter the riverside terrain, and couriers whisked ahead to Chambly to help co-ordinate the "pincer movement" envisioned by General Colborne, the supreme commander in British North America and an officer who *had* fought at Waterloo.

But eager to make his mark on something other than a requisition form, Colonel Gore had decided on his own merit to choose the age-old tactic of surprise over the more reliable deployment of scouts and dispatch riders. Thus, instead of filing into a warm barracks and a cold supper, the five companies and cavalry troop were commanded, without ado or explanation, to wheel back onto the main street and make for the road to St. Denis. The fog had already begun to turn traitorously into rain and, as the night-cold pressed down upon them, to intermittent snow. Any initial excitement on the part of the soldiers was quickly dampened by the hostile weather. Half a mile out of town, the sprightly music of fife and drum unraveled and died altogether when lips froze to mouthpiece. Then the standard-bearer had tripped on a rut, pitched cap-first into the muck, and watched in helpless horror as the Union Jack sank out of sight in a puddle.

"How are the men faring?" Marc asked his sergeant.

Ogletree, with a face as gnarled and craggy as a habitant woodcarving, peered up at his superior officer. "I spent two years on the Peninsula with the Iron Duke, sir, and I don't recall anythin' as bad as this. The lads are toughin' it out an' keepin' their mutinous thoughts to themselves, but damn it to hell, Lieutenant, if it's much farther to St. Denis, they won't be fit to fight a banty rooster with rickets."

"It's a good ten miles from here, Sergeant."

"An' we're makin' about two miles an hour, luggin' that blasted cannon over this peat-bog of a road. We can't possibly spend another five hours out in this stuff an' then be expected to make a surprise attack on an enemy, who're warm, an' well fed, an' just waitin' fer us to show our mugs."

"I agree, but that seems to be the master plan at the moment." Marc swung down from his mount and dropped beside Ogletree. "I'm going to walk with you and the men. Hilliard can look out for himself. If anyone gets a sniper's bullet, it's likely to be one of those fool militiamen hopping about like hares on a griddle."

Marc immediately felt his right boot being sucked into the mud. The continuous wet snow and rain had begun to turn the stiffened ruts into oozing slime, more liquid than solid. Walking was reduced to slithering, with repeated pulling at one boot or another to prevent it from being sucked away in the stubborn undertow.

"Welcome to our world, sir!" Private Higgins called out behind his superior officer. But there was no malice in the remark. The men increased their pace a little. Twenty minutes later Hilliard and several others of the mounted vanguard drew to a halt.

"What's the problem, Ensign?" Marc said. "Rebels ahead?"

"No, sir. There seems to be two roads instead of one." He looked perplexed, as if a fork in the road were an alien thing, inscrutable as the habitant's lingo he did not comprehend beyond a curse word or two.

"I don't recall our map showing the river road dividing

anywhere near here, sir," Marc said to Captain Riddell, the company commander, when he rode up to see what had caused the stoppage.

"Neither do I, Lieutenant. But then we have not been provided with proper military maps. My instinct is to stick to the river. The *frogs* usually do."

Marc was about to agree when Colonel Gore arrived, looking like a waterlogged peacock. The issue at hand was explained to him. No advice was sought. The deputy quartermaster-general simply waved them towards the narrower road to their left—away from the river and through a dense bush. Officers and men obeyed, as they must.

As he wheeled to ride back to his rear position, the colonel snapped at Marc: "Lieutenant, please get on your horse at once. Your uniform is a disgrace, and you are in danger of demoralizing your men!"

Marc obeyed, as he must.

Along the road to the right that the colonel had disdained to take, an incident was to occur less than half an hour later, one that would be significant in determining the course and nature of the rebellion. Neither the deputy quartermaster-general nor any of his officers or men would be witness to it, but it was recounted to them, again and again and in such horrific detail by those claiming to have been present, that they felt themselves to be not merely witnesses but guilty, even prurient, bystanders. It gave them just cause for revenge and reprisal.

An hour after Gore's brigade departed Sorel, Lieutenant

Jock Weir of the 32nd Regiment arrived there with urgent dispatches from General Colborne: Colonel Gore was to delay his advance on St. Denis until Wetherall arrived from Chambly in two or three days, and even then, should he meet with any resistance, he was to retreat. But Gore was already gone, and with him Jock Weir's uniform and weapons. Undaunted, Weir commandeered a calèche and its driver and, disguised as a Quebec City merchant, set out in pursuit along the river road. But the weather, the near-impassable roadway, and his periodic interception by curious habitants en route made his passage only marginally faster than Gore's column. In the stormy darkness he did not notice the fork in the road beyond St. Ours and so continued on the route that hugged the river.

Two miles outside of St. Denis, and puzzled that he had not yet overtaken Gore's column, he was arrested and soon found himself face-to-face with Dr. Nelson in the rebel leader's living room. The ruse was immediately admitted. Still uncertain about the possibility of an armed clash, Nelson was courteous and conciliatory. He ordered Weir to give his parole, after which he would be taken to St. Charles and kept under house arrest. Old Captain Jalbert, white-haired veteran of the War of 1812 and now a different kind of patriot, was put in charge of the transfer.

Weir was placed in the back of a wagon and bound with a leather belt. Captain Jalbert rode a few paces ahead, resplendent in scarlet sash and upraised sword. The driver was a reluctant conscript, Migneault the postmaster. Beside the prisoner and clutching the belt sat Maillet, a local firebrand. In his right hand he brandished a rusty two-foot bayonet. They set off. It was almost dawn. The road was alive with shadowy male figures making for St. Denis and Nelson's fortification. Others—crouched, wary, female—hurried the other way. The wet snow had softened to a cold mist. Suddenly, several gunshots rang out somewhere behind them. Had it started at last?

Weir flinches, notices that Maillet is dozing, and leaps off the wagon in an attempt to free himself and join the battle he has been waiting for all his life. But Maillet's grip on the belt about his prisoner's waist is unbreakable. Weir gasps as if he has been kicked in the stomach and tumbles against the rim of a rear wheel, face up. Citizen Maillet, fired by the pain of a thousand slights at the hands of the *maudit Anglais,* drives the bayonet through the conqueror's neck. Weir collapses onto the road, blood spouting from his wound. Then he scrambles on hands and knees under the rear wheels. Crazed by the deed he has begun, Maillet reaches down and stabs at Weir through the spokes of the wheel. Weir screams like a gutted cat. The cowled figures on the roadside pause, stare, glower, and close in, like a Greek chorus coming awake in the third act. Postmaster Migneault, horrified, tries to rein in the spooked horses, but they lunge forward, dragging Weir with them under the wagon, tumbling and spraying blood like a grotesque Catherine wheel.

"Officer! Officer!" The chant is taken up, and turned malevolent: among these witnesses there are old wounds and fresh hurts aplenty. As Maillet continues to hack at the helpless Weir, they cheer each blow, dazzled by hate, astonished at its unstoppable irruption.

Three severed fingers lie on the road, the mutilated hand clutches at air, while the bayonet, avid as any guillotine, continues to hack and slash. Weir's moans are liquid, unhuman. Captain Jalbert is trying to bull his way through the maddened throng back to the carnage, but no-one will give way. A young schoolteacher leaps from the mob towards the victim, huddled and groaning under the stalled vehicle, and begins to stab at him with a carving knife.

"For Christ's sake, kill him!" Jalbert screams.

A volunteer, on his way to Nelson, steps up, puts a pistol to Weir's blood-smeared forehead, and pulls the trigger. Nothing happens. He tries again. There is no sound but the ventilation of Weir's agony. A sword whips at the air and reaches Weir's neck. The body pitches forward. But there is breath in it yet. Enraged, the mob drags it across the grass to an alley between two houses. Then in sudden, awed silence they keep vigil until there is not a twitch of pomp or imperialism left to defile the morning breeze.

Days later, Weir's corpse will be recovered from a frozen creek where it had been dumped. There will be no truce now, no negotiated settlement. Rubicons were made for crossing.

TWO

Light was seeping through the mist when Marc's skirmishing party emerged from the rutted morass of the winding pathway Colonel Gore had chosen for his troops. Known locally as the Pot-au-Beurre, it lived up to its name. The grey of exhaustion on the faces of the men matched the mud that coated their tunics and sullied the bright image of the British regiment of foot. No-one had eaten since noon the previous day. The threat of snow and a wintry day lay ominously on the morning air.

"They've seen us!" Hilliard shouted, but there was no alarm in his voice. "Over there, just past that little bridge."

"Which they've just destoyed," Marc observed, urging his mount forward.

Distinguishable as the enemy only by their flowing capotes, the retreating figures suddenly stopped and turned.

"They're going to shoot!"

The pop of musketry was heard, three puffs of smoke rose above the enemy horsemen, and one of the soldiers behind Marc cried out.

"Form up and fire!" Marc called out to Sergeant Ogletree.

Ogletree assembled half a dozen riflemen, and seconds later they fired off an ineffectual volley at the snipers. But it was sufficient to send the rebels scampering south. Three of the British rifles had misfired: damp powder or frozen fingers, no doubt. Colonel Gore and the company captains arrived moments later to survey the situation and develop a plan of attack. Marc and Hilliard, along with the other junior officers, dismounted and stood nearby, hoping for an order to pause, rest, eat, and re-group.

Hilliard had his scope to his right eye. "I can see the tops of the distillery buildings, sir. And there's a huge stone house in front of them. They've knocked loopholes in the walls. And there's a makeshift barricade of broken wagons and farm implements ringing it. The riverbank is close to the right, so that flank can't be used to approach or enfilade. On the left there's a small woods and a group of barns and outhouses. They'll be nested in there and difficult to take out."

"What's the good news?" Marc asked wanly. He found himself leaning against his horse, suddenly faint from hunger and fatigue. Where would the infantry, who had struggled for eight hours on foot, find the resources to mount an all-out attack on a well-fortified position? In an open-field engagement, the superior training, ingrained discipline, and proven weaponry of the British troops would make short shrift of any collection of rebels—whatever their advantage in numbers and however committed they might be. But the rebels would not be foolish enough to come out and fight, as Montcalm had.

"There's a coulee about a hundred yards in front of the stone house," Rick enthused. "It will give us all the cover we'll need. The Frenchies certainly won't abandon their fortification to attack us there, not with a cavalry unit to protect our flanks. And they don't know, poor fools, that Wetherall is moving up the river road from Chambly. If our pincer movement goes as planned, all we need to do is dig in here and wait for Wetherall and his gunners, and then hit the buggers from three sides."

"I agree," Marc said. "We can hunker down and wait. And cook ourselves an English breakfast."

"You look as if you'd fall asleep in the middle of it." Hilliard's own eyes were as bright as a baby's after a nap. The thrill of what was to come was keeping him alert and eager.

"We'll need time for the men to check out their rifles and dry their powder. It would be suicidal to send them out there now."

"What are the odds of that?" Hilliard asked glumly.

"The odds are very good." It was Captain Riddell, who had just ridden over from the colonel's briefing. "All companies, including the cavalry and the artillery crew, are to move immediately into that coulee ahead and prepare themselves for an assault on the stone house. Our company will form up on the right flank, and then escort the gun and its crew up to a big barn on the riverbank. We'll clear out any skirmishers and snipers, secure the area, and protect the gunners at all costs. From that position we'll blast that farmhouse to the far reaches of hell!"

"Yes, sir," Marc said. "Ensign, will you—"

But Hilliard was already seeking out the sergeant and the men he would, at long last, lead into battle.

It took almost half an hour to get the twenty-four-pounder and its ammunition wagon across the creek at the bottom of the coulee. Thick limbs had to be cut from a nearby copse of hardwoods—by hands already stiff, swollen, and frostbitten—and jammed into the shallow, icy stream to form a makeshift bridge. All the while, the enemy took potshots from a variety of vantage-points close by, harried but not silenced by the loyal volunteer cavalry from Montreal, who lunged and darted fearsomely at the sound of any metallic click.

"They're more likely to shoot us or each other," Marc muttered, as he lent his shoulder to those already heaving the gun carriage onto the far bank of the creek.

"Let them know we're here!" the colonel barked.

Minutes later, with the gun unlimbered, entrenched, and loaded, the air shuddered as a solid shot whizzed in a deadly arc towards the stone house. It sailed unimpeded through an open window on the second floor. The thundering crash of its havoc and the terrified yelling inside indicated a successful hit. The men cheered. Spirits rose. Sometime soon they might even be warm.

Captain Riddell gathered his company of sixty about him on the right sector of the coulee they were using for cover. The enemy had littered it with broken plough shares and rusted harrows that could slice a foot or leg in two if one were careless.

But crouched low or kneeling on the half-frozen ground, the men were safe from snipers.

"We're to go up and clear the skirmishers out of that barn and secure a permanent position for the gun," the captain announced again. "Lieutenant Edwards will lead his squad out first. The other three will accompany the gun."

Marc noted that a ploughed field ran all the way from the right edge of the coulee to the river. They would have to cross it to get to the barn. The relimbered gun and ammo carriage would have to traverse the same terrain. They were all on foot now. Anyone above saddle height would soon be dead. The inexperienced cavalry unit was back in reserve, guarding their rear and their exposed left flank.

With swords drawn and held aloft, Marc and Hilliard began sprinting across the furrowed field. Ogletree and his troop of fifteen came scampering behind. It had started to snow. The furrows were as slippery as rain-slicked ice. The men skidded, toppled, staggered upright—keeping their Brown Besses aloft as best they could—and followed their officers. Grim and determined, Sergeant Ogletree kept a step behind the men to encourage any malingerers. A ragged volley of shots poured out of the barn twenty yards ahead. Marc could hear the plump and sizzle of lead balls and pellets in the ground around him. One of the men was hit and collapsed, clutching his left calf.

"Get down!" Marc yelled. The riflemen, who could do so only when commanded, obeyed instantly. "You, too, Ensign!"

As soon as the next volley whistled harmlessly over their prone bodies, Marc gave his next order. "Fix bayonets and prepare to charge."

"Ready, sir!" Ogletree said.

Marc raised his body as gracefully as his stiffening limbs would allow, then his sword, and brought it down as the signal to move forward. The men began to shout and ululate, their razor-sharp bayonets pointed straight ahead, and in a double line made a dash for the wide door of the barn. The rebels broke and ran from the barn without firing another round, retreating towards the barricade in front of the stone house.

"Advance rank, kneel and fire!"

A wave of bullets rocketed over the ploughed field, and several rebels screamed and fell. They were dragged, twisted and howling, to safety. All but one. His right hand rose slowly, as if in supplication, then dropped. No further movement was seen.

Hilliard hurled himself against the barn door and bounced backwards. Marc pulled it open and stepped inside, bracing for the bullet he expected from the sniper who would have been left behind to make them pay for this ground. His own pistol was already drawn. Something flickered in the gloom above the loft. Marc wheeled and fired in the same instant as the sniper. There was a single deafening explosion, and the stud behind his shoulder crackled. Then came a second explosion nearby. The sniper pitched over the edge of the haymow and fell wordlessly to the floor. His throat had been blown out. A few twitches and he lay still in a grotesque pose.

"He had a second pistol," Hilliard said quickly. "I had to shoot without aiming."

Marc smiled his thanks. "Have the men search this place thoroughly, Rick. I'll go out and signal the gunners to move up."

With a full company of sixty men firing timed volleys over the barricade, the gun was dragged and bullied over the ploughed field to the side of the barn, which would provide partial cover. But as soon as the enemy saw the twenty-four-pounder being settled into position and pointed straight at the stone house, they began firing upon the gun-crew from isolated bits of cover beyond the barricade. With the rebels' fire erupting randomly from several directions, organized volleys were of little use against them.

"Fire at will!" Captain Riddell shouted.

But it was too late for three of the gunners who had dropped against the barrel of their weapon and now slid slowly to the ground.

"Get a stretcher for those men!" Marc cried.

"Move up! Move up!"

Four more members of the gun-crew clambered warily up to the cannon, and began preparing it to fire. The rammer took several shotgun pellets in his back, writhed in pain, but still managed to get the wadding in. The shot that had been taken from below had provided the crew with the approximate range, and with some confidence the fuse was touched. The earth itself seemed to recoil. Marc saw but did not hear the cannonball clang against the lower part of the stone wall of the rebel headquarters. It bounced off. There wasn't a dint in the stonework: it was three feet thick.

Two more shots produced a similar result. Another gunner was hit in the face, his lower jaw blown away. The men protecting him were also exposed and vulnerable. Captain Riddell ordered the gunners to hunker down and fire only when they thought it safe to do so. He waved all but six men back down to the coulee. It was obvious now that they would have to attack the stronghold directly or re-group and wait for Colonel Wetherall to arrive from Chambly. But their own colonel—safe in the coulee, invigorated by an infusion of brandy, and determined to do his duty—called upon Major Markham, his most experienced officer, to take three companies and mount an assault on the house from the left flank. That it was now midmorning, that the troops hadn't eaten in twenty-two hours, that they had been exposed to the wet and chill for twelve hours, that they were exhausted from their forced march, that rebel reinforcements could be seen crossing the river below the village—none of this could deflect Colonel Gore from his sacred responsibilities.

Major Markham offered Marc's company the opportunity to cover themselves in glory.

While the rolling ground to the left of the stone house and the village that sprawled behind it were unploughed, they were dotted with small outbuildings, haystacks, capsized wagons, and clumps of dwarf cedars—any of which would provide perfect cover for enemy riflemen. And while the rebel group was not an army in any conventional sense of the term, many of its members were hunters and, of necessity, expert marksmen. They would have to be dislodged one by one, by troops moving against them over open ground. Had they been British regulars, the cavalry might have been given the task of an initial, harassing charge, but there was no thought of sending in the unseasoned Montrealers: they were best deployed patrolling the flanks of the units still hunkered down in the coulee. The only positive aspect of Colonel Gore's hastily devised tactic was that enemy enfilading fire from the stone house itself would not reach Markham's attackers on the left. The fight there would be hand-to-hand, face-to-face.

These thoughts were running through Marc's mind as he crouched at the edge of the coulee, shivering and waiting for the major's command to advance. The trembling that now rippled through his entire body was not wholly due to cold and hunger. The implications of his narrow escape up there in the barn on the riverbank had struck him suddenly and unawares. He had come under fire more than once since his arrival in Canada two and a half years ago, and had, in his own mind at any rate, acquitted himself honourably. His courage had been severely tested, and proved to be both stout and durable. Then why was he now shaking so hard he could not draw his sabre out of its scabbard? The sniper's bullet had slammed into a beam not two inches from his right ear. If Rick had not shot the man dead an instant later, the sniper's second shot would surely have hit the mark. And he would be dead, too, or as good as. He had promised Beth that he would live, but that vow was out of his hands: however brave he might be, however righteous his cause (and that was increasingly moot), however dedicated to his duty he might be, any random bullet might end his life at any moment and leave Beth alone and forsaken. Still, she had given him leave—commanded him, as it were, with the force of her love—to do his duty, whatever it entailed, and then return, the slate between them wiped clean and their life together begun anew.

But if he were to survive and keep his vow, should he not, in the least, be prudent in his deportment on the battlefield? Could he not be a worthy officer without trying to play the hero? Rick had flung himself against that barn door in a quixotic effort to be the first man in: he seemed to have a compulsion to prove himself heroic. Why then had he deliberately upstaged Rick by dashing in ahead of him? Had that been deliberate, too?

The trembling eased enough for Marc to pull out his sabre in preparation for the charge against the first of the outbuildings about forty yards ahead on the left. Thoughts like these—uncertainties and doubts really—had rarely crossed his mind during past dangers. Perhaps the others crouched behind him and waiting for him to lead them by his own example were suffering similar qualms. He could not tell.

"Move out!" Major Markham's cry rang through the snow-filled air.

Marc's shout joined the chorus of his comrades as they rose as one and dashed into the fearful spaces between them and death.

The first objective was a half-log cowshed from which a number of shots had been fired throughout the morning. Thirty yards to its left a stand of evergreens presented the possibility of sniper fire or a sudden assault against any force attacking the shed. Marc's troop was advancing on this left flank in the running crouch preferred by the infantry. When Marc barked out an order, his squad dropped to their knees and loosed a volley at the target ahead. A few bullets sailed through the several windows, but those striking the wall might as well have been fired into the air. Seconds after this volley, blackened faces popped into view above the windowsills and prepared to return fire.

The major had anticipated this, and the squad on Marc's right were already on their knees and aiming. But before they could unleash their volley, gunshots erupted from the copse on the left and several redcoats fell, including the lieutenant about to give the order to fire. When the volley did come, erratic and mis-timed, it scattered only a few wood chips. The snipers in the evergreen copse kept at it. Marc heard a groan to his right and turned to see Private Higgins on one knee, both hands scrabbling at his stomach, as if he were a boy searching his pockets for a missing rabbit's foot.

"Pull back!" the major called out.

Dragging their wounded with them, the men retreated. Higgins was carried to the rear of the coulee, where the surgeon had set up shop. Major Markham had a flesh wound in his thigh but waved off medical attention.

"We'll have to clear out that bit of woods if we hope to take the shed," the major was saying to his captains. "Riddell, take all of your company and have a go at them. The other two companies will come at the shed from angles left and right. Each troop will fire staggered volleys. The first unit there will go straight in."

Hilliard came up beside Marc, breathless and glassy-eyed. "We get the dangerous work, eh, Marc?"

"It's all dangerous."

"Aren't we lucky, though?"

It will be entirely a matter of luck, Marc thought, but decided not to share this insight with his friend.

Three-pronged and carefully planned, the next assault began a few minutes later. Marc's troop, along with the rest of Riddell's fifty strong company, made directly for the copse. Firing volleys blindly in staggered sequence, they succeeded in stemming the enemy fire from that source while the other two companies closed in on the cowshed. Both groups took casualties. The rebels seemed able to fire from every side except the rear. Every overturned wagon or haystack harboured a sharpshooter. With Hilliard running ahead—sabre brandished, ululating—Marc's squad roared into the little woods. It was empty. No rebel offered his belly to the bayonet.

"Keep going!" Marc called out.

They emerged on the far side, prepared to give chase. But thirty-five yards ahead stood a log rampart, hastily constructed of nearby corral railings with gun-slits arranged at intervals. A wave of shotgun explosions shattered the air above the din of the battle now going on around the cowshed on the right. Marc heard the spruce boughs on either side of him rattle, and felt a sharp blow, like a tack hammer's sting, at his waist. He dropped to his knees. There was no pain. Around him came terrified screams and low moaning. They had been ambushed. He opened his mouth to sound the retreat, but no words came out. With eyes full of righteous anger and a single rivulet of blood on one cheek, Hilliard looked quizzically at his superior officer.

Marc swung his sabre frantically.

Hilliard nodded and yelled, "Back into the bush, lads! It's a trap!"

Marc staggered into the trees. Three of his men lay writhing out in the open. He took a moment to examine his wound. There wasn't one. The bird shot had barely penetrated his jacket, with its extra armour of mud.

"Are you hurt?" Hilliard asked, kneeling down.

"I'm all right. We need to get the wounded back in here."

Sergeant Ogletree and three others managed to haul them into cover, protected by several volleys from the fellow troop next to them, which had also been strafed and had retreated to the safety of the evergreens. Captain Riddell's voice could now be heard hollering orders, encouragement, or castigation above the crackling of the gunfire, the fast-falling snow, and the smothering spruce boughs. Heavy fighting seemed to be going on over by the cowshed on their right. The odour of cordite was thickening the air around them.

Marc's squad was commanded to provide covering volleys for a full-company attack on the log-rampart. But the poor visibility—intermittent as a north wind gusted and died—made it difficult to see whether their volleys were having any effect, while the assault itself quickly bogged down before the rampart was reached. The ground was again littered with the wounded and those pinned there by the enemy, who seemed able to shoot from spots both hidden and implausible. Marc was surprised, and more than a little disappointed, that the lives of his men would be put at such risk in an assault carried out without the aid of maps, advance scouting, or any real knowledge of the rebels' terrain, battle strength, or opportunities for defence.

When the snow let up briefly, it was evident that the frontal attack on the rampart had failed. Men were being dragged back to the copse by their comrades, one of them an ensign with his arm swinging loosely, like the empty sleeve of a jacket. Then, without warning, a dozen rebels rose up above the rampart and aimed their ragtag weapons at the retreating and wholly vulnerable redcoats. Marc screamed the order for a full volley, but the rebels had figured out the timing between volleys and knew they had twenty seconds to inflict severe damage on the exposed British.

Suddenly, before the rebels had time to begin firing, the pounding of hoofbeats shook the ground nearby, and a troop of Montreal cavalry burst around the northern end of the copse and made a thunderous charge at the rampart. Several of them were now firing their pistols, so that between the shock of see-ing horses charging out of the snowy squalls like beasts from the Apocalypse and the deadly snap of pistol fire, the rebels balked momentarily, then dropped out of sight behind their barricade. Meanwhile, the wounded infantrymen and their res-cuers made it back to the shelter of the trees.

Before the Montreal volunteers could reach the rampart and bring their swords into play, the rebels had regained their gun-slits and begun firing, desperately and blindly. But a horse is a large target, and here there was no respect for the martial animal, no code of conduct to be recognized and honoured. Half a dozen of the noble creatures collapsed in undignified heaps, tossing their riders awry and shrieking piteously. Dazed, with limbs bruised or broken, the Montrealers staggered away in several directions. Only a series of sharp volleys from the riflemen in the copse kept the enemy at bay long enough for those unhorsed volunteers to find their way back. Those who managed to remain mounted had to veer around their fallen comrades or their dying beasts. They broke apart and scattered. But foolishly brave though they might have been, they had saved perhaps a dozen lives by their impetuous gambit.

"Christ, Marc. I thought these Frenchies would be a bunch of yokels and misfits," Hilliard said.

"They may well be," Marc said, "but we've chosen to fight them on their home ground. They've got muskets, rifles, ammo . . . and a cause."

Sergeant Ogletree arrived to inform Marc that the captain had decided to try to clear the rebels from the rampart by attempting to encircle it from both sides. Marc's troop was again to provide covering fire until the flanking movements were well under way, then they were to storm the barricade with bayonets at the ready while the enemy was distracted. But the company would wait ten minutes or so to begin the assault in the hope that the snow might start up again.

Marc was only half paying attention. His eye had caught sight of a horse in its death throes about twenty yards from the rampart. Its lips were foaming, and one huge eye was slowly rolling to a ghastly stop. And trapped underneath the animal's hindquarters was its rider. He was on his stomach, so the only way he could attempt to raise the dying creature's haunches off the lower part of his own body was by rising up onto his knees. But the dead weight was too much for him, and he was now clawing at the earth with both hands in a fruitless effort to pull himself free. Fortunately, he was facing the little woods, with the animal's bulk shielding his presence, and plight, from the rebels behind the barricade. Any sounds he might have been making were drowned out by the continuing fire from skirmishes going on over by the outbuildings and the stone house.

"We can't just leave him out there," Hilliard said. And he took a step towards the open ground.

Marc put a hand on his shoulder. "I'll go," he said, and, without looking back, he rushed towards the stricken man in a low, trotting crouch, well within the range of any rifles poking out of the improvised loopholes in the enemy barricade. But it wasn't until he had dropped down beside the surprised, and terrified, horseman that the first shots snapped at the breeze. One of them struck the upraised foreleg of the horse and shattered the bone.

"It's all right, I'm British," Marc said reassuringly. He realized that in his mud-caked clothes he could have been anyone: only his shako cap would be a certain sign of his allegiance.

"I can't move my legs! I can't feel my foot!" The "officer" turned out to be a corporal, a young man no more than twenty or so, beardless, handsome despite his pain-distorted features and glazed, goitered stare.

"I've got to lever the hindquarters of your horse so you can drag yourself free," Marc said. "Then we'll have to make a sprint for it. If we're lucky, one of the troops in the woods will give us a volley to get us started."

"Why doesn't Prince move? I can't get him to move!" The lad's cry was anguished.

"Your horse is dead," Marc said, as he drew his sabre carefully from its scabbard without raising his head above the cover being provided by the faithful Prince. The shooting had stopped, but Marc knew that the rebels would be waiting for the next act in this diverting little drama. Perhaps he should just wait here until the next assault began. But he was supposed to be leading a phase of it: technically, he had deserted his post. Moreover, his clambering about in the middle of the attack zone could well interfere with any covering or distracting volleys being planned. He would have to risk returning now. His concern for an individual soldier had overridden his duty to the troop and the company.

The corporal groaned horribly, either at the news of Prince's demise or his own considerable pain.

"Hang on. I'm going to lift up the horse's rump as far as I can, then you'll have to do the rest. And it's going to hurt. If you can't manage it, we're both dead men."

The lad's eyes widened. "I'll manage it, sir."

"Good. Now here we go!"

Marc wedged the flat blade of his sword as far under the horse's huge thigh as he could; then, using his shoulder for leverage, he began slowly to lift, mustering all his waning strength in the effort. Even so, he could not have levered the beast nearly enough for his comrade to pull free if the latter had not had the good fortune to lie in a small furrow. Marc merely needed to raise the dead weight up about five inches. However, as soon as the rebel sharpshooters spotted the horse apparently moving, they began firing. One bullet knocked Marc's cap askew; others slammed into Prince's body. His master gasped with each insult.

"Dig your hands in and pull!" Marc cried. "I can't hold this thing up much longer!" Cold sweat was pouring down his face.

The young man did as he was ordered, letting out a bone-chilling shriek with each inch that he moved his crushed legs. He had to extricate himself by using only the upper part of his body, as his legs appeared to be lifeless. Marc's shoulder, arms, and hands started to go numb. In another second he would have to let go. Bullets continued to whiz over his head or thud into the horse. With a wheezing gasp, Marc released the sabre. The corporal screamed as if he had been gelded.

Marc forced himself to look over at him. The young man's legs—one of them askew—were completely free. His face was grey and awash with sweat. He was trembling uncontrollably. His lips were working, but he was unable to speak.

"One of your legs is broken," Marc said. "The other is likely numb, but you may be able to stand on it. When I say 'go,' I want you to raise both arms. I'm going to haul you up, and we're going to make a run for it as if we're in a three-legged race. Understand?"

When no words would come, the young man nodded his assent.

Just then a volley of gunfire roared out of the woods. Hilliard had been watching Marc's every move. He was giving them four or five seconds of relief from the sniper fire.

"Go!"

The pounding of Marc's heart and the rasping of his breath

drowned out the corporal's shrieks as the two men rose up, crab-like, against the horizon, and started to scuttle raggedly towards the woods. There could be no more covering fire now. They were silhouetted against the treeline like ducks in a shooting gallery. *Forgive me,* Marc whispered to Beth, who was always somewhere close by, as he braced for the bullet that would end his life and break his promise. Several of them skidded through the grass at his feet. The lad's legs were useless. He had fainted with pain or terror. Marc picked him up in both arms, just as a fresh thought struck him: I will die with an enemy bullet in my back!

But there were no more bursts of gunfire. The air about him had gone ominously quiet. Yet he was still moving: he could feel his boots thudding on the frost-hardened ground. He could feel the wind gusting and pulling on his tunic. He could feel snow on his cheeks. Snow. He was running—camou-flaged—through a squall.

"This way! This way!" It was Hilliard's voice, soon joined by a chorus of others, orienting him as a rattling cup does a blind man.

Seconds later he collapsed into a tangle of spruce boughs.

"You made it!" Hilliard declared, beside him. And there was awe in his voice.

The rescued man was taken back to the surgeon. No-one in Marc's company knew his name, and he was soon forgotten as Captain Riddell's plan to take the barricade was now ready to be executed. The brief squall that had saved Marc's life was now over. The air was clear and cold again. Sporadic gunfire to the right indicated that the main battle was still progressing. Marc was grateful that his squad had been designated to provide only the covering fire for Riddell's pincered assault, as the adrenaline that had kept him going till now was fast draining away and not likely to return. He ordered Hilliard to direct the opening volleys, while he sat on his haunches and took deep breaths. Some sodden biscuit had been brought up, and he nibbled at it dutifully. Once the flanking troops had succeeded in nearing the sides of the log-rampart, he knew he would have to find some reserve of strength to lead his squad on the frontal assault and hand-to-hand fighting with sabre and bayonet.

He heard the opening volleys, then the individual gunfire of the advancing troops, left and right.

"They're pinned down already," Hilliard informed him. "We've got to go in now, or our fellows will be cut to pieces."

Marc tottered to his feet. "Sergeant," he said to Ogletree, "have the men fix bayonets. We're going to clear those buggers from that pile of poles!"

Moments later, Marc found himself leading the charge across ground that he had already traversed twice. The enemy gunfire on both flanks of the rampart had stopped abruptly. The rebels must have guessed at the plan and were hastily reassembling at their gun-slits to take on the frontal assault. Dodging dead horses and two fallen comrades, Marc's men sallied towards the barricade, bayonets brandished and voices roaring with menace and bravado. At the same time, the troops on either flank began to rise and make a dash towards the same target. This was it. Once in such motion, no British infantry unit could be stopped, short of annihilation.

THREE

Having cleared the left flank of skirmishers and enfilading sniper fire, Captain Riddell's company now turned its attention to assisting the main assault force. Major Markham had abandoned any attempt at a systematic infantry charge: all personnel were firing at will, whenever they could locate the source of enemy strafing. The battle was being waged on the rebels' terrain using their own favoured tactics: hit, run, hide, and hit again. Even so, a number of sheds and barns had been cleared, at some cost, and gradually the rebels were being herded into an ever more crowded and shrunken territory. If General Colborne had given Gore double the complement of troops—or if Gore had not exhausted the ones he had in a fruitless forced march aimed at surprise—then sheer persistence and willingness to take casualties would have worn the enemy down and eventually resulted in a bloody but complete victory. As things now stood, there were simply not enough rested and motivated regulars to do the job. Major Markham himself had been stalled but not stopped by two wounds to his neck.

"We'll take that barn over there," Marc said to Hilliard and Ogletree, who was dragging one leg behind him. Spurts of gun-smoke issued from the cracks in the rotting barn-board, and the soldier beside Ogletree clutched at his thigh and spun to the ground.

"Spread out and approach when you can!"

A dozen men dropped low, grateful for the cautionary order. While sporadic, the fire from the barn was hazardous enough to keep Marc's men pinned down. He thought of ordering a series of timed volleys, but the exposed men would be cut to pieces with little tangible result. As soon as the rebels spotted any threatening activity, they got off as many rounds as they dared, then seemed to dive into the hollows or behind stout obstacles so that any return fire or volley thundered by without harm. Again, if they had had more men, such a defensive tactic would have quickly failed: the sheer firepower and discipline of the regulars would have proven too much. Even Marc, a novice in these affairs, could see that if they took too many casualties, the colonel's base and the command post itself would be vulnerable to a counterattack. The rebels might already be moving squads across the Richelieu downstream of them to spring upon Gore from the rear. The colonel's entire strategy had been poorly conceived and hastily carried out. Moreover, even as his troops pressed the defenders back towards the fortified house, marksmen from that quarter were now almost in range. Every ten minutes or so, a solid shot from the twenty-four-pounder over on the riverbank smashed into the stone façade of the house and bounced off with a pathetic clang. Not a single stone had been chipped away in several hours of shelling.

"I don't think the men have the stomach for a bayonet charge," Hilliard said to Marc. "They're asleep on their feet."

"We'll go in first, then," Marc said.

Rick Hilliard's eyes lit up. "And this time they won't be able to scuttle off; there's only one door on that barn, and we're going in through it."

Marc motioned to Sergeant Ogletree to provide some distracting fire, drew his pistol, raised his sabre, and ran stride for stride with Hilliard towards the door of the barn. Bullets whizzed by, though from which side was unclear. But they reached the door together, unmarked. Hilliard's shoulder struck it a split second before Marc's.

At first they could see nothing. Bits of sombre November light were leaking through myriad cracks in the barn-board and irradiating ripples of hay-dust. Several bales of straw had been propped up along the walls where the rebels had squatted and buttressed their musket-barrels, but there were no musketeers now manning these posts. It was as quiet and eerie as the apse of an empty cathedral. The two men stood stock-still, perplexed.

"Where in hell did they all go?" Hilliard whispered.

"There!" Marc cried.

In the far right corner, where a sort of manger had once been, they saw the legs of a dark figure wriggling frantically. The rebels had devised a quick-escape hatch, but one of them had not quite made it out. Hilliard was the first to move.

In two bounds he was standing over the rebel with his sabre raised. Accompanied by a guttural cry of triumph or anger, its blade descended in a violent arc and sliced through the flesh of the man's buttocks till it struck bone. His howl rattled the barn-boards and sent the dust-motes aflutter.

Marc cringed, horrified. But some fury, too long pent up and whetted by fatigue and frustration, had taken hold of Hilliard. He reached down, grabbed the screaming rebel by the feet, and dragged his body back into the ghastly light of the little barn. Then he flipped it over, face up. The poor devil was choking on his own sobs and hyperventilating. The eyes were bulbous with shock and disbelief. But these grotesqueries were not what brought both Hilliard and Marc to a stunned halt: the rebel was a boy, no more than sixteen or seventeen. And he was gaunt, almost fleshless, his skin sagging on the bones of his cheeks.

"Christ," Marc breathed, "he's damn near starved. I've seen beggars outside Bedlam with more flesh on them."

Hilliard raised his sabre and drove it through the boy's ribs into his heart. He died with a long, accusing wheeze.

Marc fell back against the wall, dizzy and trembling.

"I've killed him," Hilliard said, as if somehow surprised at the consequences of his own savage action.

Just then a ragged sequence of shots came singing through the rotting walls and slammed into the nearby posts and studding around them. Marc and Rick dropped to their knees without ceremony.

"Now they've got us trapped in here," Marc said.

"We can wait for Ogletree and the men to move up."

"I've got to get back to the troop," Marc said. "They should be covering the door if they're still in position." A bullet struck the post behind Marc and sent splinters of it flying about his head. "We can't stay in here anyway."

"All right, out the door it is," Hilliard said with customary bravura, but his lower lip was trembling like a child resisting tears. Neither man looked over at the bloody corpse.

They rose together, bent low. Hilliard pushed the splintered door open and dashed boldly out into the mêlée. Marc was a step behind him. Hilliard skidded on the greasy snow and tumbled forward. Unable to stop, Marc tripped and landed beside him. Some part of Marc wanted to laugh at such a boyish pratfall, at the shared embarrassment of two playful companions at ease with their giddiness. He rolled over and came nose to nose with Rick.

"So far, so good," he heard himself say, with a barely suppressed giggle. Was he going mad? Was this the evidence of battle fatigue?

Rick, too, had a funny look on his face, as if he were about to tell a joke but had just forgotten it. "I think I've been hit," he said.

"Jesus! Where?" Marc pulled himself up over Hilliard, who had turned partway onto his back. Shouts and explosions roared wildly, randomly, insanely about them.

"Down here. I can feel . . ." Suddenly, Rick's eyes began to close, like a slow curtain at the end of a melodrama. His mouth hung open, waiting for the word that did not reach it. His head lolled back, and he lay still.

Paying no heed to the murderous fire around him, Marc

leaned over Rick, pulled his jacket open, and lay an ear against his chest. He heard a heartbeat: faint but steady. Against his own rising panic, he poked blindly about below Hilliard's waist till he felt the sticky ooze of blood. Rick had been hit some-where in the bowel or groin. And he was bleeding profusely.

Marc took a moment to survey his situation. It was quickly apparent that the assault had bogged down again. Most of the rebels appeared to have been pushed back into the fortified en-virons of the stone house, but with their backs to the wall, as it were, they were now raining a deadly and persistent fire upon the exposed regulars, who were hopelessly battered from the effort required to get this far. He saw Major Markham being dragged onto a stretcher. Marc's own squad were scattered and now leaderless. He knew where his duty lay.

But he did not go there. Instead, he picked up the uncon-scious body of his friend as gently as he could, laid it across his right shoulder, and began to trot back down towards the cou-lee, and the surgeon's tent. He had taken only ten paces or so before he had to stop, drop to one knee, and catch his breath.

Somewhere behind him a tumultuous shout rose above the roar of battle. Marc turned to see where it had come from. Could it be Colonel Wetherall arriving from Chambly with re-inforcements? Were they to be saved at the eleventh hour?

From the woods near the distillery several hundred fresh rebel troops came running across a ploughed field and a pas-ture, howling like Iroquois on a rampage. At the same time a second force materialized out of the bottomland along the river, threatening the cannon nearby. The defenders in the stone house had decided it was time to counterattack. But it was the approach of the group from the woods that brought Marc upright and incredulous. There wasn't a single gun amongst them. They were armed with pitchforks, axe-handles, and mattocks—and a fury fueled by hunger, humiliation, and the knowledge that some kinds of death are more necessary than others.

Suddenly, cries of "Fall back!" could be heard, faintly, from the lips of officers. Men were scampering backwards past Marc. He picked up Hilliard as he would a child, and joined them, Rick's breath still warming his right cheek.

Moments later, a bugle sounded the unthinkable: three hundred British regulars—heirs to the reflected glories of Waterloo, Culloden, and Agincourt—were in full retreat: beaten back by a rump parliament of farmers, tradesmen, and ordinary folk of every ilk.

Marc's horse plodded wearily but dutifully alongside the scarlet ambulance-wagon that carried several of the wounded men, including Rick Hilliard. A light snow was falling, silent and peaceful, upon the length of the retreating column. It was after midnight, and they had just pulled out of St. Ours, little more than halfway to Sorel. Fortunately, one of the foraging parties had discovered a cache of potatoes in a barn en route, and Colonel Gore had consented to let the men stop long enough to roast them over an inconspicuous fire. Now they were back on the river road, the exhaustion of defeat added to the physical and mental fatigue exacted by the preceding thirty hours. A few of the mounted militia rode in desultory loops about the flanks

of the column, but no organized pursuit or ambush materialized to harry them or provide some welcome distraction from
the brooding weight of their failure.

Rick had had his abdominal wound dressed to the point
where any external bleeding had been stanched, but what was
happening internally could only be guessed at. Rick remained
unconscious. His breathing was either shallow or intermit-
tently sharp and aching. Marc had removed his greatcoat and
wrapped Rick in it. He never left his friend's side, fearing that
a sudden pain might cause him to move abruptly and loosen
the cotton packing that had stopped the bleeding. But the
only movement so far had been the anxious rise and fall of his
breathing.

The retreat from St. Denis had been neither orderly nor dig-
nified. Once again Colonel Gore had not let the possibility of
such a manoeuvre enter his wizened imagination. As a result of
their initial haste, three or four wounded men had been abandoned on the battlefield, left to the tender mercies of the rebels.
The twenty-four-pounder was dragged down from its useless
perch (sixty of the sixty-eight rounds having been expended),
limbered, and hauled towards the makeshift log-bridge constructed earlier in the day. But after bearing the weight of
almost three hundred retreating men and a dozen wagons,
the bridge collapsed of its own volition just as the cannon was
crossing it. The gun was tossed sideways into the muddy water.
With enemy skirmishers harassing them on three sides, and the
danger of more cutting off their retreat as they crossed the river,
Gore continued to shriek commands at the exhausted men and
beasts. Half a dozen of the latter died in the traces and had to

be replaced by cavalry horses. The gun was hopelessly stuck, but Gore refused to abandon and spike it until the surgeon warned him that the men themselves would soon die beside the animals. As a result of this unnecessary delay, it had been dark before the column got started up the river road towards St. Ours and Sorel. The whoops of triumph from the rebels sang in their ears like a bully's taunt. Fortunately, they were permitted to slink away, licking their wounds.

No-one spoke. They were too numb to complain. It took energy to moan. The dried mud on their uniforms had caked and, whitened by the snow, made the men resemble perambulating ghosts. Marc was trying hard not to think about his own brush with death, about Rick's savage anger and quixotic courage, about the colonel's stubborn stupidity, about the patchwork army of half-starved youths who had humiliated them. There was nothing Napoleonic or glorifying about Papineau's forces: they were fighting only to live, and be.

"Could you spare a smoke?"

The sound of an English voice uttering a full sentence startled Marc, and he glanced about in search of its author. None of the men tramping near him had looked up or shifted his rhythm.

"I think I'd feel better if I just had a puff. . . ."

It was a soft voice, weakened by fatigue or pain. And it came from the wagon carrying the severely wounded. Marc peered over the still form of Rick Hilliard and saw that the bundle of blankets next to him had suddenly produced a head and an arm. Marc swung down off his mount and began to walk alongside the wagon. He found himself face-to-face with the young cavalryman he had rescued from under his dying horse. He was propped up on one elbow and smiling.

"Is it night, or is this Hell?"

"Both," Marc said. "You've been asleep for hours. How are you feeling?"

"Well, I've got a splint on my best leg, which is throbbing like a dozen toothaches, and I got bruises on my bruises. But I'm alive."

"And if the sawbones has set your break well, you'll live to ride another horse."

"But he won't be Prince."

"I'm sorry about that."

"It was my brother's horse. I promised to keep him out of harm's way."

"There's no such place in a war. Which is what we've started, I'm afraid."

"Did we beat them?"

"They beat the piss out of us. We're on the run."

"Ah . . ."

"You don't sound too disappointed."

"I didn't think when I joined up that we'd be shootin' up a bunch of farmers with pitchforks and old geezers with rickety muskets."

Marc said nothing to that, but thought much. "I'm only halfway through my pipe; why don't you finish it for me."

"Thanks. And thanks for what you—"

"You'd better take a drink before you start." Marc put his canteen to the lad's lips, and after a tentative sip he gulped down several mouthfuls.

"My name's Eugene Yates."

"Lieutenant Marc Edwards."

For the next minute or so Marc walked silently beside the wagon while Corporal Yates drew in lungful after lungful of smoke from Marc's clay pipe.

"I'm a bit of a farmer myself," he said to Marc, resting his head back on an improvised pillow and returning the pipe. "I grew up in Montreal, where my father is a merchant. But my older brother Stephen married a girl from New York State and moved to her family's farm just outside the village of Waddington. A pretty little farm that runs right down to the St. Lawrence. When Callie's dad died, she and Stephen took over the place, and they asked me to come down and join them when I turned eighteen."

"That was some time ago."

"Almost two years."

"And you took to farming?"

"I took to horses, mainly. So when I heard about the troubles up here in Quebec, I talked my father into outfittin' me for the cavalry unit that assembled in Montreal."

"Stephen supplied the horse?"

There was a pause, and Marc thought that the corporal must have drifted into unconsciousness again. But then he said, as if to himself, "How am I gonna tell him Prince died in a battle we lost?"

"I'm sure he would be a lot unhappier if you had died in a battle we'd won."

"I'll have some story to tell, though, won't I?"

"You will. And you're also out of the fighting, which we've

only begun. You've done your duty. And don't forget to tell Stephen that your unit's bold gambit saved a number of lives."

"Can I quote you?"

"Word for word. Now I think you should rest. We've still got two or three hours to go before Sorel."

"All right. But I want you to know that my brother is goin' to hear the whole story. And if you're ever anywhere near Waddington, just ask for the Yates place. We'll roll out the welcome mat."

"I'll remember that. Thank you."

"We'll share a pipe, eh?"

Marc smiled. It was the last thing Corporal Yates saw before he fell into a deep, seemingly painless sleep.

Marc found himself dozing with both hands gripping the pummel of the saddle and his body, bruised and benumbed, rocking softly to the sway and pitch of his horse, who kept in lock-step with the ambulance-wagon beside him. The column was less than an hour from Sorel. Its constituents—soldiers, officers, cavalry, horses—were moving like zombies across a spectral landscape, as alien as the far side of the moon.

"Your friend's awake."

Marc gripped the pommel more tightly, irritated that anyone, officer or soldier, should be so thoughtless as to speak aloud.

"Lieutenant . . . I think your friend's awake."

Marc opened both eyes. The darkness, laced with snow, assailed them. How he longed to close them for good.

"It's me, Eugene. I heard your friend call out somebody's name."

Marc slid from his horse. Pain shot up both legs, and he stumbled, then stamped about trying to get some feeling back into his feet. Finally, he was able to keep pace with the wagon as it lurched over the frozen ruts of the road.

"Is he gonna be all right?"

Marc reached out and touched Eugene Yates on the back of the hand. Then he turned his attention to Rick Hilliard a few feet away in the wagon. Tenderly, he lifted the greatcoat away from Rick's face, exposing it to the night-air.

"Are you in pain, Rick?"

Rick's eyes opened. It was too dark for Marc to see the expression in them or any signs of the story they might need to tell. With great care Marc reached down under the greatcoat and felt about for the wadding over the wound: it was dry.

"You're going to make it, old friend. We're almost home."

Rick blinked, acknowledging the voice. His lips, dry and cracked, were beginning to move. His breathing was audible, laboured but much stronger.

"I'll get you some water." Marc fumbled for his canteen, found it, and dribbled a few drops of icy water over Rick's lips. They slid down his chin, and Marc wiped it gently with the sleeve of his jacket.

Suddenly, the wagon bounced and careened. Marc watched Rick's face anxiously, but no groan issued from the parched lips. He was not in pain. The bleeding had been stopped and had not started again, despite the ceaseless jouncing of the wagon. Marc began to hope.

Once more Rick's lips moved, and this time Marc could hear breath whistling through them, elongated sighs or half-formed, weightless words.

He leaned over the side of the wagon as far as he dared.

"Papa?"

"It's Marc. I'm right here beside you. We're almost home."

"Take my hand, Papa."

From under the greatcoat, slowly and with great effort, emerged an ungloved, pallid hand, the selfsame hand that had cradled a sabre and wielded it willfully. Marc removed a glove and took Rick's hand in his own. As he squeezed it, Rick's eyes closed. His breathing softened and became more regular.

For the next hour, Marc walked steadfastly beside his friend, never once releasing his grip, not even when, as lights from the houses of Sorel winked into view, it grew inalienably cold and began to stiffen.

FOUR

Marc's request to accompany Colonel Gore and the bodies of the fallen comrades to Montreal was brusquely denied. The subalterns must remain in place in the Sorel barracks. The fractured morale of their men must be made whole again in readiness for the repeat engagement, which would come as surely as December's ice on the Richelieu River. Uniforms needed to be cleaned, boots polished, rifles oiled, bayonets whetted. A few dress parades on the barracks-ground, with the band fifing and drumming, should serve the cause nicely, as well as impressing any habitants who might have been unnecessarily buoyed by the news from St. Denis. The five dead regulars would be buried with full military honours in Montreal, and next-of-kin duly informed of their glorious sacrifice in the service of the young monarch, Queen Victoria. Marc volunteered to write to Rick's parents.

What could he tell them? He began with an account of their adventures during the investigation of the murder of Councillor Moncreiff, for that had been the first time that he and Rick had been thrown together in any but a perfunctory way since Marc's arrival in Toronto. In many respects they had been opposites. Where Marc tended towards caution and fore-thought, Rick was impetuous and free-spirited. And whereas Marc had decided, almost at first sight, that Beth Smallman was the woman with whom he would share the rest of his life, Rick's eye had roved avidly and had found itself next to the pil-low of more than one debutante (and occasionally her mother), a propensity that had cost him dearly. While Marc played up Rick's bold and fearless acts in the Moncreiff affair, he gave the ensign's parents an edited version of his escapade with the American actress that had seen him accused of murder. But whatever cause or calamity Rick Hilliard found himself en-gaged in, it was his honesty, his fierce sense of integrity, and his loyalty as friend and fellow soldier that attracted, endeared, and endured. It was no exaggeration to claim that the son of Mr. and Mrs. Hilliard had risked, and given, his life to save that of his friend.

Four days after the fiasco at St. Denis, the morale of the troops at Sorel was boosted by something more concrete and inspiring than dress parades and routine tactical manoeu-vres. Scattered but credible reports began to reach them that Lieutenant-Colonel Wetherall had, at last, moved north from Chambly and attacked the rebels in their stronghold at St. Charles, seven or eight miles south of St. Denis. Wetherall had prevailed with ease, apparently, killing dozens and taking numerous prisoners. However, he had not moved on to St. Denis for fear of being cut off and unable to cross the river back to Chambly. So he had retreated with his captives and the Liberty Pole, with its irreverent red cap, and made triumphant march for Montreal. Perhaps this sharp blow would break the will of the rebels, and there would be no more fighting—or so went the sentiment being passed from lip to ear in the barracks.

The next day, news of a more disturbing nature arrived. The mutilated and desecrated body of Captain Weir had been discovered, and the account of his cowardly assassination, wondrously swollen in the retelling, made plain to every regular, militiaman, and red-blooded Tory in the province. The mood in the barracks abruptly changed: it was now "Avenge the captain!" Marc felt obliged to call his squad together and remind them that they were British soldiers, whose duty was clear and unequivocal. They were to obey their officers to the letter: to put down the rebellion, disarm the combatants, and take into custody their ringleaders. All of this would be carried out with dispatch, economy of movement, strict discipline, and studied objectivity. There was no room for superfluous emotion. The adrenaline of battle and the will required to sustain courage were all that would be necessary.

The men listened politely.

Seven days after St. Denis, on November 30, Colonel Gore returned from Montreal on board the big steamer *John Bull,* with four additional companies of regular infantry and four field guns. Gore ordered everyone to be ready to embark at daylight; this time they would ride upriver in style and finish the job that had been temporarily interrupted. It was rumoured that both Papineau and Wolfred Nelson were holed up at St. Denis. A final blow would be struck, Captain Weir's death avenged, and the principal gangsters captured and brought back to swing on the nearest gibbet. The men cheered, even those who ought to have known better.

Unable to sleep that night, Marc sat up and wrote two letters. To Major Jenkin, sequestered in Montreal as quartermaster to the 24th, he penned a lengthy and impassioned narrative of the failed military expedition, holding nothing back. In the past year the major had proffered wise and discreet advice with the tact of a gentleman who has seen much of the world's horror and somehow managed to remain this side of cynicism. He had fought with Marc's uncle Frederick under Wellington; he knew Marc's adoptive father, Uncle Jabez; and he had even—unknowingly—met Marc's mother. These were familial connections dear to the heart of a young man who had been orphaned in more than one way during his short, eventful life.

While being suitably modest in describing his own contributions to the abortive efforts at St. Denis on the twenty-third, he depicted the courage and heroism of his comrades with stirring accuracy, especially those final moments in the little barn and just outside of it. He confessed the fears and doubts he had experienced, not only about his fluctuating courage but also about the nature of the opposing force. These were not Bonaparte's fusiliers or the hard-bitten professionals whom the major and Uncle Frederick had fought hand to hand and mile by mile across Spain and France to the gates of Paris, soldiers to be respected as much as feared. The Quebec rebels were farmers and townspeople, volunteers and amateurs—without training, tactics, or military leadership.

Whatever the shortcomings of Colonel Gore and however tenacious the citizen army of Quebec might prove, Marc insisted that the outcome was not in doubt. The ragamuffin rebels would be routed or driven relentlessly into the last redoubt of their hinterland. They would perish by the score. Yes, the brave men of the 24th would do their duty, but what glory, Marc wondered to Major Jenkin, could accrue to such a victory? What satisfaction in shooting a man armed with a hoe or rusty arquebus? Even as he wrote this, the image of the young habitant wriggling through that bolt-hole in a vain attempt to escape the fury of the redcoats hovered over his writing hand. The boy's horrific death at Rick's hands had haunted Marc's dreams and disturbed his waking hours for the past seven days.

What he said finally to his elder friend was that, even if they should strike a deathblow to the rebellion tomorrow at St. Denis, the troubles would not end, as his men and many officers seemed to believe. For the "army" they were being asked to vanquish appeared to Marc to be an entire populace whose anger, despair, and unassuaged resentments would only deepen at defeat, grow sullen and secretive, and smoulder like fire under a forest. "Pray we do not have such a rebellion in Upper Canada. Once started, it may be unstoppable. And there will be no winners."

When he had calmed down, he pulled out a fresh sheet of paper and began writing to his beloved Beth. With great tact he outlined the excursion to St. Denis, deleting much of the sad, sordid detail. He broke the news of Rick's death, as he must, but took care not to put the least romantic gloss on his friend's heroic gesture. Beth knew better. He suggested that the fighting here looked as if it would soon be over, then stressed how vital it was that she and Aunt Catherine keep well away from politics. The millinery shop that the two women—both Americans—operated on King Street in Toronto had twice been vandalized by gangs of ultra-royalists, looking for scapegoats as tensions mounted in Upper Canada amidst fears there of a farmer's revolt. In her last letter Beth had tried to reassure him by saying that their good friend, Constable Horatio Cobb, had been keeping a close watch on the premises. Beth could not hide her concern for her former neighbours in the hamlet of Crawford's Corners, who were equally in danger, though surely after a brief and near-disastrous entanglement with the rebel cause in October, Thomas and Winnifred Goodall would be lying low. Besides, there was now their baby, Mary, to consider.

"The cause of the French here is real, the injustices deep and universal," Marc wrote. "Ours in Upper Canada pale by comparison. People are literally starving in the townships, on the seigneuries, and in the back alleys of the towns. The flood of immigrants from Britain since 1832 has dumped thousands of penniless unemployed onto the docks and streets of Montreal and Quebec City, bringing cholera and other pestilences, which have recurred yearly since then. Not only that, but over one hundred thousand pounds sits undistributed in the vaults of St. Louis Castle, so that salaries and pensions have not been paid in months. Many once-prosperous people have lost their homes and enterprises as creditors close in.

"But armed revolt is not the answer. I foresee only needless death and loss and even more profound humiliation. Take care and be well, my darling. I shall be home by New Year's: that's a promise."

Marc fell asleep on his writing desk.

With sunlight just beginning to squeeze through the trees along the eastern horizon, Marc and his fellow officers finished their breakfast in the improvised mess. Many ate enough for several meals, as it could be long hours before they saw food again. As they got up from the table to go and organize their squads for their march to the steamer, Colonel Gore's adjutant came in carrying a packet of letters that had arrived the night before from overseas. One of them was for Marc.

Edwards Estate
Kent, England
October 2, 1837

Dear Marc:

It is my sad duty to inform you that Jabez passed from this world at two o'clock this morning. I was by his side during the final hours, and it pleases me to tell you that his thoughts were principally upon you, upon your faithfulness as his adopted son, upon your splendid and worthy life so far, and, more importantly, upon the prospects for your future. His only regret regarding you was that he could not circumvent the entailments of our father's will and leave you some part of the family estate. But as you know, the property and the funds to perpetuate it are indivisible and come to me and, eventually, to my eldest son, your cousin. However, Jabez did amass a sizeable sum of his own as a solicitor in London all those years ago, and as soon as the will is probated, I shall write to you with details of your legacy, which could be considerable. For the next while, though, we shall devote our energies to mourning the death of one whom we loved and who loved us, and life, dearly. We talked often of your heroic exploits in North America, and I want to assure you that he was as proud of you as a soldier as I was. Please take care: the life of an officer in the British army is dangerous and unpredictable.

Delores and the boys are coming from France for the funeral, and I must go to Dover to meet them. I'll write to you more fully as soon as I can: there is much to discuss between us.

Your loving uncle,
Frederick.

Marc stood with the letter dangling from two fingers. He felt empty inside, incapable for the moment of feeling anything: sadness, grief, or anger at the gods. Too much was happening to him all at once. Rick was dead, and yet his voice and image, the joie de vivre of his being, were everywhere around him. He himself had been within a week of his wedding with Beth before being wrenched away to a battle he had once longed for more than life itself. Now Jabez, his adoptive father, was gone, without a chance to say good-bye. And despite his faults and the secrets he had inexcusably kept from Marc, Jabez Edwards had raised him as his own, given him his name, and, against his own better judgement, had set him free to seek his own fortune.

A bugle on the parade-square sounded a peremptory blast. He had to go. There were immediate and overriding exigencies. He would find time to grieve his losses later. And for a while at least, he was not unhappy to buckle on his sabre and scabbard.

The *John Bull,* weighed down with eight infantry companies, four guns, and assorted baggage, tried to ram its way through the ever-thickening ice of the Richelieu River. Three hours and one mile later, Colonel Gore admitted defeat. So, shortly after noon on this first day of December, Gore's brigade was once again on the river road. Whereas a week ago it had been wet snow, rain, and a muddy morass that had made the twenty-mile trek to St. Denis a living hell, it was now the frozen ruts (their own, alas) that made their passage no better than travelling over a rock-strewn wasteland. A corduroy road in April would have been heaven.

Despite the bone-jarring obstacles, they made good progress. The sun shone cold and bright. No skirmishers threatened from the occasional woods they had to pass through. When they marched into St. Ours at dusk, no sniper fired on them from the shuttered houses. Not a soul emerged to greet or spit at them. This time Gore called a halt, and the troops bivouacked for the night—to eat heartily and rest for the battle expected on the morrow.

The next morning dawned bright and clear. All the omens were good. Colonel Gore addressed the assembled troops. He reminded them of their duty to the Queen, made ambiguous references to the misadventures of the previous week, and concluded by asking them to remember how Captain Weir had been slaughtered, mutilated, and tossed aside like a butchered calf. "Do not be fooled," he said in a pinched, effeminate drawl, "into thinking that because the rebels have no uniforms they are not soldiers determined to kill you in a blink. A farmer with a pitchfork is as murderous as a fusilier. And it was ordinary-looking ploughmen who stabbed Captain Weir to death and laughed at his sufferings. Show no mercy. Our orders are to defeat these outlaws utterly. Their leaders will be captured and clapped in irons. Any farmer or householder known to have taken part in the revolt is to have his goods confiscated and his buildings put to the torch. I know you will all do your duty. May God be with you."

They were within a mile of St. Denis when Captain Riddell rode up beside Marc and engaged him in conversation.

"Major Jenkin was telling me that you've been involved in several murder investigations."

"That's true." Marc smiled, relieved for the chance to talk

about something other than war or politics. "I found them more diverting than cards and dice."

"Everybody in the mess knew about how you helped catch Councillor Moncreiff's killer, but I hadn't known about the other two."

"Well, I don't boast about them, sir, because in my first investigation I managed to discover the killer, but he got away, in part because I wasn't quick enough to nab him."

"But you got him in the end?"

"With the help of others, yes. And his accomplice as well."

"What happened in the third case?"

"Well, I did manage to solve it, but the killer bolted across the border."

Captain Riddell, a jolly, open-faced Englishman, laughed. "Two out of three, eh? That may be a higher success rate than our good colonel will ever achieve!"

Marc acknowledged the point with a small, rueful smile.

"You did well out here last week," Riddell said, suddenly grave. "You're a natural soldier: no-one would have guessed it was your first engagement."

"Thank you, sir."

"By the way, I've written to Ensign Hilliard's father. We'll all miss him."

Marc nodded, and they rode on in respectful silence.

They were approaching the creek where they had had so much trouble trying to save their twenty-four-pounder. The makeshift bridge had since been blown to pieces, but the cannon lay as they had left it—snout down in the mud, now frozen solid—like an ancient beast trapped forever in ice. Beyond it, the path to the coulee was littered with tree trunks to impede their progress towards the village and its fortifications. The colonel was about to send his sappers down to test the thickness of the ice when the scouts came riding back to make their report on what lay ahead.

The news took everyone by surprise. The rebels had deserted the town. The stone house was unoccupied. Several new ramparts had been constructed but were unmanned. Even the residents of St. Denis had, it seemed, taken to the woods. There would be no return engagement: the rebels had anticipated the result and, after the débâcle at St. Charles a few days before, had more or less abandoned the Richelieu Valley to its fate.

That fate was soon decided. Colonel Gore met with a delegation from the village, who had appeared as soon as the troops had gained the coulee. One of the elders, clutching a white rag in trembling hands, assured the colonel that Nelson and Papineau had fled to the United States. There would be no organized resistance. As innocent bystanders, they wished to be left in peace.

"I'll determine who is innocent," Gore proclaimed from his lofty perch. "I have orders to destroy the property of anyone who joined the renegades or aided and abetted them." He turned to his captains. "We'll start with the distillery." He looked down at the old man. "You will point out to us Wolfred Nelson's house and any others, as required. Meanwhile, we shall need billets in the town. I want the officers to secure these, and turn out any occupants who do not fully co-operate.

If there is any real resistance, the premises are to be burnt to the ground."

"It is starting to get dark, sir," Captain Riddell said tactfully.

"Then the fires we shall start will burn more brightly, won't they?"

Marc was relieved that his squad was assigned the task of reconnoitring the outskirts of the village and nearby woods to make sure there really were no rebels waiting to ambush or entrap the invaders. However, the only people they scared up in the fast-failing light were townsfolk hiding among the trees, cold and starving. Many refused to return to their homes, awed by the spectacle of flames roaring into the sky from several houses in the distance. But the presence of the government troops soon became known to another group also hiding out in the woods: those few loyalists, most of them English-speaking Tories, who had remained faithful to the Crown and had suffered for it by having their barns razed, their crops and cattle stolen, and their lives threatened. They knew exactly which locals had made their lives miserable since Lord Gosford, the civilian governor, had left them to the mercies of Papineau and the Papists. And they wanted revenge. Now.

By the time Marc rode back into the village to report to Captain Riddell that the periphery of the town was clear of the enemy, the local Tories were already in the process of leading squads of soldiers along the narrow streets, pointing out the houses of traitors and seditionists. Moments later, these burst into flames.

"Jesus, we don't even know whether these wretches are guilty of anything," the captain said, his face dark with anger.

"A single finger pointed that way, and it's all over. I didn't join the army to burn out civilians and raze crops. Christ, these people are all starving!"

"What are my orders, sir?"

"Take your troop and clear out that log house up there at the end of this street."

"And set it on fire?"

"I'm afraid so, Lieutenant. Colonel Gore insists it was used to hide rebels."

Marc sighed, but nodded his assent, numbly. As much as he had tried to suppress such thoughts, all he could think of—here among the wailing of women and children as they fled their flaming homes, the shouts of rage and defiance among the returning Tories, the flare of sudden conflagrations against an indifferent, indigo sky—was that this sort of chaos and self-perpetuating reprisal could very easily happen in Upper Canada. With barn burnings, secret assassinations, and the rule of law frayed by rage.

Reluctantly, Marc hailed Sergeant Ogletree. Then he and five infantrymen followed Marc up the street towards the house indicated by Captain Riddell. Two of the men carried pitch-torches. The air was foul with acrid, greasy smoke. The spit and sizzle of flame bedazzled the eye, making the stark silhouettes of the buildings even starker.

There was a meagre bit of light shining through one window of the log house as they came up to it: someone had been brave or naive enough to remain there.

"Somebody's at home," Marc whispered, and held up his

hand. The men halted behind him. "Sergeant, take two men and watch the rear of the place. I'm going in, carefully. We all know what happens when we corner a rat."

"We could just fire a volley through the window and order them out," Ogletree said. "Then set the thing ablaze."

"We could do that," Marc said. "But we could also kill innocent civilians."

Veteran cynic that he had become, Ogletree grunted as if to say that few civilians in a civil conflict could be called innocent. But he obeyed.

Marc rapped at the stout door and called out in French: "Open up, please. No-one is going to hurt you. We require your house as a temporary billet for some of the troops. You will be paid for any food we consume." He winced at the lie but told himself it was better than needlessly risking lives.

There was no response from inside. Marc could hear Ogletree's group deploying behind the house. The flickering light in the window near the door was definitely that of a candle or lantern. Was it being kept alight to aid an ambush? Surely not. The town was totally in possession of the troops: any armed resistance would be suicidal. Still . . .

Marc pushed at the door. It was unlatched and swung open.

"I'm Lieutenant Edwards. I am commandeering these premises as a billet. I have not drawn a weapon." With that, he stepped into the room, his sabre in its scabbard and his pistol, primed and ready to fire, tucked lightly in his belt.

The interior was more brightly lit than he had anticipated. To his right several candles were burning, illuminating a kitchen area with a crude deal table and two log chairs, both occupied by women. Mother and daughter, perhaps, each with handsome Gallic features and lustrous, dark hair. But it was the eyes that caught Marc's attention and held it: black and smouldering, with a malevolence he did not think possible in a woman.

Marc tried to smile, touched his cap, and said hesitantly in his best French, "Good evening. I must ask you to leave. I noticed a shed out back. You could take some blankets out there for the night, or perhaps you have friends or relatives nearby."

The women remained as still as a pair of gargoyles. The room seemed colder than the night outside. It was the younger one, who would in any other circumstances have been thought beautiful in the first blooming of her womanhood, whose eyes moved first. It was a furtive glance only, but it brought Marc's gaze around to its object. To his left and in among the shadows, there appeared to be a large clothes-cupboard, its thick door half open. Or opening.

Marc reached for his pistol just as the form of a young man unfolded from the maw of the cupboard.

"No!" one of the women screamed.

The young man's right hand seemed to explode, and Marc felt something strike him in the thigh and spin him sideways. Just as a second pistol was being raised into the light, Marc fired. The gunman grunted, and sank slowly to his knees. Both of his weapons clattered to the floor. His hands lifted them-selves up to his throat, where Marc could see a grotesque, dark splotch spreading.

I've killed a man, was his first thought, just before his own pain struck and he reached out in a futile attempt to keep himself from falling. As he lay, numb and bleeding in the sawdust on the floor, the last thing he saw before he lost consciousness was a pair of black, feral eyes wishing him dead.

FIVE

Horatio Cobb, charter member of the five-person Toronto constabulary, was a worried man. And what worried him the most, perhaps, was his being worried at all. Cobb, as he was known far and wide across the reaches of the capital city, prided himself on keeping his life simple and uncluttered. But living where, and when, he did was making it nigh impossible to do so.

True, he continued to rise at seven each morning, except on the Sabbath, and checked to see if Missus Cobb was still beside him. This latter gesture was made less difficult by the fact that Dora, as the neighbours called her, was as round and pink-fleshed as nearly three hundred pounds can accomplish. Her work as midwife to the easternmost half of the city, the "old town," often took her out at all hours of the day or night, and her absence was palpable. But a hot breakfast never failed to appear on the kitchen table, either at the instigation of his goodly wife or that of his ten-year-old daughter, Delia. After which he invariably waved Delia and her brother Fabian off to school, kissed Missus Cobb or her image, then made his way along King Street into the heart of the city, nodding to familiars, scowling at ragamuffin boys contemplating mischief, and raking every brick and inch of his domain with a policeman's practiced eye. How much more at home he had felt here among the bustle and hurly-burly of the province's metropolis than he ever had on his father's farm. It was his own considered opinion—an opinion he valued highly—that he was a man in his element.

His element included his regular patrol, an area bounded by King Street on the north and the lakeshore on the south and stretching from Parliament Street on the east to Bay on the west. Within that precinct he was the law or its visible representative. His helmet, blue tunic, and belted truncheon, in combination with his stealthy swagger, were enough to keep the hooligans, roustabouts, and inebriates in suitable awe of his authority. And when that failed to impress, there were his powerful arms and hands with the tenacity of manacles, and as a last resort a persuasive fist or two. Each morning, after checking in with Sarge, the chief constable, at the police quarters in the Court House on King between Church and Toronto Streets, he would be released for the day to do as he saw fit in maintaining the Queen's peace. As luck would have it, there were a dozen taverns and grog-shops situated within his patrol, and, believing in that proverbial ounce of prevention, Cobb made his presence felt in such trouble-spots as often as his thirst and capacities would permit. It was here, too, that he picked up—by subtle threat, beery bribe, or appeal to good citizenship—those tidbits of information that aided him and his colleagues in their ceaseless quest for law and order in Victoria's peaceable kingdom. His network of snitches had become legendary.

That was now the problem, and the source of his uncharacteristic anxiousness. For despite the leisurely and self-regulated pace of most of his days—a lingering luncheon in the Blue Ox or the Crooked Anchor, a pleasant supper with Missus Cobb and the children, and the stimulation of an evening spent clearing the streets of belligerent drunks or assisting the bailiffs in serving warrants on sundry miscreants—he found himself, at the end of a twelve-hour day, dyspeptic and out of sorts. And politics was the efficient cause, first and last. The antics of William Lyon Mackenzie and his fellow radicals over the summer had put the whole province on edge. Rumours of an armed uprising were as frequent, and about as reliable, as the number of bent elbows over a bar on Saturday night. Such matters ought to be the business of the governor and his agents, not the local constabulary. But then not many governors other than Sir Francis Bond Head would have shipped every last redcoat in Upper Canada off to Quebec to fight the Frenchies, leaving Fort York deserted and Government House unprotected. And with the nearest militia across the lake in Hamilton, only five policemen and Sheriff William Jarvis of York County stood between the Queen's surrogate and a bullet from a radical's musket.

As if this were not trouble enough, Governor Head had ordered the chief constable to instruct his subordinates to act as his "eyes and ears" in the city. The least scrap of information that might be inflated to suggest potential seditious activity or the mere thought of seditious activity was to be reported as fact as soon as it was discovered. Each constable was to check in at headquarters at noon, at five o'clock, and at the end of the evening shift—to relay the whiff of rumour or tavern scuttlebutt.

And, of course, it was Cobb with his fabled network of spies who was expected to supply the chief and the governor with a steady stream of reliable data. Such an expectation had brought complexity to Cobb's life, and consequent worry. Every one of his "agents," smelling booze-money in the air, was more than happy to retail the latest rumour and spice it up for good measure. Cobb prided himself on knowing exactly how truthful and how useful any information passed to him in a pub actually was—to the penny or the fluid ounce. But no threat of withdrawal or reprisal on his part could stanch the flow of alarming nonsense. He was not averse to passing it along to Sir Francis if the governor was fool enough to give it credence. What he feared most was that some tiny fraction of the malarkey might be true.

Since the troops had left, taking Marc Edwards with them, there had been serious incidents in the streets. Shop windows of those merchants directly associated with the Family Compact had been smashed by radical sympathizers or, in Cobb's opinion, gangs of toughs out for a lark. On the other side, groups of young Tories, who should have known better, had been encouraged by their elders to deface the property of known radicals—which in their diminutive minds included respectable Reform politicians and most Americans. When not in the mood for wielding a paintbrush, they chose to threaten their victims with anonymous, poison-pen letters. But if there really were malcontents north of the city organizing and arming themselves (after all, he and Marc had exposed a gun-running operation in October, and news of an insurrection south of Montreal had just made the papers), then his life was about to become seriously complicated.

The problem was, he concluded, that he had too many friends. He was simply too susceptible to friendship, to having his good nature co-opted and taken advantage of. He felt that this must be a character flaw in a man professing to be a policeman. Against his better judgement he had found himself not only working side by side with Lieutenant Edwards on two investigations but coming to like and admire "the major," as he called him, first derisively and then with affection. Like him, the major was an arm of the law and royal authority, but unlike him, the lieutenant was a Tory, an aristocrat, and a man of learning. Why, at this very moment he might be shooting at aggrieved farmers and ordinary folk like himself or his father or Dora's kin up in York Township, who had been entangled with Reformers from the beginning. A dozen years ago his own father, still harbouring hopes that his eldest would succeed him on the farm, had pointed proudly to a lush field of wheat and proclaimed, "The soil under that crop has no politics. Remember that, son. An uppity cow ain't a Tory. Tend to yer own business, an' the world'll come out right." But the world here in Upper Canada had not come out right. Crops failed. Bankers balked. Bureaucracy and cronyism had bled the province dry.

Nevertheless, Cobb had tried to take the essential message

to heart: he tended religiously to the business of keeping the peace. Moreover, he did not see himself as an appendage of the ruling Compact and its haughty adherents. He meted out his street justice in an even-handed or (as he liked to remind Missus Cobb) even-fisted way. A menacing drunk was a drunk, whether he be dressed in velvet or homespun. A man beating his wife in public deserved a sharp reprimand on the noggin, whatever his income or lack of same. If the magistrates wished to favour their own with unmerited leniency, that was something he might deplore but could not rectify. The Lord—if He wasn't one of them—would settle the score later on.

It was through his unpolitic friendship with Marc Edwards that Cobb had met Marc's fiancée, Beth Smallman, who had dabbled in debates she had no right to as a woman and gotten her toes scalded. However, in the eyes of the ruling class, once a Reformer always a Reformer. And Beth's partnership in the millinery shop on King Street with Catherine Roberts, her aunt newly arrived from the republic to the south, did nothing to allay such fears. Several of Cobb's informants had been eager to tell him that it was now widely known that one of the aunt's relatives was a gunrunner. So what did Cobb go and do? He got to liking the old girl so much that he stopped in to the shop at least once a shift for tea and a chin-wag. Even worse, when the shop had been vandalized last month, Cobb had been assiduous in his efforts to track down the Tory scions responsible and, through one of his *agents de taverne,* had managed to bring a warrant against two of them. Unfortunately, the lads were both relatives of a rural magistrate and were let off with a reprimand and a promise to make restitution (still unfulfilled). Needless to say, Cobb's stock with the powers that be had not risen.

So here he was on the bright and wintry Monday morning of December 4, striving to tend to his own sheep, as it were, but acutely aware that others saw a man compromised by having friends in both camps. And which flag would he hoist when the revolution came? That was a question he tried not to ask himself too often.

As Cobb passed Jarvis Street, he nodded to several merchants who were sweeping the snow off the boardwalk in front of their shops. Ezra Michaels, the chemist, gave him a hearty "Good morning," and Cobb felt obliged to reciprocate. But by and large the city's most bustling street was empty. Only the energetic puffing of smoke from stoked fires, above the chimney-pots, indicated that the troubled citizenry of the capital had decided to suffer another day to begin. Cobb reached Church Street, where the Court House, set back from the north side of King among shrubs and flowers, now wimpled with snow, gleamed arrogantly at the risen sun. With its bright-red brick and cut-stone pilasters soaring two and a half storeys into the skyline, it announced to the world that here was an edifice of prospering authority. Next to it, and facing Toronto Street, stood its exact replica—with a single exception: its windows were barred.

Cobb walked along the stone path until he came to the rear of the Court House, where, just above the tunnel that connected the two buildings (the accused, found guilty, could be whisked to the cells without getting his toes cold), the quarters of the constabulary were located. Loitering about the entrance were two ragged, red-nosed urchins, hoping to be conscripted to run messages of official significance for a half penny or a maple-sugar sweet.

"Give us a penny, Cobb!"

"Shouldn't you two be in school?" Cobb asked, pushing open the door.

"They won't have us."

"I'm not surprised," Cobb said, chuckling for the first time this morning. He stepped into the welcome heat of the station's anteroom.

"Good mornin', Gussie," he said to the wee, wizened leprechaun perched on his stool and shuffling papers on the table before him. "Great day to be alive, eh?"

"Not so far it ain't," replied Augustus French, who peered out at the world from a pair of rheumy, myopic eyes with a squint of perpetual skepticism.

"Is Sarge in?" This was a rhetorical question at eight in the morning, for Wilfrid Sturges found it uncivil to let anything other than a full sun wake him from his comfortable slumbers. Even so, he was seldom seen these days in the tiny, adjoining closet that served as his office. For Governor Head, having only his aide-de-camp, Barclay Spooner, for immediate protection, thought it prudent to have a uniform of some kind lurking about Government House or popping up arbitrarily from time to time with menacing demeanour. These defenses were supplemented on occasion by the appearance of a brace of elderly militiamen brandishing swords and frightening the ladies of the house.

"Anythin' I should know about before I set out?" Cobb

enquired as he edged closer to the pot-bellied wood-stove that did its best to heat both rooms.

"You didn't make your report on Saturd'y night," French said, taking this, it appeared, as a personal affront.

"I was too busy bustin' a couple of heads in the Crooked Anchor. To no *pre-vail,* I might add."

"I gotta have yer report for Sarge."

Cobb sighed. Even though he went into the taverns now only when called on to umpire disputes or drag deadbeats to the magistrate, he could not help but hear the wild tales being bruited there. People even stuffed his pockets with notes when he wasn't looking. "All right, then. Poise yer pen."

While Cobb was the only one of the four constables who could read and write fluently, it was the clerk's job to prepare any reports that might be required in the course of policing the town. There weren't many, as all the writs, warrants, and depositions were handled by the sheriff, bailiff, and magistrate in the respectable rooms of the Court House.

Cobb cleared his throat and began, pacing his accounts so that Gussie French was almost able to keep up by scratching away as fast as he could and ignoring the blots and smears of half-congealed ink. Included were such facts as these: the rebels in Quebec had stormed the castle of St. Louis—Bastille-like—and taken Govenor Gosford prisoner; ten thousand troops, armed to the teeth, were marching up from Vermont to liberate the lower province in the name of republicanism; Mackenzie and Papineau were in Cornwall, conspiring to join forces and overthrow monarchist tyranny everywhere; the Iroquois at Brantford had thrown their lot in with Mackenzie's radicals and were seen doing war dances by three independent witnesses; the rebels here had so many American rifles, they were issuing two to each conscript. And so on.

Gussie dutifully scribbled down this nonsense.

"I'll be off, then," Cobb said. "To gather more *un-tell-i-gents.*"

"You better have a gander at this," Gussie said, thrusting out a sheet of paper.

On it was the sketch of a man's face, below which were enumerated his crimes and aliases. The sketch was rudimentary (Gussie doubling as portraitist), but likely complete enough to have the culprit identified, should he be spotted in town. The features were sharp and rugged, the eyes piercing, the hair unkempt. He was thought to be a dangerous agent provocateur from the Buffalo area, who had been caught snooping about Fort York and fully armed, but had managed to escape before he could be questioned thoroughly. Subsequently, several break-ins had been attributed to him. A fairly accurate description of the fellow had been provided by the army, along with his various known aliases.

"Any of these names his real one?" Cobb asked.

Gussie shrugged, intent on tidying up the blots on his report. "Couldn't say. I ain't paid to think."

And a good thing, too, Cobb mused. He himself, of course, had acknowledged the usefulness of the analytical only since his recent involvement with Marc Edwards and his investigations. He glanced at the list of aliases. They were all Irish, which might be significant: Colm O'Toole, Seamus Doyle, Sean Flanagan. Most likely he would be using the last of these, or a new one. Well, he would show the sketch around and keep an eye out: you never knew.

By ten o'clock, Cobb's feet were numb with cold, and the tips of his fingers tingled. Normally, he would have warmed himself in a tavern, but he did not wish to step into these smoky rooms, hostile with gossip. Most of the merchants were friendly, but they were leery of a uniformed policeman hanging about their premises too long: the notion of a permanent constabulary patrolling the streets to discourage crime instead of reacting to it was still a novel one, here and elsewhere, and was greeted with a prudent wariness. So it was with evident relief that he found himself outside the millinery shop belonging to Beth and her aunt Catherine. He peered in through the window display and noted with satisfaction that there were no customers inside. He swaggered ostentatiously to the next alley, then darted along it and came out onto the service lane that ran behind the King Street shops. He rapped on a door, then walked in.

As he had deduced, Beth Smallman and Catherine Roberts were at tea in the anteroom behind the shop proper. He was about to utter a hearty "Hello," but what he saw stopped the greeting in his throat. Aunt Catherine was in tears, her slight frame wracked by sobs. Beth's cheeks were stained with tears of her own, but her weeping was being constrained by an obvious concern for her aunt. Her left hand held a letter, but her right one was stroking Aunt Catherine's arm.

"He isn't dead, Auntie," she was saying. "He's been wounded, that's all."

"Who?" Cobb asked sharply, then realized that the women had not heard him enter and were startled by his sudden presence.

Aunt Catherine, normally as stoic as Beth, recovered enough to say with a grim little smile at her dear friend, "It's Marc. There's been a terrible battle. Ensign Hilliard's been shot dead, and Marc's been wounded in the leg."

Cobb put a hand on the back of a chair to steady himself. "So the stories are true," he murmured. "Things've started down there."

"Please sit, Mr. Cobb. I'll get you a cup," Beth said calmly, but the letter was trembling in her grip.

"No, no. Don't bother about me. Just tell me what happened."

"We just got the letter this morning. It's from Major Jenkin," Aunt Catherine said, blowing her nose and fumbling the hanky back into the pocket of her skirt. "I'm sorry to be such a blubberer—"

"Now don't go worryin' about a thing like that," Cobb said.

Beth handed the letter to him, then went to fetch his cup of tea and one of his favourite biscuits. She spilled some of the tea, steaming, on her wrist, but apparently didn't notice.

The letter was less than a page long, and the major promised a longer and more detailed one as soon as he could find time. But the rebellion in Lower Canada was in full swing, and the outcome not certain. Hilliard, he said, had died beside Marc, taking a bullet that otherwise might have killed his friend. Marc himself had risked all to save another wounded comrade in the field. Then, on the evening of December 1, while on patrol in St. Denis following the brigade's triumphant re-entry into the town, Marc had been shot by an insurgent. At present, he was in hospital in Sorel awaiting transportation to Montreal. The surgeon who had attended him on site reported to the major that, while the wound itself was not life-threatening, the bullet had severed a vein in the thigh and Marc had lost a lot of blood before the wound could be cauterized. While he had not yet regained consciousness, the overall prognosis was good.

"What do you think?" Aunt Catherine asked, as if Cobb could somehow make a pronouncement that would at least make matters bearable.

Cobb looked up, tried to smile, and was relieved to be able to turn to Beth and take the cup from her hand.

"Sounds like he might come home with a bit of a limp," he said at last.

"Thank you," Beth said, and her look indicated that she was grateful for her aunt's sake, not her own. Beth, he knew, did not require constant reassurance from others to bolster her own views or quiet any anxieties she might harbour.

"Beth says she must go to him," Aunt Catherine said, appealing to Cobb's masculine judgement, "even though Major Jenkin expressly warns her not to."

The major had indeed ended his letter by discouraging any such gesture. The province was in turmoil. No-one was safe. Travellers were being stripped of their money and goods. To be English in the wrong quarter was enough to get one beaten, or worse.

"It don't sound like Quebec's a place for ladies," Cobb offered.

"My place is by my beloved's side."

Aunt Catherine blushed, and Cobb uttered a protective cough.

"You oughta wait till you hear from Major Jenkin again," he said, glancing at Aunt Catherine for support. "Montreal might be safe, when Marc's moved there."

"Mr. Cobb's right, you know."

Beth said nothing.

"Besides, darling, I don't know as I could manage here alone, what with our own troubles and all."

Beth's look said, *That isn't really fair, Auntie,* but she replied in a soft, firm tone, "I'll wait for Major Jenkin's next letter." Then added: "But I won't wait long."

Cobb had decided to have lunch at home, thus avoiding the taverns. The news about Marc had unsettled him more than he was willing to let on. Seeing its effect on the ladies had been equally unsettling. He had grown inordinately fond of them both, and was now paying the price for such attachments. It was a hard world they lived in, and one could survive only by being as hard as one's humanness allowed. That was not the way Cobb himself would have arranged affairs, but then no-one had ever asked him to assist in that business. Such unnerving speculations were skittering through his mind when a sound familiar to his policeman's ear assailed it from the direction of the alley he had just passed near Front Street and Market Lane. He moved quickly towards the grunts, wheezes, and general scuffling noises.

Two bulky men, unknown to him, were thumping their fists on a smaller creature, well known to the constabulary, on any part of his wriggling body that presented itself. Other than a groan or sigh as the blows struck, the victim did not cry out for help; he expected none. Cobb drew his truncheon.

"Stop that *now!*" he shouted, as the adrenaline rush hit him. "You're both under arrest!"

The two toughs halted what they were doing, more in astonishment than fear. Finally, the taller one barked, "And just how's a tub o' lard like you gonna make us?"

Cobb's girth was often the object of amusement among the lower life of the city, often to their instant and eternal regret. For it nicely disguised the fact that he was quick, nimble, and strong as a bullock. Before the tall fellow could snicker or blink, he took Cobb's truncheon above the left eye and tumbled backwards, gasping in disbelief and pain. The shorter one was able to get a forearm up, but the truncheon-blow broke it without remorse. Unfortunately, at this point the victim decided to try to get up. In doing so, he got himself tangled in Cobb's feet, and the latter's momentum caused him to pitch forward and fall onto his side. But the toughs had seen enough, and they took the opportunity to scuttle down the alley and into King Street. Cobb struggled to his feet in order to initiate pursuit when he was once again upended by the object of the assault.

"Christ, Nestor, can't you do anything right?"

"I'm hurtin' all over. Whaddya expect me to do, lay here an' get punched to death?"

Cobb got up and hauled Nestor Peck to his feet.

Nestor, who would have been described as gnome-like if his

sallow skin had not begun to sag on the bones, essayed a toothless grin. "I guess I gotta thank you fer this."

"I do my duty, even fer scum like you."

Rubbing his cheek gingerly with his ungloved fingers, Nestor looked hurt. "How can you say such a thing, after all the help I've given you?" Nestor thought of himself as Cobb's number one snitch and, on rare occasions, came up with useful bits of information about the underclass he guzzled among.

"Why would those guys waste their knuckles on the likes of you?" Cobb asked. "I ain't seen them around here before."

Nestor wiped the blood from his nose and said, "I don't know their names, but I know who they are."

"I may be sorry for askin', but go ahead and tell me."

"They're from Thornhill, up in the County. They followed me from the tavern, but I heard them talkin' in there when they didn't know I was listenin'."

"Your only talent."

"They come down here to teach me and all the other snitches a lesson, they said. Some fellas up that way paid 'em."

"Paid good money to have you beat up?"

"They thought I'd been tellin' tales about the big meetin' of Reformers comin' up. I think they meant to kill me."

"But you've been spreadin' nonsense about the radicals for months now. Nobody in their right mind would pay the least attention to it, let alone offer cash to have your mouth shut forever—though that'd be a service to the *bawdy politic*."

Nestor looked coy, or at least as coy as a battered and shivering man could manage: "This time I got the real goods. But I ain't told a soul, I swear to God."

"And He'd swear right back at you." Cobb turned to go. "And I ain't in the mood for any more of your gimcrack gossip."

"I gotta tell *some*body!"

"Go to the station and tell Sarge. He'll probably give you a medal."

"You know I can't go there—Jesus, they loosened my tooth!" Nestor was poking at the single molar that graced the lower back portion of his gaping mouth.

"Stay out of sight for a while," Cobb said, not unkindly, walking away.

"Hey, what's this?"

Cobb turned to see Nestor clutching a sheet of paper.

"Give me that, that's police property." Cobb could see that Nestor had picked up the broadsheet that Gussie had thrust upon him earlier, the one with the sketch and description of the suspected Yankee agent.

"I seen this fella," Nestor said. His eyes widened larcenously.

Very slowly, Cobb took the paper from Nestor's hand. "Where?"

"In the Tinker's Dam."

The Tinker's Dam was a dive up beyond Jarvis and Lot Street, a hangout for fugitives and their admirers. "You did, did you?" Cobb asked, trying not to reveal his interest. "And when would this've been?"

"What's it worth to ya?"

Cobb smiled menacingly. "You'd sell your granny for sixpence. I'll give you enough for one beer now, and a quarter if anythin' comes of it."

Nestor pretended to think this over. "I saw him a coupla

days ago. I sat near him up there on Friday, I think. A Yankee with a phony Irish brogue, by the sound of him. He was quite pie-eyed, an' braggin' about gettin' even with some swell who had done his family a grievous wrong."

"You're sure? It's a pretty skimpy sketch."

"It's him all right. And I know the name he was usin', though up there it weren't likely the one his mama give him."

"A second beer, then, for the name."

Nestor grinned, winced at the discomfort doing so caused, and said, "Silas McGinty. Can you believe it?"

"I'm beginnin' to believe most anythin'." Cobb sighed. He turned once more to go.

Nestor's voice, with its wheedling whine, followed Cobb out of the alley: "They're all meetin' up at Montgomery's tavern tonight! They're plannin' ta kill us all in our beds!"

Cobb carried on to King Street. He had no doubt who "they" were. But he was trying desperately not to give the least credence to Nestor Peck's so-called "facts."

SIX

Dora had gone out to deliver a baby somewhere on Newgate Street, but Fabian and Delia had come home from school early enough to heat up a stew and butter some of Saturday's bread. They watched their father eat with that mixture of revulsion and awe that children have for the peculiar capacities of adults. Father and offspring were getting ready to leave the house when Dora Cobb came stumbling up the kitchen steps, breathless.

"You run all the way?"

"Don't start, Mister Cobb."

"Trouble, luv?"

"False alarm," she said, puffing and flushing as the children each took hold of a coat-sleeve and pulled.

"Why're you lookin' so grim, then?"

Dora nodded meaningfully towards Fabian and Delia.

"You kids run along to school," Cobb said, and the

youngsters reluctantly left. "Now, what's so grim the kids mustn't hear?"

With her coat removed and her tuque and mittens set adrift, Dora shifted her bulk onto the nearest chair. "I met my sister May on Yonge Street. She'd come in on the coach from the township just to see me."

"Strange time to be visitin' your relatives."

Dora flinched, but was in no mood to defend her turf, which alarmed Cobb considerably. "Her eldest's run off."

Cobb relaxed. "Again?"

"It's serious this time."

"You know darn well young Jimmy's been sniffin' after that Hartley girl ever since threshin' time. They've probably run off together."

Dora gave her husband a withering look. "I ain't no foolish woman, Mister Cobb."

Now it was Cobb who flinched. "What's he done?"

"He run off after supper last night. He took two dollars from the pickle jar—and his daddy's gun!"

"But that old musket ain't been used since the Wars of the Posies."

"It could get him killed." She sighed. And they both knew what she meant.

Cobb began to think that the well-ordered parts of his life had started to come unglued. Could there be any truth to Nestor Peck's story about a radicals' meeting tonight at Montgomery's tavern north of the city on Yonge Street? If one were planning an invasion of the defenceless capital, that would be a logical place for rebels to gather and conspire. Still, there had been many such rumours over the past few weeks. Jimmy Madden's leaving home with money and a gun, however, was both oddly coincidental and ominous. It didn't have the sound of an elopement. He knew now that he would have to pass Nestor's information along to Sarge, though he would give the tale no particular coloration; it was his betters who were responsible for the safety of the government and the province, not a lowly police constable. He certainly would not mention anything about his nephew's unexplained exploit. That was family business, wasn't it?

At any rate, while Dora had raced home with her news, May Madden had made for the police station to enlist Cobb's aid. He agreed to hurry back there himself to see what, if anything, he could do, other than pat her hand and see that she got safely onto the afternoon stage to Thornhill. He was nearing Jarvis Street when he spotted a small person skidding towards him along the snow-slick boardwalk. He stopped and waited, braced for anything.

The messenger-boy known only as Scrawny came huffing straight up to him. "I got this note fer ya, Cobb," he announced.

"That's *mister* to the likes of you."

"Some old lady come bustin' inta the station!" He thrust the note into Cobb's hand.

May Madden could never be described as an old lady, even by Scrawny. "What're you waitin' for?" Cobb asked irritably. "I know you've been paid at the other end. Now git!"

The boy, gloveless and draped in cast-off rags, held his ground—unintimidated. "I thought ya might wanta send some message back."

"Back where?" A cold chill was creeping along the nape of his neck.

"I'm pretty sure it was the old gal from the hat store what brung the note fer ya."

Feeling guilty about rushing past the Court House but more than alarmed at the one-sentence summons from Catherine Roberts ("Please come as soon as you can"), Cobb found himself breathless outside the front entrance of the shop. A hand-written sign in the window read: CLOSED FOR THE DAY.

His fingers had not quite touched the handle when the door swung open.

"Thank God it's you," Beth said. She was pale and shaken.

Aunt Catherine was standing, as if in shock, in the middle of a bonnet display. This time it was she who held a letter stiffly in her left hand.

"He's dead," Cobb said, failing to make the remark a question.

"Oh, no, no, no," Beth said. "This isn't about Marc."

"What, then? Someone in the family?"

Beth took the note from her aunt's grip, guided the older woman to a bench, and sat her gently down.

"I think you'd better read this yerself. It was thrown through the little window in the workroom wrapped around a stone. It nearly hit one of the girls. I had to give them all a sip of brandy before I sent them home. Auntie insisted on going out to look for you, but I shouldn't have let her."

Too startled to respond, Cobb took the wrinkled sheet of quarto-paper from Beth. The message was written in deliberately crude, black capitals:

**YOU HAVE 24 HRS. TO LEAVE TOWN.
THERE'S NO ROOM FOR YANKEES
AND RADICALS IN THIS PROVINCE**

THE LEAGUE FOR JUSTICE

P.S. WE MEAN BUSINESS: GET OUT!

"It could be them young fellas that broke yer front window last month," Cobb said without much conviction. This message had the stamp of more desperate men. The news of the Quebec uprising had given the extremists on the right the upper hand among the moderate Tories, and respectable people without an army or militia to protect them from their enemies and their own fears could do things quite out of character.

"What do you think?" Beth asked, echoing her aunt's question earlier this morning, but the doubt and confusion on Cobb's face, however momentary, gave the game away.

"You ain't seriously thinkin' of leavin'?" he asked.

Beth said, "I've stood up to much worse than this, but—"

"Good. 'Cause I guarantee I'll have the names of these *blaghordes* by tomorrow mornin'."

"And I believe you, Horatio, but who's going put them safe behind bars?"

"I'll do it myself, if I haveta!"

During this brief exchange, Aunt Catherine had remained

seated on the bench, staring straight ahead. Her skin was pasty grey and covered with a sickly sheen. Beth put a hand on her shoulder and looked Cobb resolutely in the eye. "I've got to get her away from here," she said.

"I got family near Woodstock—"

"Out of the country, I mean."

"For good?"

Beth gave him a wry smile. "I wouldn't leave Marc. You know that."

He nodded, still perplexed. "I think yer auntie needs a doctor."

"It's all been too much for her, what with the wedding being called off at the last minute when the troops had to leave for Montreal, the damage to the shop, Rick's death, Marc's getting shot, and now *this*."

"But you can't just up and leave your shop, your *lively-hood* and all."

"Our new tenant next door, Mr. Ormsby, will close it up proper, store the stock, keep an eye on the place till I can get back. I'll see our girls get some severance pay."

"But where can you go?"

"Pennsylvania, where we both have family."

"But it could be risky for two unescorted ladies to travel, the way things are outside the city." Cobb could not bring himself to mention his true fears about what might be about to happen, with all its potential dangers and uncertainties.

"We won't be travelling as two ladies."

"I don't get it."

"My plan is to leave today as soon as it gets dark. Auntie and I'll put on some of Marc's clothes and cut our hair. We'll be two gentlemen on horseback."

"*Horse*back?"

Beth gave him a guilty smile. "We'll need your help."

"The best way I can help is by talkin' you outta this foolishness. Your aunt here is in no shape to ride, and you won't get a mile before some *howl-i-ganders* on one side or the other'll stop you."

"We need two sturdy horses who can get us all the way to the Niagara."

Cobb was about to remonstrate with her again when Aunt Catherine seemed to awaken out of a trance to say, "I rode like a man when I was a girl in Pennsylvania. I will do so again."

"I'm determined to take Auntie home, and I intend to stay with her till she's got her life settled again."

"What about Marc?"

Beth's face darkened. "He knows me," she said quietly. "I've got a letter for him right here. I'd like you to mail it. As soon as we get to Pennsylvania, I'll write you and Major Jenkin and give you our mailing address."

"This still sounds crazy to me."

"Horatio, I know I'm asking a lot from you. I know how desperate you are to stay clear of politics—"

"I'll get the horses from Frank's livery and have a lad bring them around the back about six o'clock."

"Thank you. I'll give you some money for them. We'll leave them at the Central Hotel in Manchester."

They discussed a few more details of Beth's bold scheme; then Cobb allowed himself to be bussed by both women and turned, sadly, to go.

"Goddamn politics," he muttered to an astonished shopper.

What on earth could happen next? Cobb wondered as he headed towards West Market Lane and Ogden Frank's livery. After arranging for the horses to be brought to the shop just after dusk by a trusted stableboy and concocting a cover story no-one at the livery actually believed, Cobb hurried to the station to find his sister-in-law.

"She just left," Gussie intoned without looking up from his copy-work. "Can't wait fer certain people forever."

"She say where she was goin'?"

"To catch the coach home—where she belongs."

Cobb turned to go.

"You ain't give me yer report for the—"

Cobb slammed the door only slightly harder than he intended to.

May Madden and the stagecoach had left a few minutes before Cobb arrived at the depot on Yonge Street. By now he was craving a drink, but not enough to drive him to any of the nearby bars. He had a jug of whiskey hidden in the chicken-coop, but Dora might still be at home, alert and probably on the warpath. Young Jimmy was her favourite nephew. But what could Cobb do to help? The lad certainly wasn't in the city. And if Nestor's talk of a general mustering up at Montgomery's tavern were true, Cobb wasn't about to poke his nose in there and get it shot off. But what if that mob, with or without Jimmy, came storming down Yonge Street tonight or tomorrow? What would he do then? What could anyone loyal to the Crown do?

At six o'clock Cobb slipped into the laneway behind King Street near Bay. Unobserved, he watched two male figures emerge from the millinery shop, peer anxiously about, toss their bulky bundles across the withers of the waiting horses, swing up into the saddle—boldly astride—and trot softly west until they vanished. Cobb cursed the goblins of all politics.

The rest of his evening was blessedly uneventful. The taverns were eerily subdued, with fewer than half their regular customers. Pub talk was carried on in low murmurs, and the very sight of Cobb's uniform, festooned with portions of the omelette Dora had cooked him despite his confession of having missed her sister at the station, was enough to silence men for whom silence was as feared as the heebie-jeebies. Where *was* everybody? After a while he gave the question up, grateful for a few hours of peace after the roilings of the day. As he walked towards his front door and the lamp-lit interior of his home, it began to snow. He thought of Beth and Catherine riding without escort in such weather, in such darkness, along roads congested in all probability with other muffled-up riders galloping towards one kind of mischief or another. He thought about Marc lying in pain in the fetid gloom of some hospital, ministered to by strangers. Then Dora opened the door, filling the rectangle of light with her generous, robust, motherly presence.

They whispered together far into the evening and early morning. Then, at last, they fell separately into an unquiet sleep.

* * *

The knock that repeated itself with blunt insistence upon the front door did not wake Cobb. He had long ago become immune to such interruptions, for it was Dora who was always wanted to ease some squalling infant into the world, to survive hardy or weaken and die. Nor did he notice her roll off the bed and pad in her nightgown off to the cold rooms beyond the coziness of their cocoon. In fact, it took two jabs to the ribs to bring him awake and muttering.

"Jesus, it can't be mornin' already!" he growled.

"It ain't. But there's a fella at the door who wants to see Mister Cobb, an' last time I checked below yer belly button, you was still he."

"Tell him to bugger off and come back when the sun is shinin'."

"He says he's been sent by the governor."

"Jesus!"

Cobb tottered into the kitchen, pulling on his trousers and feeling about for his boots. The dampened fire barely glowed in the grate. He could see his breath.

"Constable Cobb?"

"I'm comin', I'm comin'!"

With his shirt misbuttoned and his jacket, helmet, and greatcoat in hand, he staggered to the door and out onto the stoop.

"You're the governor's stableman," he said accusingly.

"You're to come to Government House right away, sir."

"What in hell's happenin'?"

"I don't know. They just rousted me outta bed an' sent me here with the horses."

Cobb soon found himself cantering through the deserted

streets of Toronto at six in the morning, shivering, unfed, and fighting back a feeling of dread.

As they neared Government House on King Street west of Simcoe, Cobb could see other figures, mounted and on foot, speeding down the long lane that wound its way up to the verandah of Francis Head's sprawling residence. No-one was speaking. Something serious was afoot. Cobb hobbled up onto the porch in the wake of a very familiar rump.

"Wilkie?" he called.

Constable Ewan Wilkie kept on going towards the double-doors that had been swung open to let those summoned enter with dispatch. In the ample foyer Cobb bumped against several bundled-up bodies. All were staring at the door of the governor's office at the far end of the visitors' vestibule. Under a quarter-lit chandelier stood Lieutenant-Governor Sir Francis Bond Head in his nightshirt. His hair looked as if it had been dragged through a briar bush against the grain. His normally handsome features were distorted by the glassy stare of his eyes. His jaw was moving, but to no effect that anyone present could determine. Beside him, pistol *à la main,* quivered his aide-de-camp, Lieutenant Barclay Spooner, similarly disheveled, and blinking anxiously at the arrivals.

The latter, Cobb could see even in the shadowy light, included Wilfrid Sturges, his chief; the other three constables, Wilkie, Brown, and Rossiter; Sheriff Jarvis of York; and half a dozen of his petty officials.

It was Barclay Spooner who broke the silence. "Thank you all for coming. Sir Francis has requested that I deliver the news to you as delicately as I can."

Sir Francis looked as if he would have a difficult time even recognizing his aide-de-camp, let alone dictating instructions to him. Beneath the silk nightwear, his limbs trembled, and it was quite apparent that his agitation had left him catatonic.

"I regret to inform you—officers of the Crown, all—that we are now in a state of apprehended insurrection."

Spooner paused to let the collective gasp rise and ebb.

"Seven hundred armed rebels have gathered around the outlaw Mackenzie at Montgomery's tavern two miles up Yonge Street. Several thousands more are said to be on their way to join them. They have set up pickets along the road to stop any innocent citizen from entering the city and giving the alarm. About midnight Colonel Robert Moodie, a militiaman and one of the finest gentlemen in this province, tried to evade the pickets and run the blockade. He was shot dead by the rabble."

Shocked murmurs at this, and several angry outbursts.

"Two hours ago, I am happy to say, Alderman Powell was making his way north along Yonge to visit his ailing sister in the township when he was illegally detained by the same thugs. But he made an heroic escape, killing one of the ringleaders in the process, one Anthony Anderson. It was John Powell who arrived here less than forty minutes ago to raise the alarm. The rebels' feeble attempt at surprise has been thwarted!"

If Spooner expected the assembled officials to break into a cheer at this news, he was quickly disappointed. To a man they were more concerned with the mustering of thousands of armed insurgents, who were, no doubt, already marching southwards with murderous intent. And the first line of defence for the besieged capital now stood here in the governor's anteroom: groggy, dazed, horrified.

"The governor and I, you will be pleased to learn, have not been idle in the face of imminent danger. While you were being fetched from your slumbers, we have been busy developing a stratagem for delay, until we can get word through to the nearest militia in Hamilton."

Among the mutterings consequent on this stirring revelation—not all of them patriotic—Cobb had his own particular thoughts. Had Catherine and Beth reached Hamilton? Would they find themselves in the midst of a military confrontation? Would any general alarm now raised not put them in danger of being stopped and challenged? And if so, what plausible excuses could they concoct for riding in disguise at night towards the United States, where sympathy and support for the rebels was widespread?

The governor had finally found his voice, and briefly explained that he was organizing a party of loyalists to ride north with the intention of parleying with Mackenzie. An offer of amnesty would be made if the rebels would agree to disband and return peacefully to their homes. Working out the details ought to buy the city's defenders—all twenty of them—some valuable time. In the interim, each man in the room would be assigned an area of the grounds of Government House and its park, where they would act as sentries and, if required, lay down their lives for the Queen's representative. Loaded pistols would be handed out to each loyal watchman.

Sir Francis then wheeled and marched smartly back into his office, unaware that he was still in his frothy, bedtime attire.

* * *

As the sun rose on the morning of Tuesday, December 5, Horatio Cobb found himself squatting on the stump of an elm tree somewhere in the park of Government House. In actuality, it was six acres of unreclaimed bush, a city block of it that stretched out behind the gardens and farm buildings of the house proper. In spots, much of the scrub had been cleared so that Sir Francis and his Tory chums could enjoy a sleigh-ride when the snows really arrived. At the moment there was just enough of it to cover the desiccated fall grasses and mantle the limbs and boughs of the trees. And there Cobb sat, pistol cocked, as the sun climbed above the horizon and shone belligerently in a blue sky, while offering little warmth to anyone trusting enough to admire it. It was a cold day, near zero, and Cobb stamped around the stump like a Mississauga shaman around his campfire, then lay down the pistol and smacked his leather mitts together.

Despite the cold and discomfort, Cobb discovered that he was sweating. He wasn't overly worried about assassins sneaking up through the park from Market Street on the south; in fact, by noon Cobb would have gladly given them a map to the governor's sitting-room. What made him nervous was the fact that no armed force or authority stood between him and the rebel mob on Yonge Street. Surely, they would take advantage of the defenceless city and this cold, clear day to march down the frozen road into the heart of the capital, wheel to the west along King (looting the fashionable shops as they advanced?), and storm the seat of government. Time and again he caught himself listening for sounds from the distant north—the crack-ling of musket-fire or the boom of a field gun—knowing how foolish this was because the insurgents would have no need to deploy their weapons. There was no-one left worth shooting at!

It was well after noon when one of the Government House servants, armed only with a half loaf of bread, a chunk of cheese, and a partly consumed bottle of wine, came noisily up behind and hailed him.

"I'm Colson, sir. I've brought you some luncheon."

Cobb thanked him, had trouble removing his mitts, but managed to bite off a bit of cheese and flush it down with a swig of bitter wine. Colson turned to go.

"Any news?" Cobb asked.

Colson, his English as buttery as any royal butler, stopped and said, "I was thinking of asking you the same question, sir."

"Have they sent a *dele-whatever* up to parley with Macken-zie yet?"

"They've just left, sir. About six of them, I think. On fast horses."

"Jesus, what've they been *doin'* all mornin'? The rebels'll be here by now."

"A scout just returned as I was coming out here, sir. The insurgents have indeed begun to march on the city, but have stopped at Gallow's Hill for some reason not known to us."

"Who've they sent to parley with them?"

"That was the problem, sir. It took several hours of debate among the governor's privy councillors to sort that out. The two men finally chosen to do the bargaining were Mr. Robert Baldwin and Dr. John Rolph."

"Reformers!" Cobb dropped his bread.

"My sentiments entirely, sir."

And with that editorial remark, Colson departed.

Cobb decided he would simply stop thinking and do his duty as a policeman and as a citizen. There was no fathoming the ways and means of politicians, so it was fruitless to try. But once having practised the business of pondering, he discovered that it was no easy task to keep the mind free of such incursions. Fortunately, the snap of twigs off to his right provided a helpful diversion.

With all of his senses alert for the first time today, Cobb hopped off the stump and trotted soundlessly towards the noise. Someone was running hastily through the park—but away from the house, not towards it. Could it be an assassin who had already carried out his contemptible deed? Cobb's heart began to pound. Suddenly, he burst out into a clearing and stopped in puzzlement. Where was the bugger? He looked towards the house and saw that he had come out just behind the modest farm-grounds in back of the residence, where there were several small barns, pens, and coops. A loud crashing noise at the south end of the clearing brought him upright and sent him scampering in that direction. The culprit had fallen. And from the high-pitched cursing, it appeared he had injured himself. Cobb closed in for the capture, charging out of a clump of spruce to surprise the felon.

What he saw was a wiry-looking fellow stumbling back into

cover about fifteen yards away. Under his right arm, in screeching protest, wriggled a suckling pig.

"Stop!" Cobb hollered. "You're under arrest!"

Which command, though ringing with authority and threat, had contrary effects on the hog-thief and his prize. The man seemed to take wing, and the piglet, terrified, shut up. Cobb glanced down at what he took to be his trusty truncheon in his right hand, was surprised to note that it was a loaded pistol, and, squeezing his eyes closed, fired it into the air.

The felon stopped, about twenty yards away. He turned slowly to face his assailant. His eagle eye spotted the smoking pistol. A huge grin spread across his visage. He wheeled nimbly and sped off. But in doing so, he relaxed his grip on the piglet, and it scurried away, zigzagging and bewildered.

Cobb had glimpsed the face for no more than a second or two, but he recognized it. He plunged ahead into the trees in hot pursuit. When it became obvious that the fellow was gaining ground on him, Cobb halted and shouted loud enough to be heard on Gallow's Hill.

"You won't get far! I know your face and your name, Silas McGinty!"

But, of course, Cobb realized the moment he said it that McGinty would indeed get as far away from the city as possible, since he was now aware that his latest alias was known to the police and his mug would be popping up on posters all over town.

Cobb was just about to return to his post, empty-handed, when he spotted something dark against the snow, next to one of the thief's footprints, something that had fallen unnoticed during his frantic escape. Cobb picked it up. It was a billfold. Inside he found a wrinkled American dollar, tucked forlornly into a much-thumbed envelope. But it was the inscription on the envelope that arrested his attention:

SERGEANT CALVIN RUMSEY
FORT NIAGARA, NEW YORK
XOXOXOXO

Silas McGinty, my fanny! Cobb thought. Could this fellow be related to the man who had been involved in a crime that he and Marc Edwards had investigated the previous year, one Philo Rumsey? What was he doing skulking about Toronto? Spying? Or looking for some sort of payback on behalf of his "wronged" brother? If so, then Marc might be in danger—were he not lying wounded in a hospital somewhere in Quebec.

It was dusk when the intrepid band of twenty, under the command of Sheriff Jarvis, turned north off King Street onto Yonge. They were a motley crew of policemen, bailiffs, deputies, and half a dozen ordinary citizens co-opted or "volunteered." Each had been handed a British rifled musket, scavenged earlier by Lieutenant Spooner from Fort York, and two bullets in paper cartridges. Jarvis and his men were to establish a picket on Yonge Street just above College Avenue. A force of five hundred militia, who knew how to load and fire a musket, were on their way by steamer from Hamilton, and were expected to arrive around midnight. Jarvis's orders were to stall the rebels' advance, if possible, and otherwise watch their movements and send back reports to Government House.

Much had happened since midafternoon, but Cobb had learned only bits and pieces from a variety of unreliable sources. Members of Cobb's class were not routinely briefed by officialdom, after all. What was known for sure was that Sir Francis had placed his wife and family and that of Chief Justice Robinson aboard a steamer on Queen's Wharf with instructions to flee to Kingston should the capital fall and the fast-forming lake ice permit. The first truce up at Gallow's Hill had lasted for two hours, with Mackenzie demanding a constitutional convention and the governor offering only amnesty.

The rebels then moved farther down Yonge Street, past Bloor. A second truce and parley—with the governor refusing to put his amnesty offer in writing—broke up in disarray. Now it seemed that if the rebels could somehow be tricked into further delay, the militia would arrive to save the day and do honour to the Queen.

Jarvis had ordered his pickets to remain silent as they trudged over the snowy, rutted roadway through the chill of a December twilight. There was a bright half-moon about to ascend in the East, but scudding clouds made its illumination uncertain. Cobb wasn't sure whether it was safer to see where he was going or to be obscured in total darkness. With fellow constables Wilkie and young Rossiter on either side of him, Cobb fingered his musket nervously. It had been twelve years at least since he had fired a gun at his father's side, hunting rabbits or grouse. And he had certainly never used one of these new-fangled paper cartridges. Besides that, there was the question of killing someone anonymously. There was every chance that one of the rebels up ahead was his nephew, Jimmy Madden, clutching his father's stolen gun. What could have driven the boy to such a pass? To jettison his family, his new-found love, his own future? Something had gone terribly wrong, that was all Cobb knew. And good men, young and old, were about to die because of it.

It was pitch black when Sheriff Jarvis called a halt and ordered the men to set up their picket behind a snake-fence a few yards above College Avenue. But even with the moon blocked by thick cloud, the snow on the ground conspired to make their hunched silhouettes alarmingly visible. Cobb set his rifle down and tried to thaw his fingertips under his armpits. Stretched out on either side of him, his colleagues-in-arms stamped their feet incessantly, in a vain attempt to keep the blood circulating or ward off a numbing terror. There was little else to do but wait.

Just after six o'clock the white ribbon that was Yonge Street began to disappear into a tumble of shadows and to echo hollowly with the tramp of several hundred boots.

"They haven't seen us yet," Jarvis whispered. "When I raise my sword, I want everybody to fire at once. Take aim at a single figure. Do not shoot blindly. If we kill a dozen of them with one volley, we may stall the advance. God be with you."

Which was precisely the prayer going round the rebel side, too, Cobb thought with a grimace. Soundlessly, those next to him laid the barrels of their rifles on top of the log-fence and began sighting a target. They had the advantage of being partially hidden and of being able to fire effectively without having to stand. Just then the moon made an untimely appearance. The front rank of the rebels, armed with rifles, had spotted them and dropped to one knee in preparation for a killing volley. The two groups were now no more than thirty yards apart. A wild susurration rose up from the rebels. Sheriff Jarvis raised his sword in defiance.

As the air was shattered by the roar of nineteen muskets exploding around him, Horatio Cobb, loyal officer of the Crown, levered his rifle aloft, took dead aim at the alabaster belly of the half-moon, and pulled the trigger.

SEVEN

With considerable difficulty Marc forced his eyes open, then snapped them shut. Someone was shining a bright light directly into them: they throbbed with the pain of it. He felt another throb in his left thigh, and remembered the gunshot and the indignity as the bullet struck. He listened for the sound of footsteps; surely Sergeant Ogletree had heard the explosions? He could discern only a low murmur of voices and someone groaning through his teeth.

Marc tried to get a sense of where he had fallen. He was definitely on his back, even though he recalled pitching forward as he lost consciousness. He had no memory of hitting the floor. His thought now was that he ought to roll onto his side and try to get up. He didn't want Ogletree and the men bursting in here and blazing away at civilians. But he couldn't move. It wasn't only his injured leg; it was the other one, too, and both his arms. He just seemed too weary to move, even lifting his eyelids had been an effort. What had happened to him? Mustering as much courage as strength, he opened his eyes again. Blinking away the intrusive light, he kept them open. He had been staring into a thin sunbeam angling into a shadowy, dank room of some sort through a crack in the siding.

"Nurse, come quickly! He's awake!"

The voice, off to his right, was excited, and very Scottish. He didn't recognize it. Then came the pounding of several feet on a wooden floor. The groaning, farther off, continued, muted but piteous. A sequence of odours struck his nostrils: privy-stink, animal gore, a dankness of rot and mouldy decay, his own fetid sweat. Two shadows suddenly blocked the sunbeam. He opened his eyes wide but found he could not raise his head to see who was now hovering over him. He tried moving his lips; the ghost of a voice emerged, but no words. A woman's moon-face swam across his vision. A stubby finger brushed his upper lip and came to rest under his nose.

"You're right, MacKay. He's awake and breathing. I wouldn't've given a farthing for his chances."

"I'll fetch the doctor and the major."

"Don't go bothering Dr. Wilder. Major Jenkin will do."

"He's tryin' to tell us somethin'."

Marc heard a voice somewhat like his own say, "I'm co—ode."

"It's okay, Lieutenant. I'll fetch ye another blanket."

"You'll do no such thing, Mr. MacKay. Do you want all these other wretches crying out for one?"

* * *

The next time Marc opened his eyes, Owen Jenkin, quartermaster of the 24th and his loyal friend, was seated beside him and smiling as if he could do nothing else. Marc felt tears hot upon his cold cheeks. The major reached over and pulled a fresh-smelling blanket up to his chin.

"Don't expend your energy trying to talk, lad. You're going to need it all for putting some flesh and muscle back on your bones—now that you've decided to live."

Marc shaped a question with his lips, cracked and dry though they were.

"Well, you may think you're in one of Hell's vestibules when you get a chance to look around you," Jenkin said, "but this is what passes for a military hospital in Montreal these days. We've been practically suffering a siege for two weeks, but things've quieted down now."

Marc's puzzlement must have shown.

"There's a lot you'll want to know, and I'll do my best to fill you in. It's hard to know where to start, but I'll begin with you and go from there. In a day or so you'll be peppering me with questions and correcting my Welsh grammar!" He took a few moments to laugh, which was only a slight exaggeration of his smile. "You were shot in the leg down in St. Denis late on December 1. Ogletree figures you passed out from shock. They carried you back into the village after making sure the habitant you shot dead was the only armed Frenchie in the house or on the property. But the surgeon had been called out to a place on the other side of town, and by the time he got to you, you'd lost a ton of blood. He told me he had to tie up some cord or other in your upper leg, then cauterize the wound. He told Captain

Riddell that if you survived the shock of the blood-loss, you'd be healthy as a cart-horse, though you'd have a slight limp on the left side."

Someone groaned from the nearby shadows.

"Poor bugger." Jenkin sighed. "He's praying to die. And that's what everyone thought you'd be doing—dying, that is. They put you on the ambulance-wagon and left you there, thinking you'd never last the trip to Sorel. But you were still breathing when they got there, so they kept you at the barracks for three days, waiting for you to stop. When nothing changed, the doc had you put on a steamer with half a dozen of the hopelessly wounded and three dead. Again, he was surprised to find you alive that same evening in Montreal. There've been so many casualties, military and civilian, here in the past two weeks that the health officials decided to set up this temporary hospital in an old immigrant holding-shed down here near the wharf. It used to be a warehouse for fur traders: you can smell the musk, among the other stink."

Marc moved his lips with an urgent question.

"It's December 17. You've been unconscious for sixteen days."

The major leaned down and, with his handkerchief, wiped Marc's cheeks dry. Then he wetted a corner of it in a bowl of water at his feet and dabbed at Marc's parched lips. "I engaged young Davey MacKay, the attendant with the brogue, to keep a close watch on you. This place is a mecca for thieves and mischief-makers, though your uniform and accoutrements are safe in a trunk in the officers' quarters of the Royal Regiment.

As soon as you can be moved safely, we'll have you taken up there for rehabilitation."

A young woman flitted past Major Jenkin and out of Marc's vision.

"That's one of the nurse-attendants. You'll get used to them scooting about here, emptying the pans and slops, scrubbing the human messes off the floor, and trying to avoid the foghorn bellow of Head Nurse Cartwright. All the female help here are French: they work for a shilling a week and all the bad food they can stomach."

As if on cue, the foghorn boomed from some distance: "Py-ette! Take that pail outside, now! *Vite! Vite!*"

Marc uttered his first pure word: "Beth."

Major Jenkin smiled reassuringly. "There's so much to tell you about Beth and all that's happened, but she's fine, fine. Meanwhile, you've managed to sleep through two rebellions!"

Which one of these topics the major was about to choose went unresolved, for the patient was once more asleep.

Marc's head was propped up on a greasy pillow, and Davey MacKay was spooning a surprisingly tasty soup into his mouth.

"This ain't the gruel they give to the poor souls on the other side of the room. The major has yer food sent down from the Royal's mess. He's been attached to them until the fuss dies down and all the froggies are back in the pond. The rest o' yer fellas have gone back to Toronto, where they shoulda stayed in the first place."

Marc nodded towards the shadows and prone silhouettes on the far, windowless side of the cavernous room.

"You're the only officer here, sir. Them fellas're just foot-soldiers who got in the way of a rebel bullet. Since nobody here expects them to live, it'd be a shame to waste good food on them."

Ravenous, and with little shame, Marc ate.

"Here comes the major. I'll leave ya to him."

Owen Jenkin settled in beside Marc, and took out his tinder-box, pipe, and tobacco pouch. Cautioning Marc not to attempt to speak, he picked up where he had left off yesterday. Or was it an hour ago? Marc had no idea.

"There's no tactful way to say this, Marc, so I won't try. Beth and her aunt are now in Bedford Valley, Pennsylvania. Don't fret yourself: they're both in good health and reasonable spirits, considering what happened. To make a long story short, Catherine felt she could no longer safely live in Toronto, so Beth—well, you know how her loyalties work—arranged to accompany her to where they both have relatives in Bedford, way down in the south part of the state. They got there about a week ago, and I've received two letters from her, even though the mails, and most everything else, is in turmoil and chaos. You'll be able to read them for yourself in a day or two. But the ladies are looking to set up a business for the aunt—they smuggled out a fair amount of specie, it seems. Beth will stay there until Catherine is on her feet, perhaps only a few weeks if all goes well. She learned about your wound just before she left, and I've written her in Bedford to let her know the wonderful news of your recovery. My guess is that you'll each arrive back in Toronto about the same week, in time to tie the knot."

The major beamed, while Marc tried to absorb what he was hearing and suppress the dozen questions he couldn't yet speak aloud.

"Now I see Davey heading this way with a bowl of hot water and a razor. Even Beth wouldn't recognize you with that Viking's bush!"

Once clean-shaven, scrubbed raw, and settled on fresh sheets, Marc dozed and half woke, dreamed hazily, and tried to interpret the eccentric sights and sounds that coloured his waking moments. Beth appeared to him in both venues: in her bridal dress and veil, smiling and beckoning, and floating by in her drab nurse's clothes like an earth-bound but loving angel. He called out to her in English, then in French, but she merely smiled beatifically and moved on.

"Mr. Edwards, I would be grateful if you didn't try to speak to the hired help and interfere with their duties. What's more, they're expressly forbidden to use that lingo of theirs above a whisper in this hallowed place."

Once, he was almost certain, one of them paused at his calling out, turned to say something back in her own tongue, then shuddered under the head nurse's bellow and skittered away.

"Pay no attention to the old troll, sir. Her first name's Magda, but everybody 'round here calls her Magna Carta—behind her back, that is!" The soap and razor felt wonderful on Marc's chin. And even as he dreamt and lolled hazily through the day-nights, he continued to eat. His hands and arms began to move where he wished them to. The throbbing in his thigh was ebbing. He remembered to say thank you to Davey.

* * *

"You'll want to know what's been going on in the wars," the major was saying one afternoon.

"Yes. Tell me everything."

"Well, your brigade finished off the rebels in the Richelieu Valley. Most of them fled into Vermont to re-group. Then, a couple of days before you woke up, General Colborne organized and led an attack on their stronghold north of here at St. Eustache, with three thousand troops. It was a slaughterhouse. More than fifty rebels died. The church was levelled, then burned. The village was looted and razed. They moved on to St. Benoit, which surrendered without a fight. The ringleaders' houses were destroyed. But when the regulars left, the militia and English locals burned down the church and sacked the entire village. Reprisals are still going on all over the province, despite the general's decree that they be stopped. It's not a pretty sight out there in the countryside. I've been having nightmares about Spain again for the first time in years."

Marc pictured barns in flames, haystacks ablaze, families huddled in the cold woods. He saw the houses of St. Denis with smoke pouring out of smashed windows. He saw the young habitant in that shadowy room, his throat blown out and his hands lifting to it as if to pray.

"And I don't wish to alarm you, but you'd best hear the news from me. There's been an uprising in Upper Canada as well. A few days after you got shot, Mackenzie and about seven hundred credulous farmers, led by one Samuel Lount, made a run at the capital."

Here the major amazed Marc by chuckling. "I know it isn't funny, Marc, but it really was a curious contretemps. Our friend, Sir Francis, had emptied the province of regulars, as you know, and stationed the principal militia group at Hamilton to ward off any Yankees raging across the frontier at Niagara. The city was defended by a gaggle of volunteers and citizen conscripts—about twenty in total—who bumped into Mackenzie's army on Yonge Street. In the dark! The loyalists fired first, I'm told, then dropped their rifles and ran for their lives, due south. Lount had ordered his front rank to kneel and fire a volley, which they did, to no effect except to spook those behind them, who thought they had all fallen dead. At which, the rebel regiment turned and ran as well, not stopping till they reached Montgomery's tavern. A day and a half later, Colonel MacNab led the militia and a marching band up Yonge Street and scattered the rabble for good. Mackenzie's already in Buffalo, they say, trying to rouse the Americans to mount an invasion."

"Were there casualties?"

"A few on both sides. But the devil of it is that reprisals and barn burnings have started up, as they did here. No roads outside the towns are safe, as fleeing rebels and vengeful loyalists take pot-shots at one another. The jails in both provinces are filling up, and there's talk of treason trials and hangings."

"Maybe Beth is safer where she is."

"I believe so, lad. And so are you in here. We've crushed Papineau and Nelson, but the border threats down in Vermont are real, and no Englishman dares walk the streets or byways alone or unarmed. You can taste hatred in the air."

"What's going to happen now?"

The major shook his grey head. "I wish I knew. It's going to be a damn sight harder to put the pieces back together than it was to scatter them by force." He puffed on his pipe, and offered it to Marc, who declined with a shake of his head. "I saw the letter from your uncle Frederick," the major said slowly. "I recognized my old friend's handwriting right away, and, not knowing if you'd ever regain consciousness, I opened it."

Marc smiled to let him know it was all right.

"I am deeply sorry about the death of Jabez; he was, in every practical way, your father. I wrote immediately to Frederick to offer my sympathy and to let him know why you yourself had not written back. Some military and official mail is getting out through Halifax or New York, but its arrival time, as usual, is uncertain. Nevertheless, I've already dispatched a further brief note informing him of your miraculous recovery."

Marc had a suitable reply on his lips, but sleep once more supervened.

Beth was coming to him, her sinuous shape darkly sensual in a silken chemise, her copper-blond hair haloed around her head. He seemed unable to lift himself towards her, but his arms stretched out in invitation, his loins stirred deliciously. There was something in her right hand, a love token perhaps. No, it was long and sharp, and it was rising. . . .

He woke, awash in his own sweat. The room, as usual, was cold, damp, and dark, the smoky heat from the fireplace at one end being more cosmetic than real. His teeth were chattering.

"Davey!" His voice was a hollow croak, despite its desperation.

Owen Jenkin arrived with Davey MacKay in tow and a scowling head nurse. The major was unable to hide the concern in his face. "You've been thrashing about with a fever, lad. You've had us all worried sick."

Davey began sponging the sweat from Marc's face with a damp towel. "But the fever's broken now, I'm happy to say."

"All this fuss in the middle of the night. You'll be expecting the doctor to show up next," Magda Cartwright grumbled, then hustled off, her capacious bosom intimidating the air before it like the prow of a galleon.

"It's actually dawn," Davey said. "We been snoozin' in the next room, waitin' fer you to rally." He went off to fetch warm water and more towels.

"We've got to get you out of here soon," the major said. "Three men died of the fever yesterday. But Doc Wilder thinks you're still too weak." He helped Marc sit up and watched him drink half a cup of cold water before pulling it away.

A little while later Marc was able to say, "I had the strangest dream, Owen. Beth was coming to me, and I was reaching out to her, when suddenly there was a sharp and menacing object in her right hand. I thought she was going to strike me, but—"

"You woke up, thankful it was a nightmare."

"It seemed so real."

"Yes, but you were hallucinating with the fever."

Davey MacKay came up on the other side of the crude bed, a mere pallet on wooden slats. As he set the basin of water on the floor, he let out a startled cry. "What the hell is this?"

He held up into the dim light a long, sharp-pointed instrument.

"A bayonet," the major whispered, as Marc turned to look at it. "Old and rusted, but recently honed. How did it get here?"

Davey was examining the wooden edge of Marc's bed. "This board's been splintered. Bits of it are still here on the floor. Fresh."

The major came around to see for himself. "And whatever did it sliced through Marc's blanket first."

There was a stunned silence.

"It looks as if somebody's tried to murder you," the major said.

When Marc had been bathed, shaved, fed, and provided with a clean nightshirt, Owen Jenkin returned and sat down on his familiar stool. He waited for one of the French aides to move away towards the moaning forms across the room, then said, "We figure it was a thief hoping to get something valuable from an officer's kit. The Frenchies'll steal anything. Many of them are starving, or their families are. When he couldn't find anything worthwhile, he probably got enraged and stabbed at you in the dark. Or you may have been muttering in your delirium, and he took it as a threat and just lashed out."

Marc nodded in agreement.

"What puzzles Davey and me the most, though, is how he managed to get past us. We were asleep on cots right beside the only door into this area, and Magna Carta herself sleeps standing up like a horse in her little stall by the main door, which she swears was latched."

"One of the nurse-attendants could have left it unlatched before turning in."

"Or done so deliberately."

Marc thought that over. "I think a fly would terrify them," he said.

"Well, herself is giving them all a tongue-lashing for good measure. They won't understand a word, but they'll get the message."

"What should we do about this? It's not likely to happen again."

"True. But I've put Davey, on twenty-four-hour alert. And doubled his wages."

"You mustn't do things like that, Owen."

"Your uncle Frederick and I went through the wars together for ten years," the major said, and left it at that.

Marc's strength began to return slowly. He ate regular meals, and could sit at the side of the bed and waggle his legs to simulate walking. He, Davey, and Owen Jenkin celebrated Christmas quietly together. Marc managed to slip each of the five habitant girls a half crown without being seen and up-braided by Magna Carta, who refused Marc's largesse with a cold sniff.

"That wasn't too wise," Davey said when he found out, "if you'll excuse me sayin' so, sir. If the Frenchies think you got money here, they may tell their friends, if you know what I mean. They don't know you had Major Jenkin bring the coins down from the barracks."

Marc thanked him for his concern.

The day before New Year's Marc reread Beth's letters and, with the major's help, wrote her a one-page reply. A third letter arrived from Beth soon after, more detailed and upbeat than the first two. Marc was now grateful that Beth was so frank and unflinching in her assessment of people and circumstances. When she told him that Aunt Catherine had purchased a ladies' haberdashery in Bedford Valley, and that it would be only a matter of weeks before she returned home, he could believe it without reservation. He only hoped that his own strict account of his progress towards full health (he even mentioned the attack of fever and the possibility of his limping to gain credibility) would be accepted at face value and provide her with the comfort she deserved.

The only dark note in her recent letter was her continuing concern for the well-being of Winnifred and Thomas Goodall, baby Mary, and her brother Aaron, who lived with them on Beth's farm in Crawford's Corners. She had heard of Mackenzie's coup and the ructions following it. She wondered whether the manhunt for fleeing rebels and known sympathizers would turn up the facts of Thomas's earlier and recanted involvement in the radical movement or, for that matter, Winnifred's brief fling with Reformist politics a year ago? She had written Dora Cobb in Toronto and Erastus Hatch, Winnifred's father, in Crawford's Corners, but had received no reply. Marc was to write her every day as soon as his strength allowed and to let her know what was happening—by which she meant the unembroidered truth.

This time Marc awoke out of a dreamless sleep. The musty, acrid odour of the darkness all about him let him know instantly where he was, and that he had indeed wakened. Someone was moving, stealthily, it seemed, among the cots to his left. While it was unusual for the head nurse or any of the male attendants or female aides to tend to one of the stricken men in the middle of the night, it was not implausible that some wrenching cry for help might have tempted one of the latter out of an exhausted sleep. Too bulky surely to be female, the figure was sliding, hunched over, from cot to cot, pausing ever so briefly at each. Marc braced himself, knowing that whatever was about to unfold, he was helpless to prevent it. When the figure rounded the last of the cots and aimed itself at him, Marc opened his mouth to call for assistance but discovered his throat and lips were too dry to utter anything but a hoarse croak. But it was enough to bring the intruder up short. He halted in midstride, peered haplessly into the shadow above Marc's bed, and decided to bolt.

He didn't get far. Up from a straw pallet where he had been stationed rose Davey MacKay, and, with a low growl that would have made his Highland ancestors proud, he set off after the fleeing figure. A clattering tackle was made at the open entranceway, knocking the wind and all resistance out of him. Marc could hear the ensuing commotion of raised voices, male and female—shrill, accusing, abusive in both languages—but could make little sense of any of it.

A few minutes later one of the aides slipped up to Marc's bed and whispered urgently in his ear, in French. "They have arrested my brother, Gilles. They say he tried to kill you with a knife last week. That is not true. He came in tonight only to steal, to buy food for his babes. But it was not I who left the latch undone. I swear, m'sieur. The big nurse, she's dismissed me. Now we have nothing."

Marc reached over the edge of the bed and under the mattress. He drew out three silver coins and dropped them into the girl's hand. "That's all I can do. I'm truly sorry."

The girl thanked him tearfully and vanished, though she had no inkling of what had prompted the English officer to such generosity.

EIGHT

I t was the middle of January when Dr. Jonas Wilder deemed Lieutenant Marc Edwards fit enough to travel by coach to Toronto. Winter had set in with a will. Only the most rapid-ridden sections of the St. Lawrence remained unfrozen; every other creek and stream had been sealed tight. Three feet of snow fell and accumulated in the bush. The unreliable autumn roads were now snow-packed, icy smooth, and conducive to swift transport. Complicating matters, however, was the general lawlessness of the rural and less-populated areas of both provinces, as reprisal and counterreprisal continued apace, exacerbated by threats of invasion—from Vermont by land, and across the St. Lawrence and Niagara Rivers. While Wolfred Nelson was now in jail and Louis Joseph Papineau sulked in Albany like Achilles in his tent, Robert Nelson and other rebel leaders like Gagnon and Coté were gathering support on the lower Richelieu.

Then, on December 29, Colonel MacNab, asserting his authority in the face of the still-dithering and about-to-be-recalled Governor Head, had ordered a bold nighttime attack on an American ship, the *Caroline,* which had been assisting Mackenzie from Navy Island, a small redoubt in the Niagara River. The ship was boarded, taken over, set on fire, and put adrift towards the falls. A U.S. citizen had died during the boarding, and several others had been injured. The resulting furore had brought the jingoists out in full, frothing panoply. The Hunters' Lodges, American-based groups conspiring to invade Canada, expanded tenfold. Sabres were rattled. And everywhere along the thousand-mile border, fear, tension, and paranoia had begun to replace common sense and past precedent. So it was that the highway that hugged the shoreline of the St. Lawrence and Lake Ontario from Cornwall to Toronto was no longer a sure or safe road to travel.

Just after New Year's, and about ten days after the thief and would-be murderer had been manacled and imprisoned (habeas corpus having been suspended and martial law declared), Marc had been carried on a litter up to the barracks of the Royal Regiment and installed in the officers' quarters. Davey MacKay came along and remained. Marc heard from Beth often, though her letters did not always arrive in sequence, and he dutifully kept her informed of his daily progress. ("The limp, my darling, is slight, and the pleasure—the pure joy—of walking again, however unsteadily, is more than I could have hoped for when I first awoke in the noisome darkness of that hospital room.") Beth had heard back from Dora Cobb, with a brief narrative of her husband's "military adventure" appended, and while Dora and Mister Cobb had learned joyfully of Marc's recovery, they had no knowledge of anything or anyone at Crawford's Corners. Some of the rebels, certainly Samuel Lount and Peter Matthews, were about to be put on trial, charged with treason. And the capital was naturally a tense and divided town. Finally, Dora had suggested that their home would be open to Marc if he needed a quiet place to convalesce.

Dr. Wilder laid down strict criteria for Marc's travel arrangements: he was to move no more than forty miles per day, the going rate for this time of year, after which he was to remain for at least a night and half a day at the staging inn to rest, eat, and take moderate exercise before moving on. However, because many of the regular stagecoach schedules had been abandoned for the present, it was not likely that such intermittent arrangements for Marc could be smoothly executed. Nonetheless, he optimistically estimated that the four- or five-day trip could be accomplished in less than two weeks, which would bring him into Toronto by the end of the month. Happily, Beth's most recent letter suggested that she, too, would arrive there at about the same time.

Major Jenkin began looking about for a coach-sleigh leaving Montreal for Cornwall, one that would be both secure and comfortable for his young friend. Two days after the doctor had pronounced Marc fit to travel, Major Jenkin arrived with good news. He had taken a place in a coach that had been chartered by several worthies and was going as far as Kingston, from which spot Marc could easily arrange public or private transportation to Toronto. There would be five fellow passengers in a luxurious, roofed carriage fitted out with runners, with a reliable driver and four of the best horses money could lease. There would be overnight stops at Cornwall and Prescott. Moreover, for a suitable fee, the passengers had gladly agreed to extended stopovers to accommodate the "hero of St. Denis." Marc winced at this characterization of his rescue of a single soldier from the battlefield, but he did not interrupt Jenkin, who went on to explain that the head of this party was a captain in the Glengarry militia. The fellow carried a weapon and was capable of providing additional security, should it become necessary.

"He's travelling home to Kingston from his sister-in-law's funeral here this week with two other members of his family," the major informed Marc. "The fourth fellow is a wealthy wine merchant on his way to Toronto, as English and Tory as one might wish. The fifth chap is a notary or solicitor, I'm told, en route to Cobourg, your sometime stamping ground."

"I don't know how to thank you," Marc said. He was seated on the edge of his bed, not yet dressed.

"I do: be well, and get yourself married."

"And what are these?" Marc asked lightly, pointing to a bundle of clothing piled on top of a large trunk that dwarfed Marc's own modest box. "Extra layers of wool in case of blizzard?"

The major almost blushed. "I want you to forget about your uniform and put on these things I've laid out for you. There are several other ensembles and gentleman's accessories inside. I bought the works from a tall but impecunious barrister yesterday morning and had Davey haul them in here last night."

"Go in disguise, you mean?" Marc was laughing as he held up a finely tailored suitcoat and worsted trousers.

"I'm serious. You are defenceless—unless you agree to carry a loaded pistol everywhere you go. You are still very weak, and with your game leg, you couldn't outrun a duck. I hate to be so blunt, but—"

"It's all right, Owen. If you insist on this, I'll go along with it. But remember that you've already told my fellow passengers they're accompanying the 'hero of St. Denis,' so my identity won't be secret for long. And where on earth did that ridiculous appellation come from?"

"It's not the passengers or the innkeepers I'm worried about. But we've heard tales of sleighs and wagons being stopped randomly and searched for fleeing rebels and, on the other side, of exasperated rebels taking random shots at anybody in uniform, particularly officers like you, who have been made instant heroes by the English populace."

Marc was still eyeing the haberdashery. "I'll look like the wine merchant's partner," he chuckled, holding up the ruffled blouse and chequered vest. "And why this monstrous dull greatcoat? My own is perfectly fine."

"Yes, with the gold and green trim of the 24th Regiment, recognized everywhere in the province. Besides, Davey's already packed it with your uniform."

"My God, where did you come by this?"

"That, sir, is all the rage in Montreal and New York." He plunked the fur helmet on Marc's head and pulled down the flaps.

"Did you liberate this from some Cossack?" Marc grinned like a lunatic and flapped the fur wings of the hat.

"It'll keep your ears warm and aid your disguise."

"I agree: no officer in the Queen's army would be caught dead in this."

"And I want you caught alive: by your long-suffering bride."

Marc said good-bye to Owen Jenkin and Davey MacKay at the barracks, where a cutter had been hired to take him over to the Royal Arms hotel to rendezvous with the stagecoach.

"I'll be joining you soon, I trust," the major said. "In the meantime, I'll pass this news along to Beth and forward any of her letters to you in Toronto. I may even give them to the military courier who rides daily between here and Kingston. Privileges of a quartermaster, eh?"

"Thank you for everything, Owen. I'll write you as soon as I get home."

Davey now stepped respectfully forward, his open, freckled face grave: "May the Lord bless you, sir."

"He's more likely to bless *you*," Marc said in farewell.

In front of the Royal Arms on a cold but still winter's morning, Marc spotted a splendid coach sitting on a pair of formidable runners and in the reliable grasp of four, shiny-coated dray-horses. The driver, a craggy-faced fellow of in-determinate years, was arranging several bags, portmanteaux, and small trunks on top of the carriage. Watching him with proprietorial interest from the boardwalk in front of the hotel were four well-turned-out gentlemen and a lady. All eyes swung towards the sound of Marc's cutter pulling up behind the coach. One of the figures detached itself from the group and sprang forward to help Marc out of his seat. Marc took the gloved hand and raised himself onto the snow-packed street.

"Thank you, sir. My name is Marc Edwards."

"Oh, we know, Lieutenant. We know all about you! I'm Captain Randolph Brookner of the Glengarry militia." Of that there could be little doubt, for despite the subfreezing temperature the good captain had disdained either greatcoat or hat—the former draped over one arm and the latter, a fur helmet, tucked under the other—in order not to deprive the onlookers or his travelling companions of the resplendency of his tunic and trimmings: a livid green broadcloth with mustard piping and vermilion epaulettes. An officer's sword was ostentatiously buckled on and glittering, and a pistol sat perky in its studded holster. His boots gleamed, begging to be admired.

"Thank you, sir, but I'm quite able to walk unaided." Marc smiled as he politely removed the captain's hand from his elbow. "But don't ask me to sprint to the corner!"

"Then the word of your miraculous recovery has not been exaggerated. What an honour it is to meet an officer who fought at St. Denis and to be able to assist you on your way back to your glorious regiment."

Marc limped resolutely towards the other passengers. It was at this moment that Captain Brookner noticed that Marc was not in uniform: even his boots were low-cut and quite ordinary, and the fur hat demeaning his manly brow was exactly like the one seen on a hundred pedestrian heads in town—and on two of his companions.

"But you are not in uniform, sir!" he declared to Marc's back.

Marc paused. "It's in my luggage. There'll be plenty of time to put it on when I reach my regiment, as you say."

Brookner swallowed his disappointment, and said brightly, "What does the symbolism matter, eh? It's the grit and valour of the man. And I am proud to have been able to offer you a seat in my chartered coach. My desire is to maintain a pace to Kingston suited entirely to your fitness to travel. Please introduce yourself to the others while I sort out our driver and the mess he's making of our bags." He spun on his heels like a drum-major and began barking instructions to Marc's driver and then to the one already up on the coach. As he did so, Marc noted that he was tall, athletic, and fair-haired: a picture-postcard soldier.

Marc hobble-walked to the group on the boardwalk, who had been observing the scene before them without comment. He was delighted with the strength in his legs, and the little wobble to the left grew less noticeable as he found the appropriate pace and rhythm for it. A portly, soft-fleshed gentleman with round, uninquisitive eyes stepped forward with his hand out. He was attired, Marc noted with an inward chuckle, in a smart grey overcoat and fur helmet exactly like his own.

"Good morning, sir, and welcome," the man enthused with a loose-lipped smile that rippled all the way to his jowls. The accent was flamboyantly English. "I am Ainslie Pritchard, wine merchant of London and Montreal, presently on my way to Toronto. Let me introduce you to these fine people who shall be accompanying us to Kingston and beyond."

As Pritchard introduced them, Marc acknowledged each with a short bow.

"This is Mr. Percy Sedgewick, gentleman farmer from the Kingston area. And Mr. Charles Lambert, a solicitor from Cobourg on his way home. And, pardon me for addressing you last, madam, this is—"

"Adelaide Brookner," the lady said in a flat, listless voice, as if she were hoping that by stating her name she would not be obligated to say more. Marc bowed, and gave her a quick, scrutinizing glance. She was all in black—her boots, the skirt beneath the black coat, the scarf at her throat, the fur cap, and the veil attached to it. Behind the latter, Marc could just discern a face with handsome, regular features, solemn blue eyes, and a wisp or two of tawny hair.

"A precious soul has recently passed from us," said Percy Sedgewick beside her, the black armband on his grey coat now more meaningful. "We attended the funeral yesterday."

"Please accept my condolences," Marc said.

Sedgewick was short and stocky, made even more so by his standing beside Adelaide Brookner, who was very tall for a woman, probably five feet seven. But the raw-boned, weathered face signalled without doubt that this was a farmer, one who worked the plough and drove his own cattle.

"Thank you," he said to Marc while unconsciously patting Adelaide's mittened hand. "I do hope our sorrow doesn't make the trip too uncomfortable."

"I am afraid it is I who am likely to be the dull companion," Marc said, "because I am destined to spend a good deal of the time asleep. I am still some way from recovering my former strength."

"No need to apologize, sir," Pritchard said affably. "We understand, don't we, Lambert?"

Charles Lambert glanced up, took a second or so to absorb the question directed at him, then said in a guarded tone, "Yes."

"Mr. Lambert is inordinately quiet for a solicitor," Pritchard said with a sort of genial disapprobation, "but I expect he'll open up once we get rolling."

Marc looked to Lambert for a response, but the dark, sallow-skinned little man had turned his eyes away as if it were simply too much bother to enter the polite chatter or dignify its importance by contributing to it.

Randolph Brookner hallooed them towards the coach. The cutter had disappeared, all the luggage was stowed and tied down, the ostler was standing beside the lead horse ready to release it, and the coach-door had been swung open.

Marc turned to Adelaide Brookner. "It was very kind of you and your brother to agree to take along a semi-invalid."

From under the veil came a voice that was richly alto yet tinged with some private and painful ambiguity. "Randolph insisted, as he usually does. And he is my husband, not my brother," she said and, Marc thought, added as a near-inaudible aside, "alas." But there was no way of assessing her expression behind the black wisp covering her face. She stepped hesitantly towards the carriage as if she were, as a lady, reluctant to accept the privilege of entering first.

"I am Mrs. Brookner's brother," Percy Sedgewick explained, watching his sister closely as she approached her husband, who was standing beside the open door as rigid and self-important as a brigadier-general taking salute. "But you are not the first to make that mistake, sir," he added.

"Don't you think we should let Lieutenant Edwards choose a comfortable seat after madam is settled?" Ainslie Pritichard asked, like a squire pointing out the obvious to those not blessed with his pedigree.

Captain Brookner bristled, produced a tight smile, and said, "Of course." He clutched his wife's left elbow to assist her up into the carriage. She flinched and uttered a tiny cry.

"She fell on the ice at Marion's funeral yesterday," her brother said to Marc, who was protesting any favouritism directed his way.

Adelaide settled herself not in the right rear seat, with the large window and a forward view, but in the left front seat just inside the door, where she would be riding backwards with only the slit of the door-window next to her.

Marc was chivvied in next and, desiring as restful journey as possible, chose the right front seat where he could ride backwards, doze at will, and not be overly tempted to acknowledge the view outside. Brookner stepped in next and, to Marc's surprise, did not sit beside his wife. Instead, he folded his angular frame on the rear seat opposite Marc: the best one in the house, as it were. Their knees almost touched.

At the same time, Charles Lambert appeared to brush rudely past Sedgewick and Pritchard and squirrel himself across from Adelaide, who had tucked her skirt up and pulled the mourning veil firmly over her handsome features. That left only the two middle positions free. The very English wine merchant wriggled his bulk between Marc and Adelaide, and Sedgewick had no choice but to sit across from him. Seconds later, their driver gave a shout, cracked his whip, and the coach slipped smoothly away on its formidable runners. Before they had left the town behind, it began to snow.

Marc was grateful that a fresh snowfall would fill in any frozen ruts on the main road to Upper Canada and Cornwall, make any viewing of the scenery floating by improbable, and provide some muted light in the otherwise shadowy interior of the coach. He leaned back against the pillowed headrest and dozed peacefully, letting the sporadic conversation of the others drift past him.

"I was sorry we were interrupted in the dining-room last night, Captain, as I was most intrigued by your account of the rebellion in your province," Ainslie Pritchard began. "As a man wholly devoted to the other kind of accounts—the ones in led-gers, I mean—I have ever been fascinated by those who live a life of action and high risk."

"Runnin' a hardware store in Kingston ain't exactly Cyrano de Bergerac," interjected Sedgewick.

"You are right to correct Mr. Pritchard's misapprehension, Percy. There is some difference between myself as a mere mi-litia officer and an officer of the British army like Lieutenant Edwards here."

"But you have as splendid a uniform, a fine sword, and, I presume, a suitable steed to carry you into battle?"

"What happened near Kingston was hardly a battle, certainly not like those at St. Denis and St. Eustache. But there was danger, I must admit frankly. And the training we diligently carried out several times each year was, if I may be somewhat immodest, instrumental in the success of the Glen-garrians."

"You were telling us that your unit was asked to help track down rebels fleeing the fiasco in Toronto and local sympathizers guilty of harbouring those under warrant."

"That's correct. There was no actual uprising around Kingston, which, you will see in a few days, is well fortified, nigh impregnable. But its proximity to the American border made it attractive to fugitives looking for sanctuary in that damnable republic."

"And these ruffians were armed?"

"To the teeth."

"How did you know whom to pursue?"

"That has not been difficult. The countryside has five loyalists for every rebel sympathizer."

"Neighbour snitchin' on neighbour, you mean."

"Doing their duty, dear brother-in-law."

"So you actually got involved in the pursuit?"

"Yes. We received reliable information that the Scanlon brothers—notorious supporters of the Reform party and shills for Mackenzie and his republican gibberish—were heading home."

"They've run a farm near mine peacefully for ten years or more."

"Percy speaks part of the truth, Mr. Pritchard. But you have to understand that the uprising in Upper Canada was largely a farmers' revolt, not a racial and religious conflict like the one here in Quebec. It was so-called 'peaceful' farmers like the Scanlons who took up arms against the Crown rather than work out their grievances through the lawful instrument of their Assembly and the appointed councillors."

"Were the Scanlons in Toronto for the dust-up there?"

"They were on their way, apparently, but Mackenzie, they say, changed the date of his planned assault and they arrived too late. However, they did come in time to materially assist the mad Scotsman in escaping to the United States, where he has been threatening an invasion and encouraging cross-border forays in the southwest."

"The blackguards!"

"Indeed, sir. Well, we Glengarrians did not hesitate when we learned of this piece of perfidy. A platoon under my command rode out to the Scanlon homestead, ordered the women and children off—"

"They come runnin' to my place, terrified. I gave them what comfort I—"

"Yes, yes, Percy, no-one's faulting your charity or blaming you for harbouring women and children, even though they themselves would flout the law, and you were technically aiding and abetting outlaws."

Whatever retort Sedgewick may have contemplated, it was swallowed in a dismissive snort.

"And?"

"And we set the barn and coops ablaze, and scattered the livestock. We were just about to set the house alight when the three brothers roared out of the woods like banshees, firing upon us with pistol and musket."

"My God!"

"My sergeant was wounded in the arm not a yard from me. Without delay or any thought for my own safety, I rallied my men and we returned shot for shot. The Scanlons retreated to the bush, where they had hidden fresh horses, and took off. I concluded that they would soon circle back and look for their families at Percy's place."

"And you surmised accurately?"

"I did. There was another exchange of gunfire not fifty yards in front of Percy's gate. This time it was the eldest Scanlon who took a bullet, in the shoulder, and the other two wisely tossed aside their weapons and threw up their hands."

"I trust, Captain, that when this ruckus is all over, you will be rewarded with a well-deserved commendation, perhaps even a knighthood."

"Possibly, sir. But I am satisfied that the Scanlons are in jail and almost certain to hang for their crimes."

"Aren't you forgettin' about young Miles? He escaped last week, just before we left for my sister's funeral."

"I haven't the slightest doubt that he is in custody even as we speak. There is simply no place for him to hide."

"And you are not afraid that he might seek to avenge the destruction of his homestead, that he might hold you personally responsible?"

"I am not a man given to foolish fears, Mr. Pritchard. You see me here wearing my tunic in proud defiance of traitors and teenage hotheads. I shall continue to do so."

"Bravo!"

Marc's thoughts meanwhile drifted to Owen Jenkin and to his loving yet painful description of the funeral held for Rick Hilliard, the only officer at that time to have died in the conflict, besides the assassinated Jock Weir. He recalled the sonorous solemnity of the bugle, the dreadful hollow-heartbeat of the muffled drum, the ceremonial glory of Britain's beloved flag, and the slow march of severing and sorrow. The casket itself had not been buried, as the ground was frozen solid, but it had vanished inexorably from the far end of the parade-ground and took the brief laughing life of Rick Hilliard with it.

Pritchard was bent on conversation. "Mr. Lambert, I understand that you have just returned from the Richelieu Valley on business. Would you mind terribly giving us an account of the devastation up there?"

"Yes, I would."

Marc opened his eyes a bit and peered across at Charles Lambert in the opposite corner. Having rebuffed Pritchard's disingenuous gambit, he had turned his face to the big window next to him and was staring vacantly out at the falling snow.

"That bad, eh?" Pritchard said. "Did your wife's family escape unscathed?"

"No-one escaped unscathed, sir," Lambert said darkly, without turning his head.

"I believe the subject is too painful a one for Mr. Lambert." It was Adelaide Brookner, speaking for the first time since they had left Montreal.

"Too painful for anybody," Sedgewick said gruffly.

They travelled on in uneasy silence.

It was past noon. The journey along the roadway that shadowed the St. Lawrence, without being in actual sight of it, proceeded without incident. The chatter among those eager to talk was desultory and uninformative. Adelaide said no more, nor did the morose Mr. Lambert, even when they stopped at several farmhouses doubling as way-stations to use the facilities, have a quick dram, or purchase a stale roll with bad cheese. There was a proper inn just across the provincial boundary where they planned to have a decent meal, rest for an hour, and have the horses tended to.

They were anticipating this stop when the coach halted abruptly under the driver's excited "Whoa!" Captain Brookner flung back the greatcoat he had laid over his knees, stepped over his fellow passengers, tore open the door, and leapt into the nearest drift—feet astride and one hand on the haft of his sword.

"What is it, Todd?"

"Up ahead, sir," replied Gander Todd from his perch.

Through the haze of the snow could be seen, approaching the coach, a troop of men on horseback.

"Could be radicals lookin' fer mischief, sir. What'll we do?"

"Leave them to me," Brookner said. "Everybody stay put inside."

"My God! We're about to be murdered by . . . by riffraff!" Pritchard's cry was high-pitched, squeezed between umbrage and terror.

One of the horsemen detached himself from the group and trotted slowly up to Brookner.

"Good afternoon, Captain. We're on the lookout for rebels fleeing Quebec. Can you vouch for all aboard?"

"I can, sir. And I wish you luck."

"Thank you. Be very careful. This is a dangerous route these days. The stagecoach from Prescott to Kingston was robbed yesterday, and one gentleman assaulted for no reason other than that he was a gentleman."

"We're forewarned and well armed," Brookner said.

"Good. I'd keep that pistol primed, Captain. Good day to you."

Gander Todd urged his team onward, but with a little less enthusiasm than he had earlier in the day. There was a nervous tension inside the coach. Even Ainslie Pritchard lapsed into uncharacteristic silence.

Somewhere just a mile or two west of the inn they were seeking, the coach stopped again.

"What is it this time?" Brookner demanded, content to open his window and shout up at Gander Todd.

"Trees, sir. Across the road."

This time Marc followed Brookner out to have a look. Ten yards ahead and seemingly blocking the entire right-of-way lay a tangle of felled trees, festooned with fresh snow that was still sifting pleasantly down.

"We was warned about such tricks." Gander sighed from his perch.

"Let's take a closer look," Marc suggested, happy to exercise both his sound leg and his gimpy one.

"Let me, Lieutenant."

Brookner and Marc tramped up to the barricade. Marc gloved some of the snow away. "It's just brush and branches. No trunks. We can clear a path through it in a few minutes."

"True, Lieutenant, but this could be a trap or an ambush.

I'll have Todd get at these branches, but in the meantime, I intend to scout the woods on either side, just in case."

"You take that side then, Captain, and I'll take this."

"But you're unarmed."

"I'll roar loudly." And before Brookner could object Marc made his way into the spruce thickets a few yards from the roadside. As he did so, he heard the coach door open as the others, to Brookner's voiced disgust, decided to stretch their legs (or find a private tree behind which to perform a private function). Marc was certain that if an ambush had been arranged, it would have manifested itself by now. He urinated behind a thick elm-trunk. Gander Todd and farmer Sedgewick were now busy pulling back the impeding brush. Brookner had disappeared into the woods opposite, and the other two men were edging cautiously into the spruce bush behind him. Adelaide remained in the carriage.

Marc smiled and continued to exercise his legs and practise striding through knee-deep but fluffy snow. Ahead of him he heard the gurgle of creek-water and was delighted to come upon a pretty tributary, a section of which was spring-fed enough to be still flowing. Somewhere a half-mile or so away it would join the mighty St. Lawrence. Feeling just a little tired, Marc sat down and watched the bubbling blue-black water race on unperturbed by war and its casual inhumanities.

Fearing the others might be concerned for his safety, Marc got up stiffly and turned back towards the road. Just a touch dizzy, he half fell against a convenient tree-trunk. As he did so, he was aware of two almost-simultaneous sounds: the distinctive snap of a pistol-shot and the splintery *thunk* of a lead ball striking the trunk just above the tip of his fur hat.

I've been shot at! was his only thought as he dropped to his knees and rolled over as deeply as possible into the camouflaging snow.

NINE

The first thing Marc tried to do was stem the surge of adrenaline pummelling his body and stunting his breath. He had to think. And quickly. What he had heard was definitely a pistol-shot, which meant that the accuracy of any second shot would not be great. It also meant that the shooter had not been very far away, perhaps no more than ten or fifteen yards. If there were just one would-be assassin, it would take thirty seconds for his weapon to be reloaded, provided he did not have more than one pistol primed and ready. The light snow was still falling, further obscuring vision and aim. Soundlessly, Marc slid behind the bole of the tree beside him and sat up warily.

At first he heard nothing: no voices behind him in the direction of the road and the coach—where *was* everybody?—and no rasp of the assassin's breathing as he closed in for the kill. With a sinking feeling, Marc realized that he was helpless against further attack. He could barely walk, let alone run and dodge. He had no strength even if he could somehow surprise the assailant and try to wrest the pistol away from him. He thought briefly of simply calling out for help, but decided against this because such a cry would instantly alert the gunman as to his whereabouts, and the deed could well be over before anyone at the coach could locate him.

When nothing occurred for the next half minute, Marc had to assume that the attacker thought his victim had escaped the first attempt and that Marc was probably armed and ready to retaliate. He could not know that Marc's pistol lay packed in the trunk with his uniform and all that gentleman's finery that Owen Jenkin had purchased to provide a disguise. Marc's best hope seemed to be that the assailant, more cautious now that his ambush had been bungled, would be creeping from tree to tree, hoping to pick up footprints or other signs of his prey. The snow was falling more heavily, making disorientation even more likely. Marc began to breathe easier.

Could the assassin be someone from the coach? It did not seem probable. Captain Brookner had displayed his pistol for all to admire, but any of the others, including Adelaide, could have had one secreted under their winter coat. But they would have to have a reason to try to kill him. Brookner protested adoration of him (*sans* uniform), some of which could be genuine. But why would any of them—none of whom he knew nor had even met until this morning—want to do so? Lambert had been up to St. Denis and witnessed the carnage there, but he was a lawyer, an English-speaking Upper Canadian, and most likely a Tory sympathizer. Pritchard was a recent arrival and Tory to his toes. Adelaide and her brother were both deep in mourning for their sister.

This thought was interrupted by the sound of sudden footfalls, no more than twenty yards away, between Marc and the river. He braced himself for what was to come. But the footfalls, faint, muffled thumping of boots or raquettes on snow, were receding towards the St. Lawrence. Soon they vanished. He was safe. The assailants—there seemed to be more than one—were in all probability the gang who had barricaded the roadway and, surprised by Marc's unexpected presence, had taken a pot-shot at him, and decided to beat a hasty retreat while they could. Or perhaps that loyalist posse combing these woods had prompted them merely to hit and run.

Grateful for his good fortune, whatever the cause, he struggled to his feet, then grabbed a branch to steady himself. He was amazingly and maddeningly weak, without stamina. The cauterized wound in his thigh began to throb. Slowly and carefully he picked his way back towards the road. The fact that he seemed to have been a random target—a grey-coated, fur-capped gentleman in the wrong place at the wrong time—steadied him as he stepped through a screen of trees and spied the coach. There was no need, he thought now, to tell the others of his misadventure: it would only alarm them unduly and perhaps provoke Brookner to some rash, needless action.

The brush barricade had been moved far enough aside to allow passage of the coach through it. Gander Todd was quietly feeding the horses some bran from a feedbag. He grinned a gap-toothed grin at Marc, giving no sign that he had heard the recent commotion. Marc came up to the coach. Adelaide was seated in her place inside.

"Where are the others?" Marc asked.

She had raised the veil to reveal a face that was handsome more than it was beautiful, and a pair of blue eyes that shone with intelligence but also wariness.

"The men are off doing their business," she said, and again Marc, whose experience with colonial women over the past two years had sharpened his sensitivity to nuances in their gender he had never before imagined, detected a deliberate ambiguity of tone.

"They seem to have been rather long about it."

"Gentlemen set their watches by their own time."

Marc smiled to acknowledge the quip, and would have further engaged Adelaide in conversation had not the sound of voices from the far side of the road interrupted. Marc noted carefully that each man emerged from the woods alone, having sought the privacy of his own tree. Brookner stopped to talk to the driver, but Pritchard and Sedgewick ambled up to the coach.

"No sign of any ambuscade out there," Pritchard puffed, smacking his gloves together. "Powder'd freeze in the pan any-way!"

"Where's Lambert?" Sedgewick asked.

"Oh, he decided the scenery on the other side of the road was more conducive to, to you know what," Pritchard said. He gave Adelaide a sidelong glance through the open door.

"Here he comes now," Sedgewick said. "Safe, thank God."

"And much relieved," Adelaide said, to the astonishment of the English gentleman nearest her.

Lambert came towards them from the river side of the bush, not far from where Marc himself had emerged. He seemed to be trying to run, but the depth of the snow merely caused him to stagger.

"What the deuce has happened?" Pritchard blurted.

Brookner and Gander Todd turned their way.

Lambert stopped to catch his breath at the edge of the road. His black eyes were alive with a curious blend of fright and excitement. "I think I saw the ambushers! Heading towards the river. I heard a gunshot."

"Are you sure?" Sedgewick asked.

"I'm not positive. It was snowing pretty thick in there. But there were shadows of some kind moving ahead of me, of that I'm sure."

"Could have been deer," Sedgewick offered, ever the practical man.

"Did you see or hear anything over that way?" Pritchard turned to Marc.

"I thought I heard footsteps in the snow, towards the river," Marc said.

"It has to be the scoundrels who put these trees in our way, then scuttled off like cowards," Pritchard said with evident satisfaction. "We call them highwaymen at home, and a sad lot of ne'er-do-wells they are."

Brookner strutted up, looking smug. "Both of you are no doubt right," he said with a nod to Marc and Lambert, who was still trying to catch his breath. "While we were away from the coach, the army courier from Montreal to Kingston came riding through. He stopped long enough to inform Todd that a gang of French rebels were seen by several local people working their way up the shoreline. He himself had been shot at three miles back. He suggested we make our way to Cornwall as quickly as possible."

"This is outrageous!" Pritchard fumed, in part to conceal his fear.

"I agree, sir," Brookner said. "But the good news is that it was the Frenchies and not our own so-called rebels. We're well inside Upper Canada now, and the French traitors are no doubt skedaddlling back to their own territory."

They all got into the coach without further discussion. Gander Todd leapt up to his position, and they skittered off towards the safety of Cornwall, the next civilized town. A proper meal and a rest-stop for passengers and horses would have to wait until then.

"Mr. Sedgewick tells me that you operate a hardware store," Ainslie Pritchard said to Brookner when they were well away from the place of ambush and the silence in the coach had grown as intolerable as it was ungentlemanly.

"Indeed, I do, sir," Brookner replied with the sort of gruff affability of manner he had recently decided to affect. "My premises are on the main street and constructed of quarrystone—built to last, I tell my customers to amuse them."

"And I am given to understand that your partner in life assists you in the family enterprise."

Brookner glared sideways at Sedgewick, who was dozing, and then smiled thinly across at Pritchard. "Adelaide helps out from time to time and, if I may boast, does an excellent job."

"For a woman," Adelaide said in a barely audible voice. Her veil had come down again.

Brookner threw his wife a warning glance of some kind, but before he could say anything, Marc said, "My fiancée and her aunt run a business entirely on their own in Toronto."

"Do they?" Pritchard said with ill-suppressed surprise.

"What sort of shop?" Brookner asked.

Marc noticed that the captain had put his greatcoat on before leaving the coach earlier and had kept it on. Even in the pale light of the coach's interior, it gleamed a garish green and, with its wearer's stiff posture, could have passed for a mannequin in a haberdasher's display-window. Oddly, he was not wearing a black armband.

"Millinery," Marc said. "With a dressmaker's workroom in back." He did not think it wise to mention their recent troubles and subsequent flight.

"Aah," Pritchard and Brookner said together, with a dismissive sigh.

"She operated a farm before that—on her own, after her first husband died."

"I'm told the women out here get up to the damnedest things." Pritchard sighed, more ruefully this time. "But surely she will not carry on once she becomes the wife of an infantry officer."

"I believe she will, one way or another."

"But what will happen when the children start coming?"

"I've learned to take life one week at a time out here," Marc said. "You must remember that we are not yet fully civilized."

"Now there you speak the gospel truth, sir."

"You have no children, then?" Marc asked Brookner.

"No, I have not, sir. To my deep regret. Mrs. Brookner and I have been happily wed for almost fifteen years, but the Lord has not seen fit to bless us with children."

"Then it has been most generous of you, Captain, to allow Mrs. Brookner to participate in your commercial affairs."

"Adelaide does the accounts," Sedgewick said without opening his eyes.

"Whenever I myself am too busy to do so," Brookner said quickly. "Is that not so, my dear?"

Whether his good wife was about to answer or demur was not known, because Sedgewick answered on her behalf.

"Addie was very clever in school," he said, smiling reminiscently across at the veiled countenance of his sister. "Especially in sums. Her other brothers and Marion and me only finished common school: Addie was sent into Kingston to Miss Carswell's Academy for Ladies."

For a moment that remark, aggressive and affectionate, seemed to stop the easy flow of conversation. However, silence being anathema to the English merchant, he soon started it up again, in a fresh direction.

"If you are going on to Cobourg, Mr. Lambert, then we shall be travelling together for several more days."

Charles Lambert, who appeared to have been somewhat shaken out of his earlier trance by his fright in the woods, nodded courteously, but did not speak.

"Cobourg, I was told in Montreal, is a bustling new town on the big lake—Ontario, I believe it's called."

"It is an incorporated village," Lambert said, and for the first time a lawyerly precision of voice and cadence could be discerned. "And barely that. But we hope for more."

"You are newly set up in practice there?"

Lambert paused, as if considering whether or not he had said too much already, but eventually said, "We arrived there four months ago."

"Then you may have met my good friend, Dr. Charles Barnaby, a retired army surgeon who has a part-time clinic on King Street," Marc said, suddenly interested in a man who had resided in Cobourg for the past few months and who, being no more than five miles from Crawford's Corners, might well have information about the rebellion and its aftermath in the region.

Lambert looked momentarily puzzled by the question, but like a good solicitor in training, he recovered quickly and said, "No, I don't believe I've yet had the privilege. I'm an extraordinarily healthy man."

"It's the bracing country air!" Pritchard said, eager to draw the conversation back to himself.

"Then you and your wife must get out to Throop's Emporium quite often. It's been honoured with the quaintness award for the province, I've been told," Marc said lightly.

Lambert's dark brows came down to squeeze his eyes almost shut. "Pardon me for being blunt, Lieutenant, but I don't see how any of this is your business."

There was an embarrassed silence. *It's only my business,* Marc thought but did not say, *if you've never actually set foot in*

Cobourg. And if not, what are you doing on a stagecoach heading there? And what were you really doing up in St. Denis?

"We're merely trying to while away the boredom of the journey, old chap," Pritchard said.

"I don't find my own company boring," Lambert said uncharitably, despite the obvious truth of the remark.

And that put an end to that conversation.

Fifteen minutes later they reached the outskirts of Cornwall and pulled up in front of the Malvern Inn. It was five o'clock.

Alerted to their imminent arrival by the army courier who had passed through ahead of them, the innkeeper had prepared a sumptuous welcome for his affluent guests. A log-fire blazed in the huge stone fireplace of the reception area. Braziers had been sent up to their rooms and warming bricks placed in their beds between feather mattresses and goose-down comforters. The roast beef was almost ready in the cook's generous oven, and the wine-steward-cum-errand-boy had just scurried off to the cellar for five bottles of the best that ready money could buy.

Marc was hoping to observe each of his fellow passengers as they removed their outer clothing. He was looking for the telltale bulges of hidden weapons, but it was not to be. Everyone was exhausted, physically and emotionally, from the long journey and its troubling events, and headed straight upstairs to their assigned chambers. An hour later, with a wash and a nap accomplished, they reassembled in front of the roaring fire for sherry and pre-dinner chat. No doubt their various adventures would have been rehashed, if only in a perfunctory way, but Mr.

Malvern and his angular wife insisted on sharing their affability and stores of meaningless gossip with their captive customers. And so, with the aroma of roast beef and Yorkshire pudding wafting in from the kitchen, they had to endure the Malvern chatter for the sake of the pleasures to come. Marc found himself almost too weak to eat anyway. He had fallen dead asleep in his room and had had to be wakened by an alarmed Captain Brookner who, once more, showed his disappointment at Marc's choice of clothes for dinner, but made no comment.

As they were being ceremoniously led towards the roast beef by Mrs. Malvern, her husband drew Marc to one side.

"I did not want to trouble you, sir, when you first come in, as you looked quite peakèd, but the courier left a message for you, the one that come from Montreal." Without further explanation he thrust an envelope into Marc's hand and bustled into the dining-room.

Marc sat down in a nearby easy-chair. His name on the envelope was in Owen Jenkin's handwriting. He ripped it open and read:

Montreal, L.C.
Noon, Jan. 17, 1838

Dear Marc:

I am trusting this message to Sir John's express courier.
If he is unimpeded on his journey, he should overtake
you before you reach Cornwall. There is news here that
you must know about as soon as possible: your life may

*depend on it. Gilles Gauthier, the man who was caught
thieving at the hospital, was tried here this morning
in military court, the regular courts being suspended.
He was found guilty of theft—he had two spoons in
his possession—and was sentenced to hard labour for
ten years. But he was found not guilty of attempting
to murder you with a stolen bayonet. Evidence in his
defence was offered by a parish priest from Chambly, who
testified that Gauthier spent the night you were attacked
in a drunken stupor in the local church vestry. However,
suspicion has now fallen on someone else. It seems that
one of the French aides left the hospital two days after the
attack, supposedly sick and unable to work. Head Nurse
was too busy playing Boadecia to notice the coincidence
or mention it to Dr. Wilder or me. The young woman's
name is Isabelle LaCroix. Nothing is known of her here,
and the French will not betray one of their own or help us
with our enquiries. So there it is. It seems you may have
been attacked by a young Frenchwoman, of unknown
origin and without a known motive. Please be careful.
Further attempts may be made. Send news of your safe
arrival at each post en route.*

*Yours in friendship
(Major) Owen Jenkin*

Marc's first thought was that "a further attempt" may have
already been made earlier this afternoon. But it could not have
been carried out by a girl from the city. Most likely, whoever

it was who wanted him dead had co-opted the nurse to make the first try, when he was helpless in a hospital bed. Now it appeared that the same person had himself, or in concert with others, made a second try, and failed. Certainly Marc's disguise as an ordinary gentleman had not fooled the would-be assassin. Which meant that Marc was known by sight: he was neither a random nor a symbolic target. Someone hated Marc Edwards enough to make a concerted and sustained effort to kill him. And that person would know precisely where he would be sleeping tonight. He would have to be prepared.

Mr. Malvern, as rotund as he was orotund, was delighted to hear from Captain Brookner after dinner that, due to the fragile health of Lieutenant Edwards, the distinguished company would be staying a second night before moving on to Prescott. His brown eyes ablaze with the reflected flame from his cheeks, Mr. Malvern assured the lady and gentlemen that healthful food and supportive drink would be supplied as needed, that recreation would be found to amuse and edify (cards and partridge hunting being the foremost among many choices), and with the local militia active in and around the village, no fears for their safety should be entertained or permitted to bestir the equanimity that their station deserved.

As the men headed for the smoker to cap their day with a cigar and a brandy, Marc excused himself.

"There is no need to excuse yourself at all, Lieutenant," Ainslie Pritchard said graciously, his magnanimity expanded exponentially by roast beef and vin ordinaire. "We have already tired you today more than is conscionable."

With that, he manoeuvred his portliness towards the

smoking chamber, and the others, with varying nods of approval, followed. Even the mysterious Mr. Lambert, less than loquacious at dinner, joined them. Despite being dog-tired, Marc was hoping to have a chance to speak with Adelaide Brookner alone, but she was already on her way upstairs to her room.

Innkeeper Malvern, ever hovering, pounced from an alcove: "Anything I can do for you, sir, to make you more comfortable?" he asked.

Marc paused, thinking hard. "As a matter of fact, there is," he said.

Malvern beamed.

"Do you happen to have a pumpkin-squash I could borrow?"

Although life as a hotelier had prepared Malvern for many an odd request or demand—he was already planning to write a book on the subject—he was stunned to hear a British officer ask him for a pumpkin on loan. The intrepid lieutenant's exploits had been, to the latter's acute embarrassment, the main topic of conversation between the soup course and the entrée. It seemed that Marc's daring rescue of Eugene Yates, the young cavalryman from Montreal, had been bruited about that city by his companions of the 24th, and the tale had grown hairs in the retelling. Several variants were put forward and debated at table, but Marc had been too weary to adjudicate. No-one had noticed.

"You have a root cellar?" Marc enquired as Malvern fumbled for a sensible response to the hero's request.

"Yes, sir. And yes, sir, there are squash and turnip of several varieties stored there. You want a pumpkin-squash, you say?"

"Yes, about this big around."

With remarkable restraint and not a little aplomb, the order was duly given to one of the houseboys, and minutes later Marc trudged upstairs with a head-shaped, half-frozen orange pumpkin under his arm.

Using some of the vests and jackets packed into the big trunk by Owen Jenkin, Marc arranged his bed so that the outline of a sleeping body clearly showed under the comforter. Against the pillow he laid the pumpkin, then draped a linen nightcap over its bald pate, and pulled the comforter up over its hairless chin. The night-sky outside his window was black and star-studded. A full moon bathed the room in quicksilver light. He hoped the deception would work. If the assassin who had tried to kill him this afternoon was determined to finish what he had started, tonight would be a logical time and place.

Next, he rigged a booby-trap against the door, which, as in most country inns, had no lock, merely a brittle wooden latch that could be jimmied with a penknife. He piled up, precariously, a tin washing-bowl, his canteen cup, and a crockery chamber pot so that the least jarring of the door would create a jangling tumble with enough noise to awaken him or in the least spook the intruder. He himself planned to sleep curled up in the oversize mahogany wardrobe across the room, leaving its door ajar and his officer's pistol—reluctantly retrieved from the bottom of his own small trunk—cocked and ready.

Satisfied with his handiwork, he doused the whale-oil lamp

and folded his weary bones into the bottom of the wardrobe. It was uncomfortable, but he figured that he could sleep anywhere tonight.

He had just begun to drift into a doze when he heard footsteps coming up the stairs, which ended in the hall just outside his door. He recognized the voices, saying brief good nights: Ainslie Pritchard and Charles Lambert. He heard two doors close. Then he was fast asleep.

Something woke him. He sat up with a lurch and banged his elbow on a shelf. Christ! He was holding the pistol in that hand. He could have shot himself. Still trying to recall where he was and why, he glanced across the moonlit room. His facsimile lay undisturbed under its cozy camouflage. The boobytrap still teetered nicely. He looked towards the window. It was then that he heard voices, the noise that had wakened him. There were two of them, Randolph Brookner and Percy Sedgewick, very close to his door, exchanging unpleasantries in fierce, drunken whispers.

"I'm tellin' you, Randy, for the last time, you do that once more and you'll . . . you'll live to regret it!"

"What I do is my own business, and I won't be bullied by a bumpkin farmer like you, you cowardly son of a bitch!"

"I don't need no musket to make me a man, you prancin' peacock!"

"If you weren't my brother-in-law, I'd beat the living shit out of you right here and now!"

"You just remember what I said: no more, ya hear? I can

make your name mud all over the county. And I . . . I got a shotgun in my shed I use to kill rats and foxes and other vermin!"

"You snivelling little bastard. You think I'm afraid of you or anybody else? And don't you forget, I can have you charged with treason in the wink of an eye. Only the fact that you're my wife's favourite brother stops me from—"

"The Scanlons were my neighbours, for Christ's sake. What was I to do, turn the women and kids inta the bush to freeze! We're farmers and Christians out in the country, not—"

There was a brief scuffling sound, some ferocious panting, then silence. Finally, two doors farther down the hall opened and closed discreetly.

Marc lay back, carefully placing the loaded pistol on his chest pointing away from him. He was hoping to spend a few minutes mulling over the significance of what he had just heard but was asleep before he could get started.

When he woke up again, he found he was still tired and aching now in places he had not previously noticed. From the angle of the sun across the chamber, he could tell that the morning was well advanced. He was happy that the party would be spending the day resting here. Owen had been right about the fragile state of his constitution: he was a long way from full recovery.

Then he remembered why he was curled up inside the wardrobe with his pistol. He looked over at the bed, then the door. No-one had come in to disturb his dreams or worse. *Well,* he mused, *I've survived an eventful day and a night. What else can happen?*

TEN

When Marc entered the dining-room, it was empty except for Adelaide Brookner. She sat alone, darkly resplendent in her mourning clothes, picking at some food growing cold on her plate. While her gown was low-cut in the current fashion, she had arranged a copious crepe scarf so that it covered her chest and neck almost to the chin, giving the effect of an Elizabethan ruff. Her expression was unreadable, as if all thought and feeling had been sucked inward and she hadn't bothered to put a face on for the world. There was a slump of resignation to her posture, and it was all the more striking because there was an ingrained and obviously cherished pride in her person. She reminded Marc of the proud and intelligent Winnifred Hatch, now Mrs. Thomas Goodall. Just outside the front entrance he could hear the jangle of sleigh-bells. He walked into the breakfast-room and sat down opposite Adelaide Brookner.

"Good morning, ma'am. I seem to have overslept."

Adelaide looked up and said tonelessly, "It was meant to be a leisurely day."

"With a sleigh-ride, I presume, got up by our enterprising host?"

"To admire the sights of Cornwall," she said, looking to her food. But there was more energy in her response. "Such as they are," she added.

"I've seen them more than once," Marc said. "I shall offer my regrets."

"So you have regrets to give, have you?"

"Haven't we all?"

She did not reply.

"You're not partaking of the entertainment, then?"

"I've already tendered my regrets," she said, with a trace of irony in her tone.

Marc went to the sideboard, where the cook, having seen him enter, had piled fresh bacon and sausage. Marc filled his plate, adding bran cakes, hot rolls, and marmalade. He poured out a mug of tea and returned to Adelaide.

She appeared ready to rise when he said softly, "You must miss your sister very much."

Adelaide sat back as if she had been struck. When she lifted her face up to look at him, her eyes were filled with tears. "Marion was the only true friend I had in the world."

"But surely there is your brother Percy, and, of course, your husband."

She sniffed, as if he had just told an inappropriate joke, but she did not elaborate on that response.

Further discussion was stymied by Mr. Malvern banging open the front door and bursting into the reception area with his cheeks steaming and his eyes wild. His lips were working, like a basso rehearsing before a mirror, but no sound emerged. He spotted Marc.

"Oh, sir," he wailed. "Come quickly. Something terrible's happened!"

Marc rushed past him, winced as his gimpy leg rebelled, slowed to a measured trot, and went out into the frosty air to assess the damage. Behind him, from the smoker, he heard several others follow in his wake. A four-seat cutter and two Clydesdales stood serenely just outside the front door. A commotion to his left revealed two figures heading towards him from the direction of the stables: Gander Todd and Captain Brookner, the latter glittering in his tunic, breeches, and buckled sword.

"I warned him not to go walking on his own!" Malvern wailed again, this time behind Marc.

Brookner strutted up. "It's a lot of nonsense," he was saying to Todd, who was hobbling along beside his employer, bug-eyed and clearly frightened. "Malvern, I specifically told you not to go blabbering on about this and scaring the life out of people!"

Malvern looked abashed but still resolute. "I thought the lieutenant should know."

"Know what?" Marc asked, rubbing his arms in the cold.

Brookner, who seemed immune to cold and thrived on long, dangerous walks, snorted and said to the small throng that had now gathered around him, "This ridiculous note."

And he waved a sheet of writing paper in the air with a dismissive flap.

"I found it in the coach, pinned to the seat, when I went to sweep it out," Gander Todd said breathlessly.

"You'd better let me see it, then," Marc said, and Brookner, not disliking the attention he had attracted, preened and feigned indifference: "Here, then."

Marc skimmed the note, then decided to read it aloud. The message was printed in block capitals from hand-pressed wooden blocks. "Brookner: we have you in our sights. Revenge will be sweet. The Stormont Vigilantes."

"It's a death-threat!" Malvern sputtered. "And I warned the captain against going for his walk, I did." He glared at Brookner. "Why, you could've been murdered, sir, right here on my own property."

"Nonsense! I shall continue to take my morning constitutional, come what may."

Percy Sedgewick stepped forward, looking hungover and miserable. "It sounds like the Scanlons to me. Young Miles is on the loose, you know."

"Of course, I know. And for once I think you're right. These woods aren't brimming with rebel vigilantes: they're all busy running for their lives. Miles Scanlon's on his own, of that you can be sure. But we've got every road and ferry-crossing between here and Niagara covered. He won't escape. And if he thinks he's going to pot me before he jumps the border, he'll find himself dead or on his way to a gibbet."

A great buzzing and murmuring rolled through the crowd, along with sundry bits of advice and admonition. Finally, Marc said, "I think it best for all concerned if we change our plans and make for Prescott immediately."

"We can't get there today," Sedgewick said. "But we could make Morrisburg."

"Then that'll have to do," Marc said.

It was after eleven before the party of six and their anxious driver got dressed, packed, and otherwise prepared to leave the Malvern Inn. But the day remained cold and sunny, and they made reasonable progress. In fact, a determined push might well have seen them reach Prescott by early evening, but Captain Brookner, who seemed more pleased with the death-threat than frightened by it, insisted that they go no farther than Morrisburg, which could be reached at a leisurely pace by midafternoon. Thus, Marc would have the better part of this day and perhaps tomorrow morning to rest and regain his strength. He did not object.

However blasé chevalier Brookner might have appeared, the other members of the group had been spooked by the bar-ricaded road yesterday, the continuing reports of outlaw gangs in the region, and the menacing note this morning. Little con-versation of any kind took place. This served Charles Lambert well, for he seemed happy to remain disengaged, though his brooding eyes were more active in their furtive glancing. Sedge-wick and Brookner, after their drunken exchange of threats late last night, seemed relieved not to have to pretend to be civil to each other. What specific behaviour of Brookner's had angered Sedgewick, Marc could not even guess at, but he was pretty sure it had something to do with politics. Adelaide hid behind her veil. Only Ainslie Pritchard seemed truly disconcerted by the silence, but could find no neutral topic of conversation nor the tone required to keep it casual. Instead, he fidgeted with his fur helmet and cast wary glances left and right through the coach windows.

Whenever they made a "refreshment-stop" en route, Brookner would proceed to the door of the tavern or cabin and rap peremptorily on it with the haft of his sword. Only when he gave them the all clear were the others permitted to follow him in.

It was three o'clock when they approached the village of Morrisburg, without incident, and pulled up to the Wayside Hotel. Brookner addressed his companions with a solemn face: "A twice-weekly coach runs between here and Prescott, and from there you can get daily coaches that will take you to Kingston, then to Cobourg and Toronto. If any of you wish to leave this party, the local coach will arrive here in about an hour and then turn around and leave again for Prescott, getting there late this evening."

No-one accepted Brookner's generous offer. There was safety in numbers, it seemed.

The Wayside Hotel was a modest establishment on the edge of the village. The Battle of Crysler Farm had been fought nearby, Marc knew, and the St. Lawrence River, when not frozen, raced past not a quarter of a mile through the light bush behind the inn. The reception area was small and full of smoky heat from an eager but ill-functioning fireplace. Several cramped, adjoining chambers would serve as dining-room and lounge. There was no bar as such. A chalkboard sign announced that the Prescott stagecoach would arrive at four o'clock this day.

The proprietor bustled out of what appeared to be a kitchen, from the smells and metallic clangings, pulling a bloodied apron from his waist and letting it fall where it wished. His big black eyes were agog in his dark Welsh face. "My heavens, what have we here? Where on earth did you people come from? I heard the roads east were blocked by barricades and renegades and such."

"We are a party of six and wish supper and rooms for the night. Can you accommodate us?" Brookner asked loftily.

The initial shock of such an unexpected sight soon began to wear off, and the little man was able to say, "Pardon me, sir, I have forgot my manners. I am Iain Jones, the owner of the inn, and you are most welcome, you gentlemen and the lady. I'll have my wife take your coats, and my boy'll fetch your cases and trunks. You'll be needing a dram to drain away the chill. We've plenty of rooms, as you'll be the only guests, unless the stage brings us a surprise or two."

Within the next hour the party had been warmed with sherry and rum and shown to their modest but tidy rooms, where they chose to rest until supper at six. Marc decided he would take a nap, despite his having dozed a good deal of the way in the coach. While the threat against his life, or Brookner's—or both—was still real, he was too fatigued to attempt any entrapment this night. As he would do after supper, he now pushed his bed so that its foot rested flush against the door. Then he lay down and began to drift into a pleasant sleep.

The last thing he remembered hearing was the sleigh-coach from Prescott pulling up in front.

He was awakened by Percy Sedgewick rapping at his door and calling out his name. "Mr. Edwards! Supper is being served. Are you okay?"

"I'm all right. Tell Mr. Jones I'll be down in a while for something cold. I've got to shave and change."

"I'll tell him. You sure you're okay?"

Marc assured him. But he felt too groggy to shave or change his clothes, so he decided to slip downstairs and take a breath of fresh air to clear his head. As he crossed the reception area he could hear the voices of the others at supper in one of the rooms to his left. On his right was a tiny lounge with the door half ajar. He paused, then walked outside. The night was again cloudless, and the stars so bright and brittle they appeared about to shatter. He found his mind clearing wonderfully. A few minutes later he turned and went back in. Iain Jones was waiting for him.

"If it isn't too much trouble," Marc said, "I'll just come down in an hour or so and have some cold roast and bread. I—"

But the Welsh eyes were bulging with other news. "The lady in the lounge over there, the one that come in on the stage from Prescott, she says she wants to see you," he said, happily scandalized.

Marc nodded and headed towards the lounge indicated. He paused until he heard Jones reluctantly retreat to serve his other paying guests. Could it be Beth? Had she come across to Morrisburg en route home and spied him crossing the foyer? He knew there was a ferry somewhere near here. With his heart in his throat, he opened the door and went in.

The room was lit by a single lamp in one corner and heated by an iron stove whose fire had recently gone out. On a padded bench sat a woman, too tall and erect for Beth. Nestled in her arms was a baby.

"My God," Marc cried, falling back against the chair opposite the bench. "Winnifred!"

"How in the world did you get here? And with baby Mary? Where's Thomas?"

Although she looked haggard and careworn, the tough intelligence that had seen her through a difficult year since her marriage to Thomas Goodall still shone through, and intimidated. "I can't answer a dozen questions at once, and I have a few of my own for you. But if you'll sit back and not interrupt, I'll try to tell you what's happened to us since October. Thomas is fine, as fine as he can be under the circumstances. And he's right here. In the barn, hiding out."

"But he'll freeze!"

Winnifred reached down to the bench and picked up a thick roast-beef sandwich. "He's already had two of these—through the window over there—and there's more here if we get hungry."

"You're not going to sleep in a barn with—"

"Of course not. I've paid for a room, and supper."

"I'm baffled."

"What else is new?"

They shared a brief laugh, but Marc's pale appearance and thinness and Winnifred's desperate circumstances made it bittersweet.

"You first, then," Winnifred said, rocking the baby as she tried to come awake. "We heard you'd been wounded, but nothing more."

As succinctly as he could, and with one ear alert for noises from across the foyer, Marc gave her an expurgated account of the battles, Rick's death, and his own injuries. He told her about Beth's promise to be back in Toronto by the end of the month.

Winnifred then explained that she and Thomas were desperately trying to find their way across the border. They had come from Prescott, arriving at this inn a few hours earlier. She was as surprised as he when she'd spotted him from the window of her room while he took in the outside air.

"We've all got troubles." Winnifred sighed. "And to think that a year ago we were all happy and looking forward to living our lives peacefully and in the Christian spirit we were raised to revere."

"These wars have been ruinous," Marc said. "And they're not over yet. Tell me what's happened to you both."

Winnifred laid Mary in her bunting bag on the bench. "As you know, after his disastrous flirtation with the rebels in October, Thomas withdrew his active support and put all his energies into saving Beth's farm and looking after Aaron and us. But we lived in constant fear that Thomas would be betrayed to the magistrates for what he did—even though it failed. We even feared the radicals might think Thomas was a spy for the

Tories and burn us out. Terrible, inhuman things were happening, even before the actual revolt. But for a while matters were quiet, and we were beginning to hope that the troubles would die down. But in the second week of December came the awful news: Mackenzie and his band of farmers had attacked Toronto."

"Hardly an attack, I've been told. But it cast the die as sure as a cannonade on Government House."

"Yes. Before the week was out, rebels were running in all directions, and Mackenzie had scuttled away to the States, leaving hundreds to face the vigilante justice of high Tories and Orangemen."

Marc smiled.

"I know, I've been on both sides of the fence, and I haven't liked what I saw on either. But it was Thomas I was worried about." Her eyes misted, and Marc was aware of how much effort she was putting into maintaining her composure before him.

"Poor Thomas: honest and believing as a child. He only wanted to be a farmer. But that was not to be allowed. You can't ever know how my heart sank into my stomach when advance word came to us that there was a warrant out for Thomas, accusing him of sedition. We had only an hour to get away. We packed two suitcases and hustled Aaron and Charlene Huggan over to Father's place. Father was furious. I'd never seen him so angry. He cursed Mackenzie and all the magistrates and Francis Head. He offered to come with us, he offered to take baby Mary, but we calmed him down and told him we had worked out a plan."

"That sounds very much like Winnifred Hatch."

"The United States has opened the Iowa Territory to home-steading and settlement. If we can make it to New York State, to Buffalo and then to Pittsburgh, we'll head west and start a new life."

"You have enough money to do this?"

"Yes. Father gave us more than we need. Our problem's not money. It's getting across the border, and that's defeated us so far."

"You're a long way from Cobourg and Crawford's Corners."

"We've been on the road about a week. On the run, really. There are wanted posters with a sketch of Thomas's head on them all along the Kingston Road. Every ferryman and loyal fisherman with a boat has seen it. We've nearly been caught twice. Thomas is growing a beard, but it's not thick enough yet to disguise him. Luckily for us, the vigilantes and militia are only looking for Thomas, not a man with a wife and child."

"So you've just run eastward, hoping to find a way across the St. Lawrence?"

"The Niagara route was too risky. We travelled nonstop for four days and nearly froze to death. Then two things happened. We found a safe house near Trenton, and the couple there gave us information about a group of sympathizers in Quebec who would, if we could make it to Lachine, guide us across the ice to New York State. I suggested to Thomas that we split up."

"But I thought—"

"—and when he objected I suggested this: that Mary and I travel by coach or rented sleigh, as mother Hatch and her daughter on their way to Montreal to join relatives there. I would travel only one town east each day or so. Thomas would walk on the back trails or near the main road and mainly at night and meet me at the coach inn. He would sleep in the stables while I supplied him with food."

"Brilliant," Marc marveled, "as long as Thomas is careful."

"It's worked so far. I arrived at four o'clock, and Thomas has been here since noon. He's holed up in an abandoned hay-shed behind the main stable, warm and well fed. Tomorrow I've arranged to ride with a local farmer to Cornwall."

Suddenly, her face fell, her hand trembling as she reached out to stroke the baby's head.

"You're worried about Cornwall?"

"Yes," she whispered. "We've got to get around it. But we've heard that the militia have set up pickets everywhere to catch the French rebels coming this way and our rebels heading their way."

"It's true," Marc agreed reluctantly. "We saw them in action on our way here. Everything east of Cornwall is a minefield."

Winnifred was silent, rocking gently back and forth as if her baby were still in her arms.

"Then you'll just have to cross the river here," Marc said.

"The river's still flowing here?"

"I don't think so. But I'm sure it will have enough ice on it to hold you three."

"We can't just go wandering across the St. Lawrence hoping to land somewhere friendly on the far side, even if we don't drown first."

"I'll check with the proprietor and find out if it's a feasible plan." Before Winnifred could object, Marc went out into the foyer. He could hear Jones's wife in the kitchen scolding the scullery maid, who was lashing back in what sounded like French. He went to the door of the dining-room, eased it open, caught Jones's eye, and motioned for him to come out.

"I need to know two things, sir, if you'd oblige me."

"Anything for an officer of the Queen, sir."

"Is the St. Lawrence frozen over?"

"Yessir, in a few places, but you got to know exactly where or you'll be thirty feet under before you can blink twice."

"Is there a ferryman to take strangers across in the winter?"

"Yessir. Mr. Clark Cooper. He's got a dandy little skiff with a sail and iron runners. Quicker'n a fart, as old Coop says."

"The young woman, Mrs. Hatch, is trying to get to New York State to find some missing relatives. But I've explained how dangerous coach-travel might be anywhere east of here."

Jones nodded sagely.

"I'd like to arrange passage for her across the river. Tonight."

Jones was not as taken aback as Marc had expected. "It's possible, sir. Coop lives beside the river a quarter mile behind here through a marked trail in the bush. He's always there. Though you gotta watch him: he may try and charge you double if you interrupt his supper!"

"I'll seek him out, then," Marc said.

"But there's nothing on the other side. Just a hamlet without a hotel. She and the babe could be standing alone in the cold in the middle of the night."

Marc sighed. He hadn't thought of that. Nor the possibility that American troops, recently mobilized by President Van Buren, might be patrolling the border on the lookout for

Hunters' Lodge fanatics threatening invasion, or for fugitive Canadians likely to further embarrass the U.S. government.

"No, sir," Jones was saying, "Waddington, New York, is one sleepy little burg."

Marc was grinning from ear to ear when he returned to Winnifred. She searched his face for clues and at last ventured a smile of her own. "What's happened?"

"Everything," Marc said. He had worked out a scheme in the minute or so he had stood watching Jones rejoin his guests in the dining-room. "Listen carefully. I'm going to go upstairs and write a letter of introduction for you and Thomas to a family who live on a farm near Waddington just across the river from here. I saved their brother's life at St. Denis, so they will help you in any way they can. Just go into the first house you see and ask for directions. My letter will do the rest."

"But can we get across?"

"Yes. But we'll have to use the regular ferryman, who has a sort of ice-sled with a sail."

Winnifred gulped but said nothing.

"I realize he'll probably have a sketch of Thomas and others, but we're going to send Thomas in disguise."

"With a beard?"

"Much better. With a bonnet and a dress. He'll be your sister."

Marc went upstairs while Winnifred waited below with the baby. It was too risky to try to inform Thomas just yet. Marc wrote a compelling note to the Yates family of Waddington, to brothers Eugene and Stephen, and the latter's wife, Callie. Then he got his uniform out of his trunk and put it on—boots, shako cap, sabre, and all. He figured that Thomas in disguise, plus the sanctioning of the procedure by a uniformed officer, should be enough to deceive or intimidate someone as wily as Clark Cooper. At the very bottom of the trunk holding his gentleman's finery he found the last item he needed: a periwig. He tucked it under his jacket, pulled on his green greatcoat, and headed for the stairs.

"Well, Lieutenant, it is wonderful to see you at last in your full splendour."

It was Brookner, leading his troupe out of the dining-room.

"Thank you, sir. I thought I should give it a bit of an airing before Toronto."

"You're going out?"

"Just for a short walk."

"Splendid. Enjoy yourself. You deserve to."

Marc watched the others trail after him up the stairs, Adelaide bringing up the rear and whispering something urgent at her brother, who was more than a little tipsy. When they disappeared, Marc went into the lounge.

"Have you got a suitable dress?" he asked Winnifred, who had baby Mary tucked back into her embrace. "And a winter hat with a veil on it?"

"Yes. But he hasn't shaved for seven days."

"I hope he has a razor, then. He'll love this." Marc held up the grey barrister's wig.

Winnifred giggled. "And you're back in uniform!"

Marc explained why. "Can that window be opened?" he asked.

"Of course. I served the sandwiches through it."

"We're going out that way, then. Jones is busy cleaning up after supper. He'll assume you've gone to your room. I've told the others I'm out for a walk."

As Marc gently handed the still-sleeping baby through the window to Winnifred, her eyes lit up, as of old. "Are we really doing this?" she asked excitedly.

There was no time to fill Thomas in on the details of Marc's plan. But the man's absolute trust in his wife's judgement was both sad and wondrous to behold. In the darkened barn, he shook Marc's hand over and over, unable to stop shuffling and moving his arms about: he seemed a man on the brink. His craggy features and sturdy yeoman's body were ready to crumple. Still, he scrabbled through his kit for his razor, and Marc helped him use it as best he could with cold water and a dull edge. Thomas made no complaint when they stripped him to his long johns and began pulling a taffeta dress over his head. Its skirt was long enough to cover his work-boots. Winnifred had brought only one overcoat, so they draped "Thomasina" with shawls and scarves, and crowned the effort with the wig and a winter cap that covered most of it and held it in place. A fur muff would camouflage the unmistakably male hands.

"Now remember, you're Thomasina. You've got a cold and lost your voice. So just nod and shake your head to any questions. Winn and I will do the talking. You're the Hatch sisters, all right? And the baby belongs to Winnifred."

Winnifred had turned away to muffle her giggle when

Thomas took a ploughman's mighty step, caught his toe in the hem of the skirt, and pitched into the hay.

"We'll try a little practice first," Marc suggested.

Fifteen minutes later they came out of the woods and spotted, in the bright moonlight, Clark Cooper's log cabin. There was a candle in the window, but before Marc could reach the door, it opened and the ferryman emerged to greet them.

"Evenin', folks. You lookin' fer a sail across the ice?" He had a leprechaun's body, the head of a wrestler, and a voice like a mallard's on a windy day. His eyes flicked across the officer, the woman with the baby, and the creature behind her.

"Yes, we are. This is Winnifred and Thomasina Hatch, acquaintances of mine from Cobourg. They wish to go to Waddington tonight en route to Montreal because the roads east of here have become too dangerous for two women to travel unescorted. I met them by chance at the hotel—I'm on my way back to my regiment in Toronto—and offered to see them safely across to New York."

"You comin', too, are ye?"

"No, but I'll stand here and watch till you're on your way. I doubt you'll fail to reach the other side if Mr. Jones's account of your work is true."

"I ain't drownded nobody yet."

"How much?"

"A pound apiece."

"But that's—"

"And a shillin' fer the littl'un."

He peered warily at Mary. "That babe won't cry, will it?" he asked Winnifred.

"Not if you give us a ride worth a pound," she replied.

He chuckled throatily. "Yer elderly sister looks a bit frail to be tryin' such a trip on a night like this. How old are ya, anyway, old gal?"

Thomasina uttered a hollow rasping sound they had rehearsed.

"She's got laryngitis and hasn't been able to say a word for two days," Winnifred explained. "And she's not yet forty."

Marc had produced the money to cover the exorbitant charge.

"Well, I guess I can take ya. Them militia fellas has been pesterin' me to death about rebels runnin' this way an' that. They even threatened to put *me* in jail if I was to take one of 'em across."

"Well, Mr. Cooper, I am more than a militiaman. And I am vouching for these people."

"You got a name?"

Marc realized he had been wise not to underestimate Clark Cooper.

"Lieutenant Marc Edwards, 24th Light Infantry, Fort York. If there's any trouble, you just refer the matter to me."

Marc helped the Hatch sisters and the baby into the skiff while Cooper fiddled with the ropes holding it to shore.

Thomas looked up, shook his head, and whispered to Marc, "All I ever wanted to do was be a good farmer an' tend to my own business."

Winnifred asked only that Marc report their flight to her father and to Beth, then became too overwhelmed to say anything more. She waved farewell as the sail caught the breeze and the ice-sled skittered out onto the black ice, shorn of snow and buffed ebony by the constant wind. It seemed to Marc as if they were sailing off the edge of some soulless moon. He might never see them again, and his heart clenched at the thought. Oddly enough, it never occurred to him that he had just assisted a fugitive to escape the justice he had sworn to uphold. And given his name as guarantor.

He watched the triangular white sail till he could see it no more.

The foyer was empty and the dining-room dark when he came back in through the front door of the inn. The others had retired to their rooms. The only activity still in progress was the washing up. He could hear the maid singing a song he could not quite place, melodious and youthful. He stopped to listen. It was an old French folk song, one that his own French instructress had sung to him many years before. He found it both sorrowful and soothing.

The girl, whose tiny figure he could see moving across the opening in the kitchen door, was suddenly joined in midchorus by a male voice. They harmonized beautifully. Marc was unhappy that the duet had to end. When it did, he turned to go upstairs. Male and female were now conversing rapidly in French, but he understood little for it was in the local dialect. However, it was the male's voice that caught Marc's attention and drew him out of his reverie. It was Charles Lambert, speaking perfectly inflected *joual*.

Marc did not want to think about anything tonight except

the Goodalls and the Hatches, and those at Crawford's Corners who had, he realized with a pleasurable start, become his friends. His adoptive father, Jabez, was dead. The land he had been raised on would soon pass into the hands of cousins he had never met. England seemed an eon away. So he pushed his bed up against the door, removed his uniform, tucked it carefully back into his trunk, and lay down on the bed to let the floodtide of memory have its way.

It had hardly begun when he heard voices raised next door through the thin wall: the Brookners, having a husband-and-wife dispute by the sound of it. Fortunately, it did not last long, and by the time it had subsided he was asleep.

ELEVEN

Captain Brookner, ever sensitive to the welfare of Lieutenant Edwards, and even more so having observed him in the full glory of his scarlet tunic and tufted shako cap, saw to it that no-one disturbed the good soldier until midmorning. At which time the sunlight flooding his room did the trick, and an hour later the entourage was once again settled in their familiar seats in the carriage. Marc had had one anxious moment before boarding. As he was instructing Jones's son regarding the placement of his trunks—his uniform tucked inside one of them along with the pumpkin—Jones proper came sidling up to him, looking concerned. Marc immediately assumed that there was some bad news from the ferryman.

Jones forestalled his question: "Don't look so worried, sir. Your friend and her little one reached Waddington safely." He paused and gave Marc a sly glance. In a whisper he said, "Along with the elderly sister."

So Clark Cooper had already come visiting and spilled the beans.

"Was there a problem with that?" Marc asked, using all the authority of his rank and his lawyerly voice to put an end to the dangerous direction of this conversation.

Jones smiled with a weak attempt at a man-of-the-world demeanour. "Just a wee one, sir. Coop mentioned that you were one pound short of the fee last night, but you promised to pass it along before you left."

Marc smiled back, then slipped a one-pound note into the innkeeper's hand. "You'll be sure to deliver it," he said.

Jones almost winked his assurance.

If the militia captain was disappointed that the lieutenant had not continued to wear his uniform, he was too polite to say so. The relationship between Mr. and Mrs. Brookner had been frosty and uncommunicative from the outset, so it was hard for Marc to tell whether the dispute he had heard last night was the norm or represented an escalation of their apparent dislike for each other. Oddly, Brookner was always as courteous to her as he was to others. Even this morning he had taken her arm to lift her into the coach, and, as before, she had jerked away as if she had been pinched. She continued to sit in one corner and he diagonally opposite. The sun still shone, though cloud was building up in the southwest; the runners slid weightlessly along the packed snow of the roadbed; and for a little while the passengers could imagine they were on a Sunday afternoon outing in a snowy paradise of spruce boughs and plumed drifts.

Ainslie Pritchard concluded it was safe once again to initiate polite conversation. "Could you tell me, Mr. Lambert, whether that bustling new village of yours has a first-class hotel? One that might be interested in some of the new French wines I intend to introduce into this part of the world?"

Lambert looked up. "We have a hotel, but what class it may be, I don't know."

Marc was not surprised that Lambert had decided to answer the question. He had slowly been coming out of whatever shell he had been hiding under. What did surprise him was that he could detect no trace of a French accent in Lambert's English. Perhaps it had not been Lambert speaking *joual* in Jones's kitchen last night after all.

"Would you mind giving me the name of it? I could write the owner from Toronto," Pritchard said, then flashed Lambert a jowly grin: "Better still, I could stop over there, and you could show me the sights."

Marc thought he saw Lambert pale.

"It's the Lakeside, is it not?" Marc said to Lambert.

Lambert betrayed an instant's doubt, like the barrister whose witness has just given him an unrehearsed answer, then said with conviction, "Yes, it is."

"You've visited the place, then?" Pritchard asked, turning to Marc.

"I stayed in nearby Crawford's Corners for several weeks two years ago, and visited again last winter."

This neatly deflected the conversation from hotels in

Cobourg. Pritchard was not satisfied until he had gleaned as much information as possible about Marc's fiancée and wedding plans, many of them fabricated to keep Pritchard happy. During this exchange, Marc kept a sharp eye on the brothers-in-law seated side by side across from him. Whatever the source and depth of their drunken disagreement two nights ago, they seemed to have settled into a sort of reluctant truce, for the sake of their fellow passengers, most likely.

Without warning the coach began to slow, and once again their driver's desperate "Whoa's!" were alarming.

"Can we trust this chap?" Pritchard asked Brookner with a frightened look.

"Todd?" Brookner said as he pulled back the glass of his window and strained to see ahead. "With my life. His grandfather was an Empire Loyalist and his father fought at Crysler's Farm in 1813. They don't come any more faithful than Gander."

"I hear hoofbeats!" Pritchard said.

"What is it, Todd?" Brookner called up, as the others sat up, fully alert.

"Trouble ahead, sir. On horseback."

Brookner pushed his way over to the door, yanked off his garish green greatcoat to expose his weaponry, and leapt into a drift. Marc suddenly wished he hadn't repacked his pistol. But he felt compelled to follow, excusing himself as he bumped against Adelaide.

"Don't try to stop the old fool," she whispered fiercely. "He'll get us all killed yet."

The old fool was already stomping past the horses in the direction of the half a dozen mounted men riding easily towards them down the road. They wore no uniform or insignia to telegraph their allegiance.

Just as Brookner was about to draw his pistol, the lead horseman hollered, "Hold on! We're friends!"

Brookner kept his fingers closed on the pistol in his belt. "Prove it!" he said.

The leader of the group dismounted and walked towards Brookner with both hands well away from his body. His cohort stood at ease, watching but not looking particularly worried. Marc relaxed.

Brookner and the men exchanged a few words that Marc could not quite catch. Then Brookner took several pieces of paper from the stranger and began walking back to the coach. The latter remounted and led his troop past the carriage, each man tipping his hat to Adelaide, who peered out at them from behind her mourning veil.

"They're local men," Brookner said to Marc, but loud enough for all to hear. "They've been deputized to track down several desperadoes from Mackenzie's revolt. They've got pictures of them on these posters. That fellow there is Miles Scanlon."

Marc made a pretense of studying the posters. One of them contained a sure likeness of Thomas-cum-Thomasina Goodall.

The encounter seemed to have got Brookner's adrenaline flowing. Ever since the death-threat yesterday he had begun to cast himself in what could only be called a romantic light. His strut had become more animated and his speech more formal and consciously laboured, as if he were a character out of *Ivanhoe* or *The Bride of Lammermoor*. Without instigation from Pritchard, though richly responded to by that well-read gentleman, Brookner launched into a more vivid description of his capture of the three Scanlon brothers, and then capped off the entertainment with a narrative of the encounter south of Montgomery's tavern and the subsequent counterattack by the Queen's forces under the superlative command of Colonel Allan MacNab—with flags flying and bands tootling and drummers thumping—as if he himself had been present and the detail had been adduced first-hand instead of third or fourth.

Pritchard was goggle-eyed at all this, Marc pretended to doze, Adelaide stared out at the snow beginning to fall again, Lambert appeared to be listening but showed no particular reaction, and Sedgewick grunted and mumbled throughout but not loud enough to steer Brookner's fanciful tale off course.

"My brother-in-law's allegiance has been disturbed, shaken even, by the recent tragic events," Brookner said to Pritchard in response to Sedgewick's last snort of disapproval.

"Farmers fightin' farmers," Sedgewick said. "What's the good of it?"

"Quite right," Pritchard said amiably. "There's nothing civil about a civil war. It's like a family feud."

Sedgewick gave him a half smile but did not add to the sentiment.

"There'll be a few hangings and then folks'll begin to see things straight again," Brookner said loftily. "You mark my words. And a little war—quick and precise—isn't a bad thing every once in a while. Like a belt on a delinquent's backside."

This aphorism seemed to stall the conversation, and the

sudden arrival of snow fluttering past the windows in mesmerizing wavelets drew attention to the outdoors for a few minutes.

"I am not in the least concerned that these woods are crowded with vigilantes or foreign invaders," Brookner said, staring up at the ceiling where a larger and more discriminating audience might lurk. "Why, when my grandfather and grandmother trekked five hundred miles from Virginia through forests like these in 1783—as their home burned behind them and they paid for their loyalty to King George with everything but their lives—these woods were infested with Indians: Senecas and Osage, as primitive and vicious as they come."

"Mohawks and Onondagas," Adelaide responded, to the astonishment of all. "And up here, Algonquins—Ottawa and Montagnais. And most of them were running, too."

No-one could think of anything to say to such a mild but authoritative interjection. Marc saw Brookner's body stiffen and his lower lip quiver.

"Addie was tops in her class," Sedgewick said, ostensibly to Pritchard sitting opposite him. "Always."

Brookner ignored the remark and said patronizingly, "That may well be, my dear—you are often correct about such minutiae—but what does it matter in terms of the point I was making? One savage is like another."

"Oh, I trust, sir, that any of those remaining in the province are somewhat civilized by now," Pritchard said with such obvious anxiety and sincerity that the conversation was brought, mercifully, back to more immediate and practical matters.

"Your scalp is safe here," Marc said, looking out at the snow to hide his smile.

"Rest-stop up ahead!" Gander Todd called out.

And this time, as if to demonstrate how secure these woods were, Brookner did not approach the half-log grog-shop with his sword flashing.

Two hours later, without further incident or much meaningful chatter, the coach pulled up at an inn that sat on the river side of the road about a quarter of a mile from the village of Prescott. Marc got out of the carriage and surveyed the establishment, reputed to be the finest hostelry in these parts.

The Georgian Arms was a sprawling, two-storey clapboard edifice with a pillared verandah and false balcony above it and seven or eight chimney-pots, all of them issuing smoke. Barns and stables were set back discreetly in the rear. The village itself, on a clear day, would have been visible as there were working farms on either side of the road, dozing now under tender pillows of January snow. Just behind the outbuildings Marc could see, in blurred outline, a copse of evergreens and the telltale shadow where the banks of a creek meandered. Beyond the rim of the bush to the southwest, he knew, the St. Lawrence would be pouring blue and frigid underneath its carapace of ice.

"Well, this is more like it," Pritchard said approvingly.

The interior offered little to change the Englishman's mind. There was a spacious reception chamber that rose two storeys to a vaulted and timbered ceiling. All the guest-rooms apparently were on the second floor of the two-storey, in the rear section of the inn. Off the foyer, left and right, there were five or six good-sized rooms that served variously as smoker, waiting lounge for the coach service, public and private dining areas, and a taproom for travellers and local tipplers. Beneath the guest-rooms were the kitchen and probably the office and living quarters of the owner. Two strapping youths took their luggage and lugged it through the hall on the left and up a narrow set of stairs, while the honoured guests themselves were greeted effusively by the proprietor, Murdo Dingman.

Dingman looked as if he had been press-ganged into his clothes. Bulges of neck and waist leaked out at cuff and collar, accenting even more his globular head and a glowing pink scalp barely rescued from baldness by two grey tufts of hair standing above his ears like undotted exclamation marks. His berry-brown eyes were beady and hyperactive between beetle brow and bursting cheek, the only quick-moving parts of an otherwise phlegmatic physique. What he lacked in sprightliness, however, he compensated for by his enthusiastic patter.

"Welcome, welcome, welcome," he enthused, tumbling his fists like a baker kneading dough. "Your approach has been presaged by the governor's courier, and hence we have made estimable preparations for your comfort and pleasure. We will brook no efforts to make your stay with us a memorial one." He thrust out his chubby fingers and shook the hand of each of the gentlemen, catching and recording their names. He gave the captain an extra pump and, being informed that Marc was also a military officer, returned and pumped it again. So excited was he that he almost seized the lady's hand in a male embrace, caught himself in time, and made a bow so curt he threatened to topple over and crush her.

"Barker!" he shrieked at a wretched lad struggling towards the stairs with Marc's big trunk. "Be careful! Use both the hands God gave you!"

It being only two hours till supper-time at six, the party decided to go to their rooms, perform their ablutions (there was a bathroom at the far end of the upstairs hall and tons of hot water to be fetched at a whim), and then drift down for a pre-meal sherry in the plush chairs of the lounge. "Where you will be unperturbed till dinner be serviced," their host confided, with a trumpeting chortle that had no evident purpose.

Still aware that he must act prudently, Marc lingered behind the others a little to survey the layout. As he stood in the cavernous foyer looking towards the rear of the inn, the lounge or smoker lay to his left, and to his right was a tavern, abuzz with local barflies. Straight ahead and running underneath the second storey, where the guest-rooms were, was a long hallway ending in a rear exit. Off this hall were doors left and right, leading, Marc assumed, to various parts of the proprietor's living quarters or those of his hirelings, and next to the exit itself Murdo Dingman's office. Just to Marc's left, around the corner from the lounge, a short hall brought one to the stairs leading up to the rooms above or, alternatively, to a side exit on the ground floor. Over to the right, below the arching beams strung with coloured candle-lamps, was the open dining-room set with generous round tables draped in white linen cloth. A clattering of pans somewhere beyond it suggested an adjoining kitchen.

Marc started for the hallway to his left and the stairs to his room. But Murdo Dingman came trundelling up the hall from his office and across the foyer, waving a letter in one hand. Marc stopped and waited politely for his arrival. Dingman came to a rolling stop in front of him, glanced warily over at the open tavern-door, slipped the letter into Marc's hand with a deft gesture, and said, "Private communicado for your eyes only. From the currier at twelve hundred hours." And he scuttled furtively back towards his office.

It was another note from Owen Jenkin in Montreal.

Dear Marc:

More disquieting news. One of Sir John Colborne's spies has supplied information that Charles Lambert is actually Sharles Lam-bear (French pronunciation for both words), born in St. Denis but raised in Vermont across the border. Many relatives still in the area. Spent the past two weeks near the village, but his purpose is not yet known. His wife is English-speaking and, we believe, still in Cobourg. Watch your back. More news as it comes to me.

Owen

Well, old friend, Marc thought, *I can't look forward and backward at the same time.* But Monsieur Lambert would soon receive a face-to-face surprise, for Marc could not afford to wait much longer. Still, though it was possible that Lambert had taken a shot at him back near Cornwall—and now seemed to have a motive for assassinating him—Marc was inclined to think it had not been him. That didn't mean that Lambert wasn't looking for such an opportunity. It just meant that there could be more than one person out to kill him. And why would Lambert bother with a death-threat against Brookner?

True, Brookner was a Tory bigot and a *miles gloriosus,* but he hadn't been involved in the carnage at St. Denis or St. Eustache. His principal offense, beyond his swaggering arrogance, had been against the Scanlon brothers, one of whom could well be stalking him.

Marc decided that the coming night would be critical for any assassin, for by this time tomorrow the Brookner party could be in Kingston, where it would break up, leaving Brookner on home ground and Marc, Pritchard, and Lambert to arrange their own unpredictable schedules. He walked slowly and pensively up to his room.

Supper was delayed fifteen minutes while the group waited, somewhat anxiously, for Captain Brookner to return from his obligatory walkabout, in full military regalia "Daring young Miles Scanlon to make him a martyr," Sedgewick muttered for all to hear.

Murdo Dingman, too, was beside himself with worry: the roast chickens were cooling and the gravy with kidneys congealing on the table. But Brookner did arrive unmartyred, stamping the snow off his boots at the side exit in clear view of the diners seated across the foyer around a single, large table. He came across to them, pulling at the sleeve of his magnificent greatcoat. He was flushed and excited.

"I saw the bugger!" he cried. Then to his lady, "Pardon my French."

"Scanlon?" Sedgewick asked, wide-eyed.

"I couldn't be sure. But it was the shadow of a man—not a big man—moving through the trees to my left as I strolled along a little path beside the creek back there. I was admiring the scenery, especially a spring with the dark water bubbling up through the ice."

It was obvious that the captain was enjoying himself.

Dingman broke into the narrative: "Were you insulted, sir?"

"No, I was not. At the first flick of movement, I opened my coat and surprised the the miscreant by flourishing my sword."

Which would certainly have frightened an assassin with a pistol, Marc mused.

"Do you not think you are taking the threat from this Scanlon chap a bit too lightly, Captain?" Pritchard asked with some hesitation.

"I would turn your question around, sir: Miles Scanlon may well be taking me too lightly. At any rate, no Scanlon shall prevent me from executing my morning walk or enjoying the local scenery."

"Hear! Hear!" Pritchard cried, then blushed when he realized he was alone in the sentiment. Marc was sure he heard Adelaide utter "Fool!" under her breath. If Brookner heard, he did not let on nor allow it to modify the pose of lofty valour he had assumed and then maintained throughout an awkward, jittery supper.

It had occurred to Marc that the shadowy figure Brookner claimed to have seen—if it had been real and not imagined for dramatic effect—was just as likely to have been stalking him as the captain. After all, there had been two actual attempts on his own life and a mere threatening note to Brookner who, in his vainglory, may have concocted it himself. Reluctantly, for he was once more extremely fatigued, Marc took out the pumpkin and set up the dummy-form in his bed. Then he rigged several noisy objects against the unlocked door. There was no wardrobe in his room to curl up inside, but a dressing-screen set in front of an improvised bedroll against a far wall provided a suitable vantage-point. He loaded the pistol and laid it on his chest. He kept his clothes and boots on, prepared for pursuit and capture if need be. He was just about to blow out the candle when the first sounds of argument in the room next to him made him pause.

It was the Brookners. Though muffled by the plaster-lath wall between Marc and them, their angry words were decipherable. It appeared that they were well into the altercation, the tone and temper of which had been steadily rising.

"—didn't even have the decency to wear a mourning band!"

"At least I didn't make a spectacle of myself weeping and wailing over the coffin!"

"Keep your voice down! Do you want the whole house to hear?"

The next exchange, though vehement, was conducted in tones too low for Marc to determine the tenor or topic. But soon the voices rose again in pitch and volume.

"Don't you ever—*ever*, you hear—contradict me in public one more time. I won't have it!"

"Don't you know what a strutting peacock you're making of yourself? For God's sake, Randolph, you were once such a proud man, such an intelligent—"

"Shut your mouth this instant! I won't stand for much more of this! When are you going to start acting like a proper wife?"

"When you stop playing the fool!"

"Damn it! Damn it! Damn it!"

Marc got up, lamp in hand. He was waiting for the slap or the woman's cry.

"Take your hands off me!"

Marc eased his booby-trap aside, cursing himself as he did so, and slipped into the dark hallway that ran along the width of the upper floor. He had lost a precious minute, was not even sure what he was about to do, but he reached the Brookners' door out of breath but reasonably alert. He put an ear against it. Silence. There had been no slap, no outcry or gasp of pain at a hurtful male grip. He could hear nothing for a while, then, finally, a sequence of what sounded like snores: the deep-throated kind that interrupt themselves. Brookner had apparently fallen asleep. Marc continued to listen for another minute. The snores subsided. The swishing of sheets or cloth-ing suggested that Adelaide was slipping quietly and safely into bed. She may have been weeping.

Marc made his way back to his room, re-established the booby-trap, poked at the dying fire, re-arranged himself in his place of observation, and prepared to watch and wait for his assassin.

Outside the rear window, the snow continued to fall softly and persistently. In the peaceful quiet of the room, Marc's thoughts turned to the revelations about Lambert. Beyond the remote possibility that Lambert might be gunning for him, Marc considered the larger question of who he was and what he had been up to for the past several weeks. It seemed doubt-ful he had ever visited Cobourg, even though his wife was reputed to be there waiting for him, let alone lived in the town for four months. Was the Cobourg story he told merely a cover for secretive and seditious actions he had been carrying out for some time now? Perhaps he was a close aide of Papineau or Nelson, who had tried to establish an English identity (or had one) for some nefarious purpose. Was he possibly en route to Toronto to execute mayhem of some kind or to Buffalo to rendezvous with Mackenzie and the Patriots, as the exiles threatening invasion liked to call themselves? Whatever was going on, Marc was determined that he would get to the bottom of it before they reached Cobourg.

As he lay thinking thus, he began to realize that the element of excitement and danger, which had beset him since his miraculous awakening in the hospital, was actually helping his rehabilitation by constantly bringing him back to his senses, to a quickness of thought and decision that could easily have mouldered under the strain of coping with Rick's death, facing his own precarious mortality, worrying about Beth and whether there was any future for them, or raging futilely against the inordinate injustices he detected everywhere about him in the world. Then a more profound thought asserted itself: Could a visceral revulsion against such grim realities have been part of the reason that Rick Hilliard had courted danger all his brief adult life? Did it explain Rick's willingness to step into the path of a bullet meant for somebody else?

The answers did not come before Marc fell asleep.

Marc was not unhappy to be wakened. He had been dreaming that he and Beth were rumbling over a dusty, grasshopper-ridden prairie in a Conestoga wagon towards some Yankee paradise named after a decimated Indian tribe, and Beth was saying, "But I don't see any millinery shops!" just before a typhoon of some sort came wriggling out of the endless horizon like a rabid black cobra. He recognized it as a nightmare even before he was fully awake.

But it was not the morning sun he felt on his right cheek. In fact it felt more like snow. The pistol lay where he had placed it, on his chest, except that it was now covered with fine, white flakes. His hair was ruffled by a tiny, chill breeze.

He sat up quickly, knocking the dressing-screen over against the fireless stove. His eye went immediately to the door. The booby-trap was intact. He sighed with relief. He had not counted on the extent of his fatigue and the consequent depth of his sleep: even if someone had forced the door open, he was unlikely to have heard the intruder, who would have had plenty of time to murder both the dummy and its creator.

He turned now to the source of the draft and the snow. The lone window—overlooking the woods behind the inn—was ajar. If there had been much wind, it would have been blown completely open. With growing dread he turned slowly and made himself look at the bed. The night-capped pumpkin was still in its place, but the bedclothes had been knocked askew. He went over and examined his "head." There was a two-inch incision just below the "chin." In the deep of the night, some-one had crept in through the window, stabbed him through what should have been his throat, and crawled back out— undetected by the great investigator.

TWELVE

Despite the obvious jeopardy Marc's fatigued sleep had placed him in, it had left him feeling rested, alert, and ready to discover who was trying to murder him—and why. That he was the intended victim was no longer in doubt. Stiffly but with great determination, he walked over to the window and peered out. The snow was falling gently, drifting down with just the whisper of a breeze to suggest it was in motion at all. Marc could actually see a hazy outline of sun above the shadowed treeline to the southeast. Looking directly down, he noticed for the first time that a wooden ledge, about a foot and a half across, ran along the width of building between the two floors, all the way to the rickety fire-stairs, now mantled with snow like a derelict scaffold. He could see footprints—two sets probably, one going and one coming—stretching along the ledge to the fire-stairs. The assassin must have come up those stairs, or out onto them from the inside hall, and shuffled along the ledge to his unbarred window. From there, if one were bold or desperate enough, it would be simple to ease open the window, enter, and do the deed.

Marc noticed also that it seemed to be about nine o'clock, from the position of the sun, and that the footprints on the ledge were three-quarters filled with fresh snow. Thus, he could not determine their true size or imprint, though he guessed that they were made by a small or medium-sized person, certainly not a large man.

Dismantling his booby-trap, he went out into the main hall. He could detect no sounds from the other rooms. No doubt everyone but he was down in the dining area having breakfast. Well and good. He went to the smaller hall, where it met the main one, and followed it back to the rear exit. Again, he stopped to listen and heard no-one. He eased open the rear door, ignored the sudden chill of the January morning, and examined the landing. It was dotted with bootprints, as if someone, or more than one person, had stomped about there—impatiently? to keep warm? to get up enough nerve? These imprints were also drifted in with snow. Several pairs of prints were visible leading up and down the stairs and, at ground level, veered off in several directions. He realized that the hotel staff might use this back entrance in the course of their duties, and so it was really impossible to tell if the assassin had climbed these stairs to reach the ledge or had got to it from inside the inn.

A few yards behind the building lay several barns and sheds, with well-trod paths leading to and from. Still, intent on considering all angles, Marc walked down the steps, creaking and shuddering, and followed various sets of near-obscured prints, ending up either at one of the sheds or on a much-frequented path that led into the woods towards the creek, where Brookner had been promenading earlier last evening. Marc did not pursue these farther, as any prints there could have easily been those of staff or guests or locals enjoying the scenery. Besides which, Marc was no tracking scout.

Mildly discouraged, he went back up the fire-stairs to the second floor and scanned the carpet of the rear hall in search of wet stains. He ran his hand along its surface, feeling for dampness. He found none. But if the murder had been attempted as early as midnight, say, any telltale signs of snow having been brought back in on the assassin's boots might be lost. He upbraided himself for sleeping in. The only conclusion he could draw at this point was that the intruder had used the ledge and the landing. How he got there was anybody's guess.

Back in his room, Marc took time to scrutinize the "wound." It was a precise incision, very thin and slightly wavy, the work of a flensing-knife, perhaps, or an extremely thin dagger. Other than that, he could find no other clues. His trunks had not been opened or searched. Nothing else seemed out of place.

The next question was whether or not he should reveal this attempt to the others. If the culprit were an outsider, they could well have seen or heard something of importance. On the other hand, if it were Lambert, for instance, Marc thought he would be wise to keep his counsel and merely watch. Perhaps his sudden appearance at breakfast, like Banquo's ghost, might be enough to startle the killer into giving himself away in some manner. But if that failed, would another attempt then be made? The opportunity for it now seemed remote, as the group would be travelling together all day, with the outside possibility of reaching Kingston by late in the evening. However, if they only made Gananoque and had to put up as a group for one more night, Marc would have to come clean or be extraordinarily cautious. He decided to watch and wait.

Marc wheeled sharply to his left at the bottom of the stairs and strode across the foyer to the open dining area and the table where several of the entourage were seated at breakfast. "Good morning!" he boomed cheerfully, but his eyes darted about, seeking signs.

Pritchard, Sedgewick, and Lambert looked up from their coffee and newspapers. The Brookners were not present. What on earth was going on with those two? Marc had heard no sounds from their room. Down here, though, it was plain that his abrupt entrance had made no particular impression on any of the gentlemen. Lambert barely glanced up from his paper to nod a surly hello. Pritchard, addicted to bonhomie, smiled and stood up almost halfway to greet him. Percy Sedgewick said "Good morning" to Marc as if he were genuinely glad to see him.

"Here's my newspaper, Lieutenant," Pritchard said. "I've finished with it. I'll get Dingman to bring in some fresh supplies. There's quite a good pot of coffee on the sideboard."

"You're most kind," Marc said.

"I trust you've had a solid night's sleep," Sedgewick said. "Did you happen to see anythin' of Addie or Randolph?

They're awfully late, and the captain usually goes for his fool walk long before this."

"Perhaps I should go and knock on their door," Marc offered.

"Oh, I didn't mean to sound no alarm," Sedgewick said quickly, colouring slightly. "You go ahead with your breakfast. I'll slip up in a few minutes if they're not down soon."

"Yes, I hate to be impolite about it," Pritchard said, "but we need to leave here within the hour if we're to attempt Kingston."

"Addie's been upset with her husband over his boastin' and his damn fool walkin' out in his tunic," Sedgewick said. "I heard them arguin' about it last night."

Among other things, Marc thought.

"She thinks he'll get himself shot by vigilantes or else catch pneumonia."

"I thought I'd catch my death last night," Pritchard chortled. "How about you, Lambert?"

Charles Lambert continued to study his newspaper.

Just then they heard a clumping of boots on the stairs across the foyer, and turned as one to see Captain Brookner fully dressed and ready for his constitutional. No-one was particularly surprised that he did not greet them, but rather wheeled and headed away towards the side door.

"For Christ's sake, Randolph, listen to your wife for once in your life!"

Sedgewick's uncharacteristic outburst startled everyone, including Brookner, and brought Murdo Dingman motoring dangerously down the hall from his office. Sedgewick followed up his brief advantage by leaping up and trotting across the foyer to the hallway where Brookner had stopped and merely half turned to wait for him, in his customary haughty manner. The two began arguing, sotto voce, to the embarrassment of the breakfast table. Suddenly, Brookner pushed Sedgewick away and stomped out into the morning.

Red-faced and obviously unused to dealing with such situations, Sedgewick trudged dolefully back across the foyer.

"You did your best," Pritchard said. "But a man must determine his own fate," he added sententiously.

Sedgewick sighed and sat down. He was sweating.

Dingman decided it was time to defend the honour of the inn. "I can insure you, sirs, that the ground and previews of this establishment are as safe as a mouse in its hole. We are all loyalists in this township. We adulterate the young Queen."

"For which I'm sure she shall be grateful," Pritchard said with some amusement, "when she hears of it."

Lambert looked up from his steady perusal of the *Brockville Recorder* and said to Dingman, "I could help you with that last will and testament now, if you have a moment."

"Oh, thank you, Mr. Lambert. Mrs. Dingman's been after me to do somethin' about it fer ages, and when I learned you were a solicitor—"

"May we go to your office now?" Lambert asked with great politeness.

"Indeed, sir, indeed."

Lambert got up, nodded to excuse himself, and then he and Dingman disappeared around the corner into the rear hall from which they could access the proprietor's office. At that same moment, Adelaide Brookner came across the foyer towards them, looking, to everyone's astonishment, flushed and flustered.

"Has he gone off?" she asked her brother.

She was a changed person, and they all stared. Her hair was dishevelled, her blue eyes underscored with black smudges, as if she had not slept or slept badly. Her mourning dress was rumpled, and the black scarf she used to cover the upper reaches of her bosom and neck had been stuffed carelessly in place and flung haphazardly under her chin.

"I tried to stop him, Addie, but he's worse than ever."

Adelaide gave her brother a grateful smile. Then she addressed Marc and Pritchard. "I apologize for my appearance. My husband and I, as you may well have heard, had an argument last night. I did not sleep well. I don't think Randolph did either. We only woke up about fifteen minutes ago. My husband began dressing for his morning walk, and we quarrelled again. When he marched out, I just threw on my clothes. Foolishly, I still thought I might stop him or persuade you to—"

"No need for apologies, madam," Pritchard said gallantly, though he was quite flummoxed by all this ungentlemanly and unladylike behaviour among the colonials. "I'll fetch you some hot coffee."

"That would be kind of you." She sat down with a sigh beside her brother.

Marc was wondering what really had transpired up there last night. If Adelaide had lain awake, as well she might have after the altercation, then she may have seen the assassin shuffling along the ledge right past her window. Also, it was clear now that both husband and wife had been asleep during his investigation of the footprints on the landing and beyond.

Adelaide sipped at her coffee, bringing it all the way up to her lips, as if it were too much effort to bend down to it. Closer to her now, Marc could see the dried runnels where copious tears had fallen. She caught him staring.

"It wasn't just the argument," she said with quiet dignity. "I haven't been able to weep for Marion since the afternoon of the funeral. Then, later last night, it all came pouring out."

"Maybe I should go after Randy," Sedgewick said to Adelaide. "We do need to leave very soon."

"You'll only antagonize him."

"Then I'll go along with you," Pritchard said. "I believe I can make the man see reason. Neutral party and all that."

Marc rose to join them.

"Please, stay," Adelaide said, and Marc sat down.

The other two trotted upstairs to get their coats and hats, and came back down less than a minute later. They hurried out the side door.

Marc took the opportunity to go to the kitchen and request more hot food and fresh coffee. When Brookner came back, they would have to hurry him along. Lambert, apparently, was still closeted with Dingman, going over codicils and the like.

"The food will be right in. We need to eat well. It's seventy miles or so to Kingston. You'll no doubt be relieved to get home."

Adelaide smiled, and swallowed hard. Her hands were moving restlessly in her lap.

When the food arrived, she poked at it listlessly. But it was obvious that she did not wish to carry on a conversation.

Some minutes later, the side door was flung open. Sedgewick stood in the doorway, waving for Marc to come over.

"I hope nothing's wrong," Adelaide said, getting up.

"Please, stay here, Mrs. Brookner." Marc rushed over to Sedgewick. Pritchard was peering over his shoulder, white as an Easter lily. His jowls were quivering.

"Come with me quickly, Lieutenant," Sedgewick said. "No time for your coat. Something dreadful's happened."

"Lead the way," Marc said, fearing the worst.

Pritchard was apparently supposed to look to the lady, but whirled and followed them, in a total daze.

"I've never seen anything like it," he gasped.

"Then go back and sit with Addie."

"Oh, I couldn't tell her, could I?"

Sedgewick sighed, and then decided simply to lead Marc directly to the dreadful happening without further conversation. They walked quickly past the barn and sheds, following the path into the woods that Marc had observed earlier. The recent snow, still falling faintly on the path, was marred by a number of bootprints and scuffs, from Brookner's boots most likely, and those of Sedgewick and Pritchard having come after him and then retreated. They soon came upon the creek, frozen over and blanketed with the winter's accumulation of snow. The path paralleled the curves of the creek for a hundred yards or so with spruce trees on their left and the creek-bed on their right.

"We followed his tracks—they were the only ones to come this far—right to this here bend," Sedgewick was saying to

Marc at his heels. "And then we heard the bubblin' sounds of the spring-water Randolph mentioned last night, and we thought—"

"I can't go a foot farther," Pritchard said, halting behind them.

"The footprints stopped, got all muddled, as you can see, and I couldn't figure out why they stopped so sudden. It was Pritchard who looked down there and saw him."

Marc turned to look down over the creek-bank, noting that the snow was matted down, and there in the creek itself, where he had tumbled, lay Captain Randolph Brookner. His eyes were wide open, aghast at the last thing they ever saw. He was very dead. He had landed in the only running water in the township, a frothing, spring-fed rivulet of blue-black water only a yard wide and several more in length. The body was almost fully under water, on its side, and facing Marc. An icy stream bathed his bare head and poured over the hole in his temple where a lead ball had entered or come out, killing him instantly. Little blood was evident. The fancy fur hat lay in the snow nearby. He had either fallen or been shoved into the water. Certainly he had been murdered in cold blood.

Marc hurried along the path in the considerable wake of Dr. MacIvor Murchison. Barely an hour had passed since the grisly discovery. A lad had been dispatched on mule-back to fetch the esteemed county coroner from his palatial abode in Prescott, and he had arrived a half hour later in his one-horse sleigh. The solitary horse had to be of draught size as MacIvor

Murchison was a man of intimidating weight and girth, in addition to being a fellow of formidable height, means, and gait. His first duty had been to minister to the distraught widow, who was soon under sedation in the care of Mrs. Dingman in her quarters. The witnesses and other interested parties were ordered to sit in the dining-room or lounge and keep the peace. Murdo Dingman, uncertain as to which division he belonged, fretted and fumed on principle. When Marc mentioned to the coroner that he had been involved in no less than three official murder investigations, he was instructed to follow along when Murchison marched out the side door to view the body "*in situ.*"

Wearing floppy, flat overshoes ideally suited to trudging through snow when they were carrying three hundred pounds, the coroner with his long assured strides was keeping well ahead of Marc's limping pace.

"It's to your left about a hundred—"

"I know the terrain, laddie. You concentrate on keeping up, eh?" Murchison had a voice that could have outclassed a foghorn, and didn't seem interested in modulating it in any way for the benefit of his audience or good manners. The first sight of him filling the front entrance of the Georgian Arms had left Marc speechless. He had a huge head, side-whiskers like two stooks of fraying wheat, tufts of ginger hair sprouting irreverently from his scalp, and loose, dark features—all flap and crevasse—with eyes as burnished and staring as a pair of swollen hickory nuts. His brown tweed suit hung over his flesh with all the subtlety of an awning, and when he added a greatcoat more capacious than an army-tent and a beaver flapped-cap, he resembled nothing less than a badly tailored bull moose in moulting season.

In short order they came upon the corpse of Randolph Brookner.

"This place looks like it's been trampled by a camel caravan," he muttered loudly. "We won't find our killer's boots among this stew."

"Exactly what I concluded," Marc said. "After I sent Sedgewick and Pritchard back to the inn to break the news to Mrs. Brookner, I carefully surveyed the perimeter. We've had intervals of fresh snow all night but not enough, I think, to completely obscure any marks made in the deep snow beyond this path and the high ground. I found nothing. It looks as if the killer used the path and came from the vicinity of the hotel or one of the many sheds behind it. What do you think, sir?"

The coroner, who was teetering over the bank to get a better view of the body, swivelled his big head around without moving his torso, like a ruffled owl, smiled at Marc, and said, "Most likely. And don't call me *sir*. Around here I'm known as Mac to my equals and, to those obsessed with formality, as Doctor Mac. I answer to both, but you call me Mac and I'll call you Marc."

Marc nodded.

"Now take ahold of my hand, laddie, I've got to go down to get a closer gander at the poor bugger."

With Marc providing necessary ballast, Mac leveraged himself down until his massive bulk just seemed to settle into the snow around Brookner's upper body. He whistled, stridently enough to wake dogs throughout the township.

"Jesus Christ on a donkey! What a mess! We ain't had a real murder like this in the region for four or five years, not counting the aftermath of the odd grog-shop fisticuffs or some gelding getting revenge on its master with a well-aimed hoof. But this chap's been shot by somebody who truly wanted him dead—and quickly, if you'll pardon the pun."

Marc watched with fascination as the coroner removed his furry gloves and applied a set of surprisingly nimble fingers to examining the wound and the area around it. "He fell immediately into this ice bath, I'd say. There's still very little bleeding. He might've lain here like this for days, unchanged."

"How was he shot?"

"Small lead ball from a pistol, from the size of the wound. Entered the back of the head just below the left ear and came out through the right temple, taking some of the brain with it. The running water's washed most of the brain-matter away."

"So he was likely shot somewhat from below."

"Well, he looks like a very tall man, almost as tall as you or me. Few killers could have shot down at him."

"Can you tell how far away the killer was when the shot was fired?"

"Well, I don't see any splash of powder—the water's done a job on the hair—but even so, I'd guess from the size of these holes and the force of the blast that we're looking at three or four feet, no more."

Marc gave that some thought while Mac continued his probing: "I'd say, then, that the killer came up behind him, perhaps stepped onto the path from behind one of these spruce trees, and simply fired before Brookner could react." Marc surveyed the other side of the path. "There are no prints back here anywhere. That means the killer must have come up silently behind him and fired just as he turned. That's possible because Brookner was a stiff-necked, stubborn creature, an easy target for this type of ambush."

Mac chuckled sonorously. "Well, he isn't stiff yet. Petrified a bit from this chilly shower, but no rigor mortis."

"Not surprising. Four of us saw him head out for his walk about twenty minutes before Sedgewick and Pritchard found him."

"You don't suppose the two of them—"

"Not a chance. Pritchard is a rather silly Englishman who knew none of us before we set out together. Sedgewick didn't like his brother-in-law, but he was with me when the victim left for his walk. It certainly points to someone who may have been stalking Brookner for the last day or two."

"Tell me about it."

Marc gave the coroner a brief account of the threatening note, Brookner's involvement in the capture of the Scanlon brothers, Miles Scanlon's subsequent escape, and Brookner's imprudent behaviour in the face of legitimate danger.

Mac put both hands in Marc's and hauled himself up out of the creek. He didn't bother brushing the snow off his flanks or haunches. "Well, he's paid a high price for his arrogance. Now tell me, before we go back in, where everybody was during the twenty minutes from the time Brookner left the building till he was found here."

Again, Marc gave him a brief account. At nine o'clock or so, he had joined Sedgewick, Pritchard, and Lambert for breakfast.

Ten minutes later, perhaps, Brookner came downstairs, argued for half a minute with Sedgewick in the side hallway, then left on his own. No more than five minutes later, and just after Lambert and Dingwall left for his office, Mrs. Brookner arrived looking for her husband. Learning he had already left, she joined the others for breakfast. Perhaps ten minutes after that, Sedgewick and Pritchard went to fetch the wayward captain and found him dead—apparently murdered only minutes before their arrival.

"It looks to me as if Miles Scanlon is our main suspect," Mac said, pointing out the obvious.

Marc said nothing, however, about the attempt on his own life during the night. He might eventually do so, but his instincts told him that the two incidents were unrelated, and he did not want one complicating the other needlessly. His own stalker would surely strike again, and further opportunities would open up for catching him in the act.

Marc took one last look at what remained of the proud and audacious captain. The tumble into the creek had caused the upper buttons of his greatcoat to come open, so that the top of his militia-jacket with its gold chest-bars was just visible. His officer's boots, polished to an ebony gleam, lay out of the water upon a shelf of ice, as they would have if he had fallen on the field of battle. The rest of him lay almost fully submerged in the chattering stream whose effervescence seemed to be keeping him afloat and continuously bathed. But the greatcoat itself—his pride and joy, freshly purchased, no doubt, just for the expected rebellion—was now waterlogged and threatening to pull the body down. Its bright green sheen had succumbed to the insistent waters, which left it soggy, darkened, even shabby. It was a sad end.

"So the only one of your crowd who was actually out of sight of you or any of the others during the critical twenty minutes was this Charles Lambert fellow?"

"That's right," Marc said, his puzzlement showing. "He was. We saw him and Dingman go around the corner into the hall leading to the door of Dingman's office. They were supposed to be discussing a will."

"Where is the office? I don't quite remember."

"It's at the end of the centre hall, just beside the rear exit." Marc's eyes widened. "It's possible Lambert didn't actually go into the office with Dingman."

"Well, we'll just have to check that out with Proprietor Dingman, won't we?"

"In addition to double-checking everyone's whereabouts. And, may I suggest, Mac, that you not exclude me as a suspect."

"Ah, that I haven't, Marc, though I have given the notion a low probability. But we shall soon hear everybody's tale in detail under oath. I'm going to have Dingman's lads put this corpse into the back of my sleigh. Then I'm going to drive it to my surgery, where I can get it up on a slab and second-guess my own conclusions. Then I'll have it boxed for the grieving widow to take back home to kith and kin, should they be concerned for it. I'll have all this accomplished by one o'clock, after which I shall enjoy the fine luncheon my chatelaine will have prepared for me, washed down with a half litre of ten-year-old Burgundy. And because most of the witnesses and potential culprits are now here and hoping to depart soon, I shall hitch up Prometheus and return to Mr. Dingman's taproom for the coroner's inquest—at three o'clock sharp."

"But shouldn't you consult the magistrate first?"

MacIvor Murchison, Esquire, grinned like a moose in a mayflower swamp: "I *am* the magistrate," he said.

THIRTEEN

After the initial shock of discovery, Marc had no opportunity to study the reactions of his fellow passengers to the murder of Randolph Brookner. Adelaide remained closeted with Mrs. Dingman; Sedgewick and Lambert retired to their rooms (with luncheon being sent up); and Pritchard, ever eager to converse, found himself alone in the lounge. Of the four Marc would like to have questioned a little more closely, Pritchard, alas, was the only one who had no motive. Nevertheless, Marc did go into the lounge to take lunch there with the perplexed wine merchant.

"I was warned that the colonies lacked many of the civilities it has taken the mother country centuries to accumulate and refine," he was saying to Marc through his cigar smoke. "But I never expected to be accosted by hooligans on the Queen's highroad or discover a travelling companion brutally slaughtered a few paces from his hotel. I haven't stopped trembling since I came upon that gruesome sight."

"You and Sedgewick found the body together, I understand."

"Yes. I was no more than a step behind him, but it was I who had the misfortune to first look down into the creek."

That confirmation, as Marc had suggested to the coroner-magistrate, appeared to let both Pritchard and Sedgewick off the hook, unless they had, improbably, conspired together to kill Brookner.

"I would go easy on those brandies, old chap," Marc said, getting up. "The inquest begins in less than two hours."

"So I'm told," Pritchard said, "in the *tap*room!"

After lunch, Marc took it upon himself to interview the kitchen staff, who might have seen something or someone from one of the windows facing the stable and woods. But no-one had noticed Brookner or his stalker on the path about 9:15 or later. The stable-hands had all been indoors at the critical time and could not help. Nor had anyone, inside or outside, seen anyone lurking about the premises last night or earlier this morning. Marc re-examined the footprints between the woods and the back and side of the inn. No clear pattern emerged. He sat down and prepared a written report for the coroner and had it sent off to Mac in Prescott. Perhaps the inquest itself would turn up some useful information.

Dr. MacIvor Murchison arrived before the porticoed entrance of the Georgian Arms like the potentate of some far-flung pocket of empire. The one-horse sleigh, ribald with bells and jangling chains, glided to a graceful stop at the behest of a rail-thin gentleman, who set the reins down with a silky gesture, stepped smartly to the ground, then held out a suede-gloved hand to assist the magistrate out of his elevated seat. Although no general notice of the proceedings had been broadcast, some-how word had leaked out and the big tavern-room had begun to fill up with gawking, dry-throated devotees of the court shortly after opening time at two o'clock. The presiding justice, however—much to the chagrin of the gathering crowd—or-dered the bar closed until the inquest was concluded, in keep-ing with the dignity and sanctity of British jurisprudence. The presiding official himself, of course, had taken on sufficient quantities of fortifying liquors well before his ostentatious arrival.

Murdo Dingman bellied his way through the consider-able throng outside the inn to greet Doctor Mac and welcome him to court, as it were. "I have arranged everything just as you constructed me, your honourable," he boomed, acutely conscious of the gallery watching. "There's plenty of chairs in neat little rows and my best table up front with the big, padded captain's chair for your gracious to be seated upon."

His Honour nodded in curt acknowledgement of these amenities. "And a chair for my clerk here, Mr. Digby Parsons, with pen and ink?"

Parsons stared at Dingman with his long, horse-like face.

"Already done, sir. You've brung your own paper?"

"We have, Mr. Dingman. We have."

And without further clarifying dialogue, the cavalcade of

three swept through the awed crowd into the foyer, where they made a right wheel into the re-rigged tavern.

By three o'clock, when Digby Parsons rapped the gavel on behalf of the coroner upon the deal table before him, the make-shift courtroom was jammed, with a standing overflow crowd in the foyer beyond the opened double-doors. As many women as men were in attendance, a fact that invariably puzzled and appalled new arrivals from the more proper domain of Her Majesty's kingdom. What they would have observed on this particular afternoon was a spacious taproom from which all tables but one had been removed and the orphaned chairs set up in respectable ranks facing the official dais at the front. Behind it, his bulging bulk having been shoe-horned into its padded chair, sat the coroner-magistrate draped in a tattered red cape with furred collar and sporting a moth-infested wig, which teetered on the random tufts of his delinquent hair. To the right the clerk sat with poised pen and parchment before him. To the left was the witness chair, a spare bar-stool. Farther left, beneath the tavern windows, a bench had been cleared for the assembled witnesses, who looked on anxiously.

MacIvor Murchison opened the proceedings by announc-ing that what followed would be a preliminary and a summary hearing: to wit, without a jury. And the findings, should there be any, would be tentative and non-binding.

The clerk then swore in the first witness, Ainslie Pritchard.

Any notion, previously held, that these proceedings would be marked by a foolish and dismissible country-bumpkinness quickly evaporated, as Pritchard seated himself on the edge of the stool and turned to look into the sharp intelligence of the coroner's eyes. As Doctor Mac closely questioned the initial witness, the murmurings and whispers in the room died away and were replaced by a silence that was part awe and part reverence, but principally the intense curiosity of the disinterested in other people's miseries.

"How long had you known the victim?"

"We met five days ago in Montreal. We were staying at the same hotel. We met at breakfast. Captain—"

"I believe you've answered several questions I haven't yet asked."

"Sorry, Your Worship."

"You yourself are newly arrived in Canada?"

"Yes, I've been here less than a month. I came up to Quebec City from New York. I'm in the wine-importing business."

"Yes, yes. That is all very interesting, sir, especially to those with a fine palate, but I am trying to determine whether or not you had any conceivable motive for doing away with Captain Brookner."

Pritchard was aghast. "Good gracious, no! I merely agreed to help share the costs of a private carriage that Brookner hired to take us as far as Kingston."

"Thank you for your forthrightness, Mr. Pritchard. It is certainly hard to imagine a motive for murder on your part, unless the carriage-ride was inordinately bumpy."

The gallery reacted with appreciative titters and one muted guffaw. The coroner glared at the offenders, but couldn't keep an acknowledging smile from curling the corners of his lips.

"Tell the inquest, if you would, the exact circumstances of your discovery of the body."

With the spectators glued to his every word, Pritchard told the inquest of the morning's events, beginning with Brookner's boisterous entrance in the side hall just before 9:15 (there was a chiming clock in the foyer striking the quarters) and concluding with the ill-fated pursuit that culminated in the "hideous sight" in the creek-bed. From his seat on the witness bench Marc noted that, although nervous, Pritchard gave what seemed to be an accurate and credible account. It was Marc's view that Pritchard, without motive or opportunity, was an innocent in the case.

"Did you see any blood flowing from the wound?"

"No, sir, though I didn't really get too close to the body."

"Any sign of the victim's brain-matter on his forehead or cheek?"

A collective gasp seized the gallery.

Pritchard blinked and gulped. Finally, dry-mouthed, he said, "There was icy water running down his entire face. He was . . . washed clean."

"Thank you, sir. I do not mean to be overly gruesome, but I need to know whether or not Captain Brookner had been shot just before your arrival or a little earlier. But it appears as if the cold spring-water into which he tumbled has wiped away much potentially useful evidence. I take it that you did not hear a shot, then?"

"No, sir. There was little wind; it was very quiet and peaceful. We would've heard the slightest noise."

"Like someone thumping off into the bush?"

"Yes. But we heard nothing. It was deathly quiet."

The coroner's swift and baleful glance precluded any

tittering at Pritchard's unfortunate pun. The witness was excused. Percy Sedgewick was then called and sworn in by the abstemiously thin Digby Parsons. The coroner led Sedgewick through the same events attested to by Pritchard, confirming all of them. He expected to be dismissed, but MacIvor Murchison had a few more questions.

"You've told us, Mr. Sedgewick, that you went over to the victim in the hallway on the far side of the foyer and tried to dissuade him from taking his morning walk. Tell us why, sir."

"Because my brother-in-law had received a death-threat the previous day at Morrisburg."

Again, the gallery reacted and had to be silenced.

Sedgewick provided the details of the note found pinned to the seat of the carriage. He described, as delicately as he could with his limited facility for language, Brookner's refusal to take the least precaution and his insistence on flaunting his military status by remaining in the full uniform of the Glengarry militia.

"And this was a brightly coloured, easily recognizable uniform?"

"It was. The coat was brand new, bought in—"

"So he was a bit like a deer wearing a scarlet blazer while foraging in a farmer's wood-lot?"

The appreciative laughter was allowed to rise and fade on its own.

"I'm afraid so. And it cost him his life."

The coroner nodded gravely, knitted his intimidating brows, and said, "Now tell this enquiry about the Scanlon brothers."

Again, with the gallery hanging on every word, Sedgewick

recounted, without gloss, Brookner's capture of the Scanlon brothers—rebels all—and his curt treatment of their family.

"And was the Scanlon barn burned by the militia under Captain Brookner's command?"

Sedgewick hesitated, obviously uncertain how to answer. He looked over at Adelaide, who had sat veiled and still throughout this early testimony. She bowed her head. Was it a nod or a refusal to be drawn in?

"The militia had specific orders to do so. There was a warrant out for the three Scanlon men."

"Nonetheless, the barn got razed, and the women and children were forced to flee?"

"Yes. I . . . I took them in."

"I see." Doctor Mac's thick brows converged. "And was your brother pleased with this act of mercy on your part?"

Sedgewick stared at his fingers.

"You must answer truthfully, sir. I am obliged to get to the question of motive."

"But I had no chance to harm him!"

"We'll come to that in a moment. Please answer my original question."

Sedgewick swallowed hard. "Randolph was furious. He always thought me soft on the rebels. I wasn't, really. I've been a loyal citizen all my life. But these people, the Scanlons, were farmers like me. We suffered the same troubles. They just wanted their grievances taken seriously."

"But such arguments carried no weight with Captain Brookner?"

"No."

"Now, sir, tell us about the quarrel you had with the victim three nights ago in Cornwall."

At this unexpected volley in the interrogation, the witnesses on the bench turned to stare at one of their own, Lieutenant Edwards, seated at the far end. But he was looking respectfully at the coroner.

"How do you know that?" Sedgewick gasped. A sliver of fear edged into his eyes.

"There will be corroborating testimony later on, sir, so if I were you, I would answer the question with scrupulous regard for the truth."

"We'd both been drinkin' a little too much that evenin'. We begun quarrellin' over the usual things, the fact that I didn't support the militia or agree with the barn burnin' and all that. We were loud and very angry."

"Did Brookner threaten you in any way?"

"I wasn't afraid of him. He was all bluster."

"I don't mean physically, sir."

Sedgewick now looked not only uncomfortable but perplexed. He paused while the coroner stared at him with unnerving patience.

"He told me that takin' in and harbourin' the Scanlon family could be looked on as treason."

A curious mixture of groans and nods of approval animated the gallery.

"A serious charge, eh? And one that, if acted upon, posed a grave threat to your well-being?"

"He was all bluster! I didn't take it seriously!" Sedgewick started to get up, stopped suddenly, then slumped back onto the witness stool.

"You are not denying, then, that you had a motive to extinguish this threat? And that such threat had been made just three days before the murder itself?"

Sedgewick's response was barely audible, "No, I'm not."

"Did you place a threatening note in your brother-in-law's carriage?"

"I did not!"

"Are you now telling this inquest that, given the possibility that the man threatening to turn you in for treason might be assassinated by Miles Scanlon, the fugitive, that you went to the side hallway this morning and tried to talk him out of going for a walk in his bright green uniform?"

Sedgewick looked deeply insulted, but it was fear that gripped him and made his reply a tremulous one: "I did, sir. I love my sister dearly. I did not like or admire her husband. But she begged me to try to talk some sense into him—she'll tell you so—and I did it for her sake, not his."

With this heartfelt outburst, the witness was excused. The widow was now called to the stand. The suddenly hushed gallery watched her walk with dignity and purpose to the witness stool. Although she wore the familiar chiffon mourning dress, it was now unwrinkled, and the crepe scarf was folded demurely across her bosom and up and around her long, regal neck. The coroner turned a solicitous eye upon her.

"You are a woman of great courage with a severe sense of duty," he said solemnly, "to accede to my request that you give testimony this afternoon, so soon after the shock of your husband's death."

"I wish not to delay these proceedings," Adelaide said in a firm, almost mechanical tone. She had lifted the veil to reveal her tear-ravaged face, now dry-cheeked and steady with resolve. "I realize that they must take place, now or later, and I did not want to complicate the lives of those innocent persons who have travelled with me and offered me so many kindnesses. Which I have not always had the courtesy or will to acknowledge."

"Yes, madam. We understand that this is your second bereavement in less than a week. I have just a few brief questions for you." He turned to face the gallery. "Before I begin, however, I want to say that the reason I was probing for motive in this case is that it has occurred to me that, while Miles Scanlon is a prime suspect with motive, means, and plenty of opportunity—and may well have fired the fatal shot—it is conceivable that some other person or persons—with suitable motivation—might have conspired with Miles Scanlon to murder Captain Brookner. They might have used Scanlon as a convenient stand-in and perhaps even an unwitting scapegoat."

This statement stirred the gallery so thoroughly that the coroner had to bang his gavel three times, shivering the water in the glasses thereon and spattering ink across his clerk's pristine parchment. The witness showed no particular response.

"It is further conceivable that, failing an outright conspiracy, someone with sufficient motive might have found it expedient merely to let Miles Scanlon know when and where Captain Brookner might be on display, as it were."

The spectators absorbed this astonishing but cogent theory, and added commentary among themselves in a rustle of whispers.

"Now, Mrs. Brookner. I have information that you also quarrelled with your husband, as recently as last night."

The gallery was more shocked than the witness, who answered calmly, "Yes. My husband and I quarrelled often. Over many things. We are both strong-willed, I am afraid."

"And which of those many things did you quarrel about last night?"

"Randolph thought I showed excessive and unbecoming grief during the obsequies for my sister in Montreal."

"That seems somewhat callous, does it not?"

"I would not call my husband callous. He was set in his convictions and beliefs and he had a surplus of both. To remind me of my folly, he removed his mourning band the day after the funeral. I accused him of disrespect for the dead."

"Did you quarrel about anything else?"

"He upbraided me for correcting him in front of the other passengers. It was a subject we argued about many times."

"And you are a woman who does not easily let inaccuracies in conversation go by unnoted?"

"I have tried to do so. But, of course, I was angry with him over his removing the armband." There was the slightest trembling of the lower lip, but she quickly mastered herself.

"Let us move on to this morning. You awoke after your husband?"

"Yes. About nine o'clock. He was already dressing."

"In his parade uniform?"

"I'm afraid so. Jacket, breeches, boots, greatcoat—everything military except his ordinary fur hat. I begged him not to go out. After that death-threat was found, I pleaded with my brother to forget his differences with Randolph and try to dissuade him from such foolhardy bravado. But Randolph was stubborn and proud."

"So we've been assured. Did you follow your husband downstairs?"

"I wasn't dressed. I threw on my clothes. I didn't have time to pin up my hair properly. I'd been crying much of the night over the loss of my dear sister. I looked a wreck. . . ."

Murmurs from the gallery denied that this could ever be so.

"Was your husband gone when you did get downstairs?"

"Yes. It couldn't have been more than four or five minutes later, but he had gone out the side door, or so my brother and Mr. Pritchard told me."

"And you did not think to go immediately after him, knowing the reality of the danger to his person?"

"Not right away. It was very cold out and snowing a bit. I had no coat or hat."

"But you did subsequently persuade Mr. Sedgewick and Mr. Pritchard to do so?"

"Yes, using the excuse that the coach had to leave by ten o'clock if we were to reach Gananoque or Kingston by this evening."

"Let me review these times, then, just to get them straight. Your husband left your room, fully dressed for the outdoors, at about nine-ten or so. He arrived downstairs, we've been told, about fifteen minutes past the hour, observed by all those at breakfast with a clear view across the foyer. Mr. Sedgewick spends less than a minute, say, trying to discourage the captain from going out. He does go out, however, a little after quarter past nine. You arrive downstairs less than five minutes later and join the others at the breakfast table."

"Yes, though Mr. Lambert was heading down the back hall just as I arrived."

All eyes swung towards Charles Lambert, who had been sitting stolidly on the witness bench, staring straight ahead as if preoccupied with more weighty or more pertinent matters. He continued to do so.

"Yes. Thank you, Mrs. Brookner. We will hear testimony on his whereabouts in due course. What we have so far, then, is this: I have retraced the route Captain Brookner took this morning and, walking at a steady pace, I found it took ten full minutes to reach the spot where he was shot. However, your husband was accustomed, was he not, Mrs. Brookner, to stroll along in leisurely fashion enjoying the scenery?"

"That is right. He would march along for a bit, then pause to take in something that caught his eye, especially if he were in a new place."

"In all likelihood, then, it may have taken him fifteen to twenty minutes to reach that fatal spot. Which would bring him there about nine-thirty or nine thirty-five. You arrived at the breakfast table about nine-twenty. How long were you there before you asked Mr. Sedgewick to follow your husband?"

"Not more than five minutes. Mr. Pritchard had had time to fetch me some coffee from the sideboard."

"That means that Sedgewick and Pritchard, who took several more minutes to fetch their coats and boots, began to follow after him at about nine-thirty or so. They were obviously in a hurry. They must have reached him by, say, nine-forty or nine forty-five—not more than a few minutes after the shot must have been fired, but far enough away not to have heard the report of the pistol. A minute or two sooner and their presence might have prevented this tragedy."

The gallery took this in. Adelaide looked stoically ahead.

"It seems improbable, if not impossible, then, that anyone seated at the breakfast table from nine-fifteen to nine twenty-five could have fired the fatal shot."

Again, all eyes swung to scrutinize the only member of the travelling party who had not been present during these critical minutes. Charles Lambert looked down, fingers clasped tightly.

Adelaide Brookner was excused with thanks. She walked through the crowd and out of the room, with Mrs. Dingman one solicitous step behind her. The next witness was Charles Lambert. It took four gavel raps to quell the muttering and morbid speculation.

The coroner began by leading Lambert over some familiar territory, so that it was soon ascertained that he had not known or ever knew of Randolph Brookner until meeting him at the hotel in Montreal and joining his travelling group.

"Did you have any reason for disliking any member of the Queen's regulars or Her militia?"

"No, sir. I am a loyal citizen."

"I'm sure you are."

Marc had not yet told the magistrate about Lambert's true identity, partly because the information had been given to him in confidence by an officer of the army and partly because he thought it would throw a red herring into the proceedings. If, as a Quebecker, Lambert wished revenge for alleged atrocities, it was Marc who would have been the target, not Brookner.

"Please tell this inquest at what time you left the breakfast table, and why."

"Mrs. Brookner was just coming downstairs when Mr. Dingman and I left for his office."

"That would make it close to nine-twenty?"

"I believe so."

"Who suggested that you go there, you or Mr. Dingman?"

The spectators leaned forward to hear the witness's response to this potentially incriminating query.

"I did," Lambert said very softly.

"And did you go straight to Dingman's office?"

Lambert hesitated again. "No, sir."

"Why not?"

"The office is at the far end of the hall near the rear exit of the building. When we got there, I realized I would need one of my law books to facilitate the business Mr. Dingwall had been asking me to attend to ever since my arrival here."

"Which was?"

"To help him rewrite a complicated will involving previous entailments on this valuable property, and several new codicils as well."

"But no-one at breakfast reports seeing you return to the foyer to mount the stairs to the guest-rooms above."

"They were not the only stairs, sir."

This brought the gallery to rapt attention.

"I see. Go on."

"Because Mr. Dingwall and I were already at the rear of the building, I decided to slip out the back door, go up the outside fire-stairs, and reach my room that way. I had no coat or hat, but I did have my boots on." When Doctor Mac lifted one skeptical brow, Lambert added, "It just seemed the most convenient way of doing so."

"And you returned in the same manner?"

"Yes, sir."

"While you were outside, did you notice anyone at all using the path to the woods?"

"No-one."

"You went straight up and came right back?"

"Yes. I couldn't have been gone more than five minutes. Mr. Dingman was waiting for me in the office the whole time."

"Which would bring you back there about nine twenty-five?"

"That seems about right."

The spectators sighed as one. Here was another likely suspect, dark and mysterious, with a perfect alibi. Lambert could not have trailed Brookner to the creek, shot him, and scampered back to Dingman in five minutes. The witness stepped down, looking relieved.

Interest picked up instantly, however, when Murdo Dingman was called forward.

It was soon determined that Dingman could not corroborate earlier testimony about the goings-on at the breakfast table because he had been closeted in his office with the entrails of his last will and testament before him on his desk. He had come out hoping to ask Lambert to return with him to his office, and had been happily surprised when Lambert had suggested such a move himself.

"But Mr. Lambert did not go immediately into your office?"

"No, sir. He pardoned himself and went out the back door to fetch one of his law tombs."

The coroner blinked hugely, but said nothing.

"I went in and sat waitin' for him."

"Please answer these next questions carefully. Mr. Lambert has testified that he was away—and outside the building—for no more than five minutes, and that he thus returned to you by nine twenty-five. First of all, do you have a clock in your office?"

"I do, Your Honourable. Made in the United States. Keeps perfect time."

Some skepticism at this latter claim was evinced by the gallery.

"So, is it your testimony that Mr. Lambert returned by nine twenty-five?"

Dingman looked suddenly stricken. He glanced about him for assistance but could find only sixty pairs of eyes interrogating him with heartless inquisition.

"Could be," he mumbled.

"You are saying that you are not certain?"

"Yes. No. It's just—"

"Surely you can tell us if it was closer to five minutes than, say, twenty. For if it were the latter, Mr. Lambert would not have an iron-clad alibi for the time of the murder."

Charles Lambert did look up at this remark, and was

studied minutely for his reaction: it seemed to be a combination of startlement and resentment.

"Could be either," Dingman said, staring at the arabesques his fingers were executing. "You see, I was so absorbent in thinkin' about my will, with all its detailments and its codpieces—"

The courtroom erupted with unconstrained laughter. The coroner struggled valiantly to be unamused.

Bewildered by this inexplicable outburst, Dingman soldiered on doggedly. "Whenever I'm readin' or thinkin', I find I lose track of time. But I remember Mr. Lambert did come in with snow on his boots, before all the fuss started up in the foyer."

"And that's the best you can do?"

"It is, sir. And I blame it all on my last will and testimony."

"Then that will have to do," said the coroner with a razor-thin smile. "You may step down."

"But I ain't up, Your Honourable."

Pulling flaps of cheek, brow, and jowl into more solemn conjunction, MacIvor Murchison read into testimony his own pathologist's report, which added nothing new to his initial findings earlier in the day. He next informed the witnesses and gallery that Lieutenant Edwards, who was by dint of elimination to be the next witness summoned, had provided the inquest with a detailed deposition, which testimony tended to corroborate much of that presented by the other witnesses.

Nothing they had said prompted him to call forth the good lieutenant for further enquiry. This announcement caused much disappointment and vocal complaint from the spectators, but the coroner waited patiently for silence. After which he informed them that he was ready to offer his preliminary findings, without a recess. Digby Parsons pushed several parchment-like sheets of paper in front of his master, who took five lengthy and dramatic minutes pretending to scrutinize the indecipherable notes of his earnest clerk. Then he brushed back the errant wig, which had gradually taken root in his eyebrows, and began.

"It is clear that the most probable suspect in the murder of Randolph Brookner is the man with the strongest motive, the relevant means, and plenty of opportunity. As magistrate for this county, I have been kept informed of any sightings or successful captures of rebel fugitives in this region. I can tell you today that Miles Scanlon has been seen by more than one dutiful citizen of this township no farther than five miles from this courtroom, as late as the day before yesterday. That he is the most logical one to have fired the fatal shot is the tentative conclusion of this summary inquest, and, in my role as magistrate, I am going to issue a warrant for his arrest on suspicion of murder, in addition to the charge of sedition. That is not to say that some other individual may not have conspired with Scanlon, in whole or in part, but until the latter is apprehended and brought before this inquest, the coroner declines to point a finger at anyone in particular. Needless to say, these proceedings are merely prorogued, to be continued when circumstances dictate. All those who have been travelling with Captain Brookner will be subpoenaed to appear at a time and place to be determined later. In the meantime, all are free to go."

The gavel descended, the spectators looked thirstily towards the bar, and the witnesses appeared much relieved.

Marc sat quietly on the bench, absorbed in thought.

FOURTEEN

Marc was lying on his bed, reviewing the testimony in his mind and going over the events and conversations of the past three and a half days, when there was a tentative knock on his door. He opened it to discover Dingman's youngest boy standing expectantly in the hall.

"Yer bags, sir?"

"But we're not leaving till morning," Marc said.

The boy blushed. "Then you ain't Mr. Pritchard?"

"I am not. I'm Lieutenant Edwards."

The blush deepened. "Sorry, sir. It's Mr. Pritchard and Mr. Lambert that's leavin' in half an hour." He turned and went farther down the hall.

Marc limp-trotted downstairs and found Dingman in his office, studying a heavily marked copy of his will. "I got them a fast two-man cutter from the village," he told Marc without looking up. "There're hopin' to reach Brockville by ten o'clock."

Then on to Kingston in the morning, Marc thought. And out of his reach.

When Marc made no move to leave, Dingman reluctantly looked up and offered more details. "Mrs. Brookner is gonna stay with us tonight. Doctor Mac give her a sediment to help her sleep. She'll take the big coach in the mornin', with you and her brother—and the coffin, of course. Will you be wanting supper soon?"

But Marc was already out the door. He was still working out the details as he ascended the stairs, but he believed he now knew who his man was.

Marc passed the boy as he struggled downstairs with Ainslie Pritchard's luggage, and headed to the room at the far end of the hall. Lambert was still packing when Marc gave a single rap and entered. He was surprised, but that was all.

"You've come to say good-bye," he said. "Would you like a drink?" He indicated a silver flask on the dresser.

"No, thank you. What I want is for you to sit down while I tell you a story, one that doesn't have a happy ending, Monsieur *Lam-bear.*"

There was a perceptible flinch followed by a soft sigh, nothing more. "So you've found out my little secret, eh?"

"I've found out a lot of your little secrets."

Lambert sighed again. He dropped a shirt into his suitcase and sat down on the edge of the bed, watching with interest but no apparent alarm as Marc paced up and down before him.

"I know all about you, monsieur. I first suspected you weren't what you professed to be on the second day when I overheard you speaking *joual,* and I have been keeping a close eye on you ever since. You are a French Canadian, not a citizen of Cobourg or Upper Canada. You were born in the St. Denis district and no doubt have dozens of relatives there. It was not your wife's family you were visiting, I suspect, but your own. And the extent of the devastation and carnage left you appalled and raging with hate against all things English, especially anyone in Her Majesty's uniform."

"But I am a lawyer in Cobourg," Lambert said without inflection or emotion.

"I'll come to that ruse in a moment. I have no proof yet, but I believe you are more than an outraged habitant. I think you've been playing at the spy-game, perhaps even as a double agent. You learned fluent English somewhere, probably in Vermont when you were very young, as you have no accent—"

"Thank you. I do try."

"Most likely you have been moving about Quebec for at least the past month posing as an English-speaking lawyer from Cobourg, an obscure town suitably distant for your deceitful purposes. And I'm sure a clever fellow like you concocted a credible cover story. Any information thus gleaned by you would soon find its way to Papineau or his henchmen. But the glorious revolution went sour, didn't it? There were terrible battles and unforeseen losses. Then the barn burnings and reprisals began. Half of your so-called leaders were in jail. You could not resist the urge to see for yourself. So you left Montreal or Quebec City and ventured up the Richelieu Valley, growing more bitter by the mile. Perhaps you found that a cousin had been killed in action, another one incarcerated, a third with a razed house and barn and his children starving."

Marc could see that he was beginning to penetrate the veneer of indifference that Lambert, with his lawyer's training, had managed to keep in place. Something like pain shot through his eyes, and one corner of his mouth curled downward. He tried out an ironic smile: "You should have been a barrister, not a soldier."

"I'm just getting warmed up," Marc said, turning too suddenly on his gimpy left leg and stumbling. "You may or may not be a lawyer—I considered trying out a few Latin legal phrases on you, but I didn't want to expose my hand too soon—but after the debacle at St. Eustache and the failure of the invasion from Vermont, you were a spy without a constituency. Your dream of a French nation was dead, ashes in your mouth. Your own home ground was in ruins. The only choices left were abject mortification or the joy of revenge. And you chose the latter: any man worth the name would have done so."

"I have never denied being in St. Denis."

"True, but by the same token, you've never set foot in Cobourg."

"Oh?"

"You could not have set up shop there four months ago and not run into Major Barnaby. His surgery is on King Street, known to the whole county. And the hotel down by the wharf is the Lakeview not the Lakeside. Moreover, it was the larger and more prosperous Cobourg Hotel that you should have been able to recommend to Pritchard, if you'd ever laid eyes on it. That was all the proof I needed to expose you as a fraud. And one intent on exacting revenge whenever the opportunity arose."

"You're suggesting that I arranged to ride into enemy

territory in a coach with two military men in order to turn my rage on them?"

"I am. Moreover, I have not discounted the fact that you may still be operating under orders from the exiled rebels abroad. Even though the cause is clearly lost—there will be ten thousand British regulars in Quebec by the end of this month—it hasn't been utterly abandoned. I intend to have you detained at Fort Henry and interrogated by the army there: you could well be on a dangerous mission to Toronto or beyond. Your luggage and person will be thoroughly searched."

"So you're accusing me of espionage and indulging in a little murder on the side?"

Marc ignored the sarcasm: he was in full flight, doing what he might have done had he not taken up soldiering. "It's the murder that concerns me most, simply because it is me you have been trying to kill for the past three days."

That cold, blunt remark extinguished any lingering sarcasm. Lambert's jaw dropped in astonishment.

"Don't bother denying it, for I've worked out all the salient details. First of all, I believe that Montreal was your base of operations. It was a logical choice. You would know or have contact with compatriots from all walks of life there. You knew or were friends with an aide at the temporary military hospital, a woman named Isabelle LaCroix."

Lambert continued to stare, open-mouthed.

"My own foolish comrades bruited about the streets of Montreal that one Marc Edwards had done the enemy harm at St. Denis. When you returned from that region, about a month ago, you soon learned that this 'hero' lay unconscious and helpless nearby. I suggest that you bribed or suborned Miss LaCroix to stab me one night with an old bayonet you no doubt supplied her. Having failed, and in danger of discovery, she wisely slipped away two days later, to the protection of her countrymen. But you did not give up easily. Your intelligence network probably informed you of the date and means of my departure, so you got yourself a seat in Brookner's coach and began plotting. The months you spent playing the double-spy game allowed you to perfect the poker face: we just thought you a morose and misanthropic character and paid you little heed. Or so you assumed."

Lambert's lips began to twitch.

"Your initial opportunity came on that first day when we ran up against the barricade, set there by rebel habitants, though I doubt they knew they were helping one of their own. In fact, as a *maudit Anglais* yourself, you risked being shot by those marauding gangs. Nevertheless, when you observed me limping off towards the river, while the others went to the other side of the road, you saw your chance and seized it. You kept a pocket pistol, I believe, in your big overcoat, and you followed me till I was well away from our party. But it was snowing and you had only one shot to make, and you missed. While I lay waiting for a second blow, you returned to the coach by a roundabout route. If I had revealed the incident to Brookner, the presence of vigilantes in the area would have readily and conveniently explained the ambush. I accepted such an explanation myself until yesterday afternoon, when I received word of your true identity. But you are a clever and patient man. You knew there would be further opportunities."

Lambert, lips quivering, remained speechless.

"Your next move—diabolically clever—was to plant that death-threat in Brookner's carriage. The tale of the Scanlon brothers and the real possibility that Brookner would be the target of the escaped brother, Miles, gave you a fresh opening, for not only were there vigilantes behind every bush but a vengeance-seeking rebel who might easily mistake one military greatcoat for another. Unfortunately, despite the captain's urgings, I did not accommodate you by donning my tunic and shako. So you began to grow desperate. Here we were at Prescott, a day from Kingston and the breakup of the party. It was now or never. You knew that Brookner slept in the room next to mine. If I were found stabbed to death—a pistol would have been too noisy—it could be postulated that Brookner was the intended victim and Miles Scanlon the likely suspect. You must have been pleased, smug even, that I had not revealed the earlier attempt on my life. No-one knew that I was a potential target, except one of my fellow officers back in Montreal."

There was a rustling sound just outside the door. "Are you ready, Mr. Lambert? Our sleigh is waiting. Shall I send the lad up for your bags?" It was Pritchard.

"Give us fifteen minutes!" Marc barked, and something in his voice got through to Pritchard, for he mumbled "All right" and shuffled off.

"So we come to your penultimate act. In the middle of the night, with snow conveniently falling, you went out onto the fire-stairs, shuffled along the ledge past the Brookners' room, then climbed into mine and drove a knife into the body on the bed. But it was a dummy you stabbed. You may even have realized it at the time and decided to get out while you could. If not, your calm reaction to my appearance at breakfast would have made an Old Bailey hack proud. By now you were, despite your icy demeanour, frustrated and enraged. If you couldn't kill me, then you'd damn well kill somebody in uniform before the trip was over."

"I been sent up fer the bags," a tremulous, adolescent voice called out from the hall.

"Go away!"

A hasty scampering ensued, then silence.

Marc wheeled around and stepped closer to Lambert. "This morning at breakfast, you watched Brookner go out that side door, and when Dingman arrived a few minutes later, you saw a last chance present itself. You knew all about the rear doors and the fire-stairs. It was you who suggested that you and Dingman go to his office. You followed him into the back hall, then excused yourself on the pretext of getting a law book. You hurried outside and trailed Brookner down the scenic path you knew he'd just taken. You had your pistol on you, as I suspect you have at this moment. You crept up behind and fired into the back of his head.

"As you rushed back along the path, you likely had to side-step Pritchard and Sedgewick—they must have given you a bit of a fright coming up to the scene so soon after the event. But you found cover and returned unseen to Dingman's office where you made some excuse about not finding or needing the law book after all. If Dingman, whom you knew to be an addled soul, were to testify that you were gone overly long, you could calmly dispute his claim. And, more important, you had no apparent motive for killing Brookner, while the notorious Miles Scanlon did. You couldn't murder me, but you did manage to take some measure of revenge for the depredations of General Colborne's troops. I will not be surprised even now if you were to pull out your pistol and try to finish the job, though I wouldn't advise it."

To Marc's great relief, Lambert did not draw his pistol. The trembling of his lips had reached a crisis point, and his mouth opened wide. Then he clutched both hands to his belly, rolled back onto the bed, and shook with helpless mirth. It took him fully a minute to stop laughing and regain control of his voice. Marc looked on, incredulous: Had Lambert gone mad, broken under the relentless pressure of Marc's accusations?

"You find all this amusing?"

"You've just told the funniest, wildest, most preposterous tale I've ever heard. In fact, you've managed to get most of it completely backwards."

"What on earth do you mean? Don't try lawyer's tricks on me. They won't wash." But Marc was suddenly not as certain as he sounded.

"Now it's your turn to sit down while I tell you a story," Lambert said, wiping his eyes. Cautiously, Marc sat in a nearby chair, but kept a wary eye on Lambert's right hand.

"I am what you see, Lieutenant: no more, no less. I speak both languages fluently, and I am, in a real sense, both English and French. I was born and spent my childhood on a farm near St. Denis. But unlike most Quebec families, my parents had but two children, my sister Sophie and me. When I was six, my father inherited money and land from an uncle in Vermont.

We moved there. My father sold the farm and became a merchant. I was sent to the best English schools. My sister spent her summers in St. Denis with our cousins, but I soon became as English as I was French. I apprenticed law in New York City. It is English law I know, not the *Code Napoleon*. My sister fell in love with a local boy in the Richelieu Valley, married him, and moved back there to farm. When I was on business in Buffalo last year, I met my wife, Marie. She was visiting her aunt, but her home was in Kingston. She was of Scots Irish stock. Although I was raised Catholic, I had long ago fallen away from the Church. We were married last spring in a Presbyterian ceremony in Kingston. I was offered a junior partnership in the Cobourg law firm of Denfield and Potter. We arrived there early in October."

Marc, who had been listening with increasing interest and much chagrin, finally found voice to say, "But you can't have known so little about—"

"That is easily explained. Marie fell ill with a fever the day after we arrived. Our house was a mile east of the town. I was the one who nursed her. A doctor did come to see her and left medicines, but I was in the village then, informing my new employers that it would be some weeks before I could safely take up my post. Marie may have mentioned the doctor's name, but if so, I must have forgotten it. We had a girl from town to help out, but I still refused to leave Marie's side."

"Why didn't you tell us this? Why were you so secretive?"

Lambert coloured slightly. "I do apologize. But you were correct about one thing. I had been to the Richelieu Valley, and what I saw there appalled and sickened me. I have not been fit human company since. I just did not feel like talking to any-one, even though my fellow travellers were congenial."

"But surely you must have harboured some resentment against me, an officer who was present at both assaults on the town."

Lambert smiled, and some of the personality he might have exhibited under more sanguine circumstances peeped through. "I'm afraid you got all that backwards as well."

"How so?"

"Just as Marie was nearing a full recovery, I got a letter from my sister in St. Denis. A desperate letter. The rebellion had failed, but reprisals and acts of vengeance continued un-checked. My sister's barn was destroyed and the few harvested crops looted. Even their cows had been shot and their horses' tails cropped."

"You must believe me, Mr. Lambert, when I say that I was nearly as appalled as you at the behaviour of our troops. Sir John himself ordered—"

"It wasn't the troops or even the loyalists who burned So-phie and her husband out," Lambert said sombrely. "It was her own cousins."

"My God!"

"Incredible, eh? But Sophie and Guy had tried to remain neutral. They had friends and neighbours on both sides of the issue. But when the British army prevailed, the English began their barn-burning campaign, and the French, when they could, played turnabout. Either side might have gone after So-phie and Guy, but it was definitely her own kind who did the damage. They made a point of letting her know."

"What could you do to help?"

"Not much. But I had some cash, a wedding gift from our father. I put it in a satchel and headed straight into the chaos of Quebec in the aftermath of the failed revolt and the aborted invasion. I quickly learned to keep my mouth shut and to adopt the manners and language most convenient to the situation. I was Lambert one day and *Lam-bear* the next."

"You could have been discovered and dealt with harshly by either side."

"Yes. But I did manage to reach my sister. The cash would prevent them from starving to death and would go a long way towards purchasing seed and replacing livestock, if and when things settled down. I stayed as long as I could. But I had to get back to Cobourg: the firm had granted me an extension to the end of this month only. That's why I'm eager to be off this evening. And I want to embrace my dear Marie once more."

Marc could empathize with that desire.

"You may search me and my bags if you like. You won't find any weapons or coded messages."

"That won't be necessary." Marc knew the truth when he heard it. He took a deep breath. "I must apologize, sir, in the most sincere way possible, even though I realize how weak my words will seem."

"Please, don't. You allowed me to laugh again. I can now greet my bride smiling. And remember, it has been you who have been shot at and nearly stabbed, not me, and Brookner's killer is still on the loose. You did your duty in St. Denis. I have no quarrel with that. I have tried to remain a loyal subject, but doing so is getting to be either an impossible or an inhumane act. Allegiance has become a relative term."

"Yes," Marc said, rising and shaking Lambert's hand. "We live in terrible times."

Charles Lambert and Ainslie Pritchard left the Georgian Arms soon after. Adelaide Brookner remained in the care of the Dingmans. Percy Sedgewick took supper in his room and then went into the Dingmans' quarters to offer comfort and support to his sister. Marc ate alone in the lounge, envying the roars and whoops of boozy laughter coming across the foyer from the taproom, now denuded of its legal trappings. Then he went up to his room and lay down on his bed. He had a lot of thinking to do.

If, as it now seemed, it was Miles Scanlon who shot Brookner, then there was still a stalker out there somewhere. While it was conceivable that Scanlon may have been the one to have climbed through Marc's window in a case of mistaken identity, it had not been Scanlon back there in the Montreal hospital, and no-one could have mistaken Marc, in mufti, for the full-tunicked Brookner in the woods beside the St. Lawrence. He decided to err on the side of caution. He borrowed a hammer and nails from Dingman's boy and nailed the window of his room shut. Once again he shoved the bed up against the door, then made himself a pallet of goosedown comforters on the floor well away from the door and window. He loaded his pistol and placed it on his chest. He lay fully clothed, waiting for sleep.

It did not come easily.

A strange new notion entered his head, triggered by something that had happened earlier on their journey. From that inkling, a train of thoughts—erratic, vague, but persistent—began to move towards some possible, if astounding, conclusion. He went over a dozen events, conversations, and gestures, putting the pieces together this way and that. If his theories were valid, was there any way to prove them?

Just as he was falling asleep, he thought of a way.

FIFTEEN

The Brookner coach, now missing three of its original passengers, left the Georgian Arms at 11:30 on the morning of January 21. A light snow was falling; the air was crisp; and the sleigh's runners glided merrily. Gander Todd, none the worse for wear for having spent four nights sleeping in stables next to the horses, whipped his charges mildly and harangued them harshly. Earlier, the widow Brookner had emerged at last from the ministrations of Mrs. Dingman, clothed still in her mourning dress, though it now did double duty. Holding her right arm solicitously, her brother had led her unsteadily across the foyer and out to the waiting carriage. Murdo Dingman attempted to assist at her other elbow but was shrugged off curtly. Marc held the door open. From beneath her veil Adelaide bade him a polite "Good morning" and thanked him for his many kindnesses. Once inside the coach, Marc sat opposite Sedgewick, who took up the near seat by the window, facing ahead, and his sister was placed beside him.

As the coach pulled away, she fell back against a pillow and appeared to be staring out at the snow. She held that silent, solemn posture until they reached Prescott about twenty minutes later. Sedgewick gave Marc a rueful sort of smile, but had nothing to say, lacking the casual talk of Ainslie Pritchard or the need for it.

Unbeknownst to either Adelaide or her brother, however, was the fact that before coming down to the coach, Marc had deliberately remained behind in his room. It was only when he was certain that Sedgewick had finished packing his own things and those of both Brookners and had gone down to fetch Adelaide that Marc ventured into the hallway. He did not go immediately downstairs. The keystone to the theory he had developed before falling asleep lay in the room next door, and he had entered it with great anticipation. Five minutes later, he had found what he expected to.

As instructed, Gander Todd pulled up at the side lane of Doctor Mac's residence, where his surgery attached itself to the grandiose country home. Two stout lads were waiting for them. Sedgewick and Marc got out, leaving the widow sitting stoically inside, and watched as the pine box containing the remains of Randolph Brookner was hoisted up onto the roof of the coach and secured thoroughly with ropes and a leather belt.

During this operation, which took just under ten minutes, Marc was hailed inside by MacIvor Murchison, who insisted on his taking a quick brandy to "ward off the morning chill." They chatted briefly about the inquest, and would have continued further if Marc had not been called back to the coach. The coffin had been secured, and, if they were to make Gananoque by nightfall, they had to leave right away. Marc shook hands with Doctor Mac and left.

They rode on, the three of them, with the corpse above, in a silence that was increasingly uncomfortable. Marc closed his eyes and feigned sleep. Sedgewick stared ahead out of one window and Adelaide the other. There was nothing to see but the slanting snow and the ghostly billowing of evergreens through the haze. An hour later, Todd stopped the coach in front of a log hut that served grog and sometimes lukewarm soup to passers-by. The privy behind it was free.

When they made to depart again, Sedgewick, who seemed unaccountably nervous or perhaps merely embarrassed, announced that he was going to sit up on the bench with the driver for an hour or so. Adelaide nodded and got into the coach on her own before Marc could offer any assistance. They sat cattycorner to each other. Marc let ten minutes go by before he began.

"Like the coroner and everybody at the inquest yesterday, I concluded that, outside of Charles Lambert, no-one in our party could have committed the murder of your husband. I confronted Lambert before he left last night and came away convinced that he was not the killer. For a while I was even more compelled to accept the obvious: that Miles Scanlon had killed Captain Brookner to avenge the harsh treatment of his family. But just to play devil's advocate, as I mulled matters over in my room last night, I started with the seemingly bizarre notion that one of us was the murderer. I didn't do it. Pritchard was never a serious suspect. Lambert exculpated himself. That left you or your brother."

Marc peered over at Adelaide. She had not turned towards him, but a perceptible stiffening of her posture indicated that she was listening intently.

"But how was it possible, I asked myself. First of all, I had to establish powerful motives for one of you or both. Your brother feared that Randolph would go through with his threat to have him charged with treason. Even if the charge were a flimsy one, in the post-rebellion atmosphere around here, Percy's day-to-day life would be poisoned by suspicion. Your husband made the threat, I am convinced, because Mr. Sedgewick had in his turn made physical threats upon your husband's person—in his laudable efforts to stop Randolph from beating you."

Adelaide twisted her head slightly in his direction, but nothing could be seen behind the veil.

"I don't know how often he has done so, but I'm sure he did it surreptitiously so that no bruises were visible. After all, he was a respectable merchant, a church elder, and a proud militia officer. But abuse you he did. I recalled how you flinched whenever anyone touched your left arm. Most probably he was an arm-twister, turning it in his iron grip until you cried out. Later, I noticed that you kept that crepe scarf curled well up under your chin—to hide more bruises, no doubt. The reason for his anger also seemed obvious: you are more intelligent than he was; you are proud; and you are independent. Your very presence, let alone any public correcting of his faux pas, was a rebuke to his vanity and his foolish ambitions."

She turned back to stare out the window, as if to underline the very traits he had just ascribed to her.

"What puzzled me was why you might have chosen this particular time to lash out. But the death of your dear sister and Randolph's callous flouting of the traditions of mourning may have been the last straw. Or, by the same token, these insults may have driven your devoted brother to some sort of precipitate action on your behalf. Thus, it turns out that you both had motive and immediate provocation. Still, I was sitting next to the pair of you when the fatal shot was fired. While it was logical to enlist Miles Scanlon to do the job, neither of you appeared to have had the opportunity to arrange it."

Marc paused until the coach had finished jouncing over a rough patch of rutted road, then continued. "How could either of you have fired that shot? For some unexplainable reason, a picture popped into my head. Back at Morrisburg, when I was supposedly out for a walk airing my uniform, I was actually assisting some friends to cross the river. One of them, a man, not wanting to be recognized, had dressed up as a woman, wig and all. Then a second image leapt up beside it: you and your husband as I first saw you, when I mistook you for your husband's sister, not his wife. Percy remarked that such a mistake was not uncommon. You and your husband are both tall, walk erect, and have similar fair features."

Adelaide turned again to scrutinize him through her widow's veil, but said nothing. Her breathing seemed more rapid though.

"The question, then, of a possible disguise entered the

equation I was trying to work out. Certainly neither you nor your brother was in disguise at breakfast. But what if the murder did not take place at nine thirty but earlier, say at seven thirty or eight? The body was found submerged in ice-water. There was no way to determine when the fatal wound might have been suffered. If so, then the killer, if it were one of us, had perhaps two hours to play with, to cover his or her tracks, and to establish a foolproof alibi. Moreover, I found it hard to believe, right from the outset, that Captain Brookner would sleep in until nine. I believe he got up at seven or so and immediately prepared to promenade himself down that scenic path for Scanlon or anyone else to try taking a shot at him. But it was not Scanlon. Someone from our group followed him. It was easy to come up behind him undetected and blow his brains out."

"I could ask Percy to stop this coach," Adelaide said, in what was meant to be a cold and intimidating tone but came out more world-weary than menacing. Marc simply continued his narrative.

"While Scanlon would be the obvious suspect, none of us had any real idea where he might have been yesterday morning. Perhaps he had escaped to New York. So rather than leave it to such unpredictable and potentially incriminating possibilities, a more practical and ingenious deception was devised. If those at breakfast could be witness to the captain leaving the inn—very much alive—at nine fifteen, then alibis would be established and the entire investigation of the murder sent askew. The risks were minimal: if the body were discovered before nine, then the planned ruse could simply be abandoned with no-one the wiser. But the risk seemed worth it."

Marc paused, took a deep breath, and plunged towards his denouement. "I remembered that your husband was obsessively vain about his uniform. Two parts of it appeared to be brand new, as if he had bought them specifically to show himself off during your days in the big city, among the regulars from the Royal Regiment. Your brother suggested in court that the greatcoat was acquired recently: it almost glistened in the sunlight, as did his boots. I believe both were purchased in Montreal. And the hat he wore was much like mine or Pritchard's or your brother's. All this meant that an extra greatcoat and an extra pair of boots were available, both older and somewhat tawdry, but that was a chance the killer or killers had to take if the ruse was to work. I say killer or killers because I still do not know whether it was actually you or your brother who pulled the trigger. But one of you certainly did."

Again, Marc waited in vain for a direct response.

"I soon realized that it would take both of you to execute the deception. For if Percy had not been in on the game, he would have seen right away that you—dressed in your husband's old greatcoat and boots and wearing your brother's hat—were not Captain Brookner. We might have been fooled, but not Percy. I suspect that you planned it together. In any event, you brazenly clumped down the stairs, having waited anxiously, I'm sure, for me to wake up and go down to breakfast. I was to be your most incontrovertible witness, wasn't I? You must have been puzzled and not a little frightened by my bizarre movements, but at last I did go down, and you were able to follow, disguised as your husband. All those at the breakfast table were aware of the captain's departure. Once outside, you did not go down the path to the creek, but just wheeled behind the inn, mounted the fire-stairs, and returned to your room, doffing the coat, hat, and boots, and then coming down to breakfast as yourself, no more than four minutes after your husband had apparently left on the twenty-minute trek to his death. You joined us to secure your own alibi, and adroitly explained away your dishevelled state as grief over your sister's death. The only real risk here was that one of the stablemen or maids might see you back there, but, as it turned out, they didn't.

"There was one other possible danger, though. What if Pritchard or one of us at the table had called out or moved to stop you from going out? To forestall this, I believe you arranged for Percy to rush over and appear to restrain his brother-in-law. You and he then pretended to have a whispered arguement, he was brushed aside, and out you went. A perfect plan. Why would I or anyone else suspect that Percy was playing some devious game? Especially when even the coroner himself was satisfied that nine thirty or so was the time of death. You and your brother must have been pleased at the outcome of the inquest. Even the business with Lambert and Dingman was an unexpected gift."

Adelaide did not raise her veil, but she spoke nonetheless. "You have a remarkable mind, a nice conscience, and a penchant for kindness—the very sort of man I foolishly thought my husband would be. But then we all marry too young."

"Could you not merely have divorced him?"

"I have not admitted murdering him, Lieutenant. Your theory is fantastic, but plausible enough, I suppose, if you like theorizing. What you lack is a shred of evidence." She was speaking as if somehow she felt obligated to, the weariness still undisguised. But then, she had just suffered a double bereavement.

"True. But just as I fell asleep, I realized that you and Percy had one major problem after the fact. If, during the inquest and under interrogation, one of us suddenly had had doubts about seeing the real captain in that hallway—for example, if the coroner had thought to ask, 'Did you actually see Brookner's face?'—the first thing the magistrate would have done is gone looking for that spare coat and pair of boots, for the new ones were on the body in the creek and are now with your husband in his coffin. That was the only real evidence that could make a theory such as mine credible. The pistol, either Percy's or a second one of the captain's, was tossed deep into some snowdrift where it won't be found, if ever, until spring. And I'm sure that hat was your brother's. But you can't throw a militia greatcoat with identifying insignia on it out into the snow. The boots could be left in the captain's trunk, but not that incriminating coat. Both you and Percy would be suspects, so stuffing it in either of your suitcases would be risky. My instincts told me that you might try to leave it behind. So I went into your room after Percy had cleared it out this morning. It took about five minutes of poking and stomping about, but I soon found the loose floorboards under the carpet over by the dresser. They came up easily. And there was the coat, stuffed between joists and destined to remain there to provide nesting material for generations of mice."

Adelaide let out a long sigh.

"Even if I had not found it there, I could have got a warrant to have your luggage searched at Gananoque. It gives me no pleasure to conclude that you and your brother conspired to kill Captain Brookner, a man each of you wished dead."

"You must not blame my brother," Adelaide said, as some feeling began to flow back into her voice. "It was I who shot Randolph. You wanted to know why I did it yesterday. Well, I'll show you." With that, she undid the top two buttons of her coat to reveal the camouflaging crepe scarf. Very slowly she unwound it from around her regal neck. Even in the uncertain light of the coach's interior, what Marc saw there made him gasp in shock: purple-black bruising about her throat, with the imprint of fingers and thumbs grotesquely visible.

"He tried to kill you?"

"I don't think he thought of it that way."

"The night before last I heard you two quarrelling. I had already begun to suspect that he was an abuser, and I waited for his slap or your cry. I raced out into the hall and stood—somewhat foolishly—outside your door. I heard nothing for a long while. Then your husband began snoring. I concluded I had been wrong."

"Those were not snores. That was me gagging for breath. Randolph always thought I was being melodramatic. Once the fury passes with him, he'd pretend it didn't really happen or wasn't of any consequence. He turned his back and went to sleep, while I sat awake most of the night, knowing that sooner or later I would die in one of his rages. To suggest a divorce would be to publicly humiliate him and induce a tantrum that might prove to be the fatal one."

"Did you plot to kill him then and there?"

"I knew he had a second pistol. He bought it when rumours of rebellion began to heat up last summer. He showed me how to load and fire it. I planned to follow him on his walk and shoot him, hoping that some faceless vigilante could be blamed. I prepared the pistol in the moonlight and hid it in among my clothes. But I fell into an exhausted sleep, and when I woke up, he was nearly dressed and ready to go out. I threw on my coat and boots and used the outside fire-stairs to gain a minute or two. By the time he reached that spot in the creek where the spring is, I was right behind him. He never once looked back nor to either side until that bubbling spring caught his attention, and he stood gazing at it. I almost lost my nerve, but my throat ached and my skin burned from his assault. I raised the pistol and fired. He fell into the cold water. I was surprised there was so little blood."

A shudder passed through her body, but she did not lower her head. The veil swung delicately above her ravaged throat.

"So you returned to your room via the back way?"

"Yes, though I went straight to Percy's room. I still had the pistol in my hand. I was in shock. Percy took the thing, climbed up on his dresser, and dropped it down under the eave of the roof. After I had calmed down, we discussed the possibility of an outsider being blamed. But we couldn't be sure that Miles Scanlon had not already been captured. It was I who eventually proposed the deception which we played out. I did not want to involve Percy, but he insisted that the ruse would work better if he were seen talking to Randolph in the hallway. I could not dissuade him. He felt he was partly to blame because he had not been able to protect me from Randolph's cruelties."

"But there was the problem of the boots and greatcoat."

"Percy wanted to hide the coat in his trunk, but if it were found there during any investigation or as a result of something raised during the inquest, he would hang with me for sure. I refused to let him take that chance. I remembered the loose floorboards I had noticed the day before. I had no time to hide the coat when I first came up the fire-stairs, but I slipped back up about noon on the pretext of getting some night-clothes. You and Ainslie were in the lounge. I got the floorboards up far enough to stuff the greatcoat in there. The boots I put in Randolph's trunk. The hat, as you guessed, was Percy's."

"But when no suspicions were raised later on, why didn't you or Percy remove the coat and pack it in your trunk?"

"There was too much coming and going up there by then. I was with the Dingmans, and Percy decided to leave things as they were."

"Yes. It was the uniqueness of that coat that could give away the show."

Adelaide had turned back to gaze at the snow and at the eons-old landscape it made pristine for a brief season. After a long while, without looking at him, she said in a muted, uncertain voice he had not heard before, "What are you going to do now?"

"I'm going to carry on to Toronto, where I shall wed my fiancée."

* * *

Percy Sedgewick rejoined them shortly thereafter. A quick but telling look was exchanged between brother and sister. Percy relaxed visibly and began to tell stories of the homesteading Sedgewicks who pioneered Landsdowne Township, where men were men and women their helpmates and companions, working side by side in field and fallow. Much later in the afternoon Percy went back up on top to smoke a pipe with Gander Todd, and Adelaide returned to the subject of their earlier conversation.

"I will not ask you why, but only thank you for such an unexpected gesture," she said with feeling. "But are you not worried that by not turning Percy and me in to the magistrates you are perhaps putting Miles Scanlon's life in danger? I know for a fact that he was not involved with his older brothers in the rebellion. He helped them after the fact, as Percy did their wives and children. He will not hang for that, but he could hang for murder. I would not want his death on my conscience. Nor would I permit it to happen."

"Do not be concerned for Miles Scanlon. When I went into Dr. Murchison's surgery this morning, he told me that word had reached him late last night that Scanlon had been captured and held in custody on a farm many miles north of here, twelve hours before your husband was shot. There is no way that he will be accused of that crime."

"I am relieved to hear that."

"Apparently, he admitted planting the death-threat in the

coach, but swears he never planned to do the captain harm. He just wanted to frighten him. According to the doctor, the poor bugger was bushed."

"So then you were certain I had done it?" Adelaide actually smiled.

Marc smiled back. "It was either you or Gander Todd!"

It was dusk when the coach bearing the living and the dead neared the village of Gananoque. Percy was back on top with Gander.

"With Miles Scanlon out of the picture," Marc said suddenly, "the coroner told me that he would have to enter a finding of 'murder by person or persons unknown.' He will add a comment in his summary to the effect that the motive appeared to be political and the assassin a vengeance-seeking vigilante from the rebel camp. He feels that Captain Brookner may have been a symbolic target picked at random."

"Why did you not give him your theory and your evidence back there? Or had you already decided on a course of action?"

"I had not made up my mind either way. The greatcoat would still be where you put it and I left it. And I wanted to be sure I was right." Marc thought it prudent not to mention the acute embarrassment of the scene in Lambert's room yesterday afternoon and the fragility of theories.

"And?"

"And I saw the murderous bruises on your neck."

After a pause, she said, "I suppose his regiment will insist on giving Randolph a funeral with full military honours."

Marc gave her a wee, ironic grin. "Why not? He died as a martyr for the people's cause, did he not?"

She didn't smile, perhaps couldn't, but she did reply: "Like Rob Roy or Bonnie Prince Charlie, you mean?"

They crossed the long bridge over the Gananoque River and swept down into the village in the snowy darkness of a late January evening. The town boasted two hotels, only one with a livery stable. Outside the larger one, Marc shook hands with Percy Sedgewick. Adelaide Brookner leaned over and kissed him on the cheek.

"Your fiancée is a lucky woman," she said, and walked with elaborate dignity into the lamp-lit interior.

Marc carried on down the street to the one-storey inn and tavern. Gander would deliver his luggage later on. Among the many thoughts rippling through his mind was this one: he was beginning to believe that the notion of justice was just as ethically muddled as that of allegiance.

Marc was so exhausted that he planned to sleep in until noon and then catch the regular coach to Kingston and Fort Henry. A couple of days to rest and rejuvenate among fellow officers of the regiment there, then it would be on to Cobourg and Toronto. And there, with any luck, Beth would be waiting.

His room was cramped and ill lit but clean and warm enough. He undressed and got ready to sleep, making no preparations to thwart an assassin. He did realize that because Adelaide and Percy had done away with Brookner, there was still one stalker unaccounted for, unless he were to accept the near-absurd proposition that each attempt on his life—the bayonet in the hospital, the shot in the woods, and the stabbing at the Georgian Arms—had been a case of mistaken identity or the result of independent, random opportunities. But he was suddenly beyond caring. He was now more than a hundred miles from Montreal and the Quebec border. The passions surrounding St. Denis would surely be waning with each mile separating him and those grim events.

Refusing to become a slave to his own fears, he raised his ground-floor window six inches to let in the bracing night-air, then lay down on the bed immediately beneath it. He also removed his tunic and breeches from his trunk and laid them out on the table next to his sabre, pistol, belt, and scabbard. If he were going into Fort Henry tomorrow afternoon, he would march in—stiff leg and all—in proper military attire. He fell asleep almost immediately.

It was 10:00 the next morning when he woke up. Adelaide and Percy had left long ago. Marc knew that Adelaide's life would never be the same. She was deeply intelligent and, he surmised, innately moral. She had tolerated the indignities and assaults her husband had meted out with stoic determination, instinctively understanding that he was really the weaker of the two and conscious of her duty and the vows she had taken. She might suffer remorse; she might excoriate herself from time to time; she might lead a constrained, perhaps even a quiet and reclusive, life. But she would live. And she deserved to, like the long-suffering horse who turns on his tormentor with a justifiable kick.

Marc began to dress. And for the first time since his training days at Sandhurst, he found no joy in donning his officer's uniform. The jacket did not feel right. He had, of course, lost thirty pounds and regained but fifteen, and it hung limply upon his shoulders, as if it belonged to someone else. Was he even still worthy of its lustre and long tradition? He put his pistol into its holster and shuddered. Tears burned at the edges of his eyes, unbidden and shaming.

On his way out, he had to lean against the wall to steady himself. He thought of Beth and carried on.

SIXTEEN

Three days later Marc reached Cobourg in the company of two officers of his own regiment returning to Fort York from an assignment at Fort Henry. They had hired a fast cutter, and pulled into Cobourg late in the afternoon of January 24. The weather had been clear and just cold enough to make sled-travel swift and smooth. Marc's companions decided to stay overnight at the Cobourg Hotel. Marc, of course, was eager to go five miles farther to Crawford's Corners, where he would stay with his old friend, Erastus Hatch, and his family at the mill. He wanted very much to reassure them of the safe arrival in the United States of Winnifred, Thomas, and baby Mary. He had also considered taking Beth's brother Aaron along with him to Toronto, though the lad could be sent for a bit later on when he and Beth were settled. At any rate, he waved good-bye to his fellow officers at Cobourg's main intersection, assured by them that they would pick him up in midmorning in Crawford's Corners for the final leg of their journey. Meanwhile, Marc would hitch a ride with someone going west along the Kingston Road.

Pausing on Cobourg's main street, Marc was assailed by memories. Voices echoed in his mind: Willy Mackenzie's booming and erudite rhetoric as he swayed the locals in the town hall just a block away; the banshee imprecations of the Orangemen rioting and purveying mayhem, fuelled by ancient grudges and ingrained prejudice; the voices, too, of the poor and the disenfranchised as they cheered their champion on to . . . to what?

"You lookin' fer a ride, sir?"

It was a gap-toothed farmer, ruddy and smiling, seated on the bench of a small cutter with reins slack in his ploughman's grip.

"I'm heading for Crawford's Corners," Marc said.

"Then hop aboard, son. I'm goin' right by there. I just have to pick up a bag of feed over at the Emporium. You can hang on ta Jasper's reins fer me."

Marc was happy to oblige. While he waited for the farmer to return, Marc spotted a familiar figure strolling eastward along King Street: Charles Lambert. Beside him and holding his hand was a small woman, obviously his wife, Marie. Every few yards Lambert would lean down and brush the top of her fur hat with his lips. They did not see Marc. He watched them until they were out of sight.

It was growing dark when Marc thanked the farmer and hopped off the cutter at the intersection of the Kingston Road and Miller Sideroad—Crawford's Corners. A light valise was his only encumbrance. For a full five minutes he stood in the middle of the crossroads and allowed more memories to rise. It was here he had come just two years ago to investigate the mysterious death of Joshua Smallman, and found not only a group of friends—Dr. Charles Barnaby, James and Emma Durfee, Erastus and Winnifred Hatch—but the first woman he had loved more than his own life: Bathsheba McCrae Smallman, his Beth.

Marc noted the lights in the Durfees' tavern and their quarters behind it. Two sleighs drawn up outside indicated the presence of some customers inside. He would drop in later or first thing in the morning and pay his respects. And incidentally catch up on the local gossip. Dr. Barnaby had not been keeping a surgery in town, so Marc was surprised and disappointed when he looked across to the house on the southwest corner and saw that it was in darkness. Perhaps Barnaby was out on a call and would return this evening. He hoped so.

With an unexpected sense of trepidation, Marc now walked northward through the snow up the Miller Sideroad. On his right and occupying many acres lay the estate of the local squire and magistrate, Philander Child. Marc recalled his former encounters with the squire with distaste: he was a man whose allegiance had led him as far astray as any man could wander. Something drew Marc right past the miller's evergreen-shrouded house and on up to the lane that led to Beth's place, so recently occupied by Thomas and Winnifred Goodall. The lane was free of footprints.

Very slowly, Marc approached the cabin. It was dark inside, abandoned. Beth's brother Aaron, of course, would be next door with Erastus. As he came up beside the house, Marc got a shock: every window had been smashed, and across the front door someone had painted in crude whitewash: TRAITER! With mounting dread, he carried on past the house towards the sheds and barn. Their shadows were still blunt against the horizon. Not burned. Yet.

Marc decided to take the path that linked Beth's property with the Hatch's to the south of it. He and Beth had walked it more than once, deep in the conversation that began as friendly argument and ended in love's banter. He would go past the mill, starkly visible up ahead in the waxing moonlight, and approach the miller's house from the rear, as he had done so many times before. It imparted a sense of permanence and stability that he knew to be illusory but nonetheless necessary.

No lights greeted him. Surely they couldn't all be abed at six-thirty in the evening? He came up to the door of the summer kitchen. It was open and swinging crookedly on one hinge. Snow had drifted into the big back room. With a pounding heart, he rushed through to the main house. It was cold and dark. He felt his way over to the stove. It had not been used in days. Beside the fireplace no kindling or split-logs were neatly piled, as they had always been. He looked in every room before stumbling out the front door, ignoring the protestations of his gimpy leg, and raced back up the sideroad to Durfees' tavern. He felt as if a horse had kicked him.

James Durfee, tavern-keeper, postmaster, redoubtable Scot, sat back in his favourite chair in his favourite room, sipped at his brandy, and cast a concerned and avuncular eye upon the young lieutenant seated across from him. Emma, it turned out, had gone out with Doc Barnaby to an ailing woman five miles away on the far concession of the township, and neither was expected back before noon the next day. But Emma had left a pot of stew and fresh bread, which Durfee was happy to share with Marc. Over supper, Marc gave him an account of his adventures in Lower Canada. Later, the two men returned to the den. It was Durfee's turn to provide explanations.

"I'm sorry you had to go over there and find the place like that, without any warnin'. I was hopin' you'd come in here first," Durfee began.

"But I still can't believe Erastus would just pull up stakes and leave like that. It's completely out of character. Why, he's been miller here for a generation. He's respected by every honest man in the district, Tory or otherwise. He always managed to keep his head above the fray, he had no enemies—"

"All that's true, lad. But for the last year or more, as you know, it hasn't been a question of makin' enemies. Suddenly, you just become one."

"The windows are all broken in Beth's house, and there's that ugly word plastered on the door."

"Thomas Goddall became a wanted man. He lived in that house, owner or not. He had no place to hide. When Winnifred and him and the bairn packed up and took off for parts unknown, it damn near destroyed her father. Erastus was distraught. He'd put up with some of the farmers, men he'd helped and carried with credit over many a rough spot, when they threatened to take their business all the way to Port Hope just to spite him. He was philosophical about that, figurin' time would heal those wounds. But when the warrant was issued for Thomas, it nearly broke him. His grown daughter and grand-child just fleeing, with an hour to say their good-byes. And bound for Iowa."

"So you think he's gone after them?"

"I do. The gathering point for the Iowa expedition is Pitts-burgh. From what you've told me, Thomas has made it into New York State and will head straight there."

"How do you know all this?"

"You been away for more'n two months, haven't you? Well, two weeks ago a group of well-off Reform supporters—not reb-els, mind you, but people like young Francis Hincks and Peter Perry—started up the Mississippi Emigration Society to help folks get out of this place."

"My God. Matters are worse than I'd imagined."

"They're sayin' up to ten thousand farmers might leave, sellin' out at ruinous prices and headin' west."

"But why did Erastus take Beth's brother? She'll be devas-tated."

"Emma and me offered to take Aaron in till we heard from Beth down in the States; we knew she'd be there a while. But the boy's seventeen or more, a grown-up lad. The only life he knows is farming. He begged to be taken along, and in the end, Erastus agreed. They couldn't keep young Susie Huggan from goin' along either. 'I'm Baby Eustace's aunt!' she said, and that was that."

"And what of the other Huggan sister, Charlene? She wasn't with Winnifred and Thomas."

"Of course, there's no house to keep over there any more, so Barnaby's taken her on till we can find somethin' permanent for her."

Marc stared into his brandy glass. "Does Beth know all of this?"

"Yes," Durfee assured him. "The mail is irregular, but we've written to give her any news."

Marc looked up at his friend. "Why am I wearing this uniform, James? Can you tell me that? I was sent into Quebec to put down a revolt against the Crown. And I helped to do so. I acquitted myself as a soldier ought to. We were sent also to bring about order. And we did. But we did not re-establish the law. We walked away as soon as the smoke of battle had cleared and left thousands of innocent citizens to the ministrations of vigilantes and vengeance-seekers. We brought order but no real peace. And certainly no justice. Sir John issued decrees against looting and reprisals but refused to send troops to enforce them. The Queen's writ is gall in the mouths of the people. And that is all they have to feed on. When a farmer burns out his neighbour, you know how deep the poison has penetrated."

James reached over and placed a hand over one of Marc's. "I don't believe you would've actually set a torch to that house in St. Denis."

"That is a question that's been haunting me for seven weeks. I do not know what I would have done if I had managed to clear the inhabitants out of that house. But I didn't. What I do know for sure is that I'm glad I was shot, for it prevented me from finding out how far my allegiance would've taken me from my own humanity."

"Well, things are bad here but nothin' like Quebec. After the first surge of reprisal and payback, a lot of the steam's gone out of the vengeance game."

"I'm happy to hear that. Revenge is a grim and self-defeating business."

Durfee grunted. "Tell that to the extreme Tories and Orangemen. They've been callin' for a hundred hangings. There've been a few down in London, but the trials that are goin' on now are havin' a hard time findin' believable witnesses. The only ones likely to hang in Toronto are the two ringleaders, Peter Matthews and Samuel Lount. They were convicted last week and sentenced to hang on Saturday morning. Most responsible people now expect that'll be the extent of the blood-lettin'."

"But there's still the threat of invasion."

"True, but it's mostly a bunch of Yankee freebooters and opportunists lookin' to liberate the natives from despotism. Nothin' to worry about really. All bluster and no muster, as we say up here."

Marc was staring grim-faced at his untouched brandy once again. "Still, somebody's got to do the actual scaring off, don't they?"

"You thinkin' seriously of takin' off that uniform?"

"I've been thinking about a lot of things, dear friend—and that's one of them."

Marc was caught by a wave of emotion as the cutter sped across Scaddings Bridge and curved southwest along King Street extension towards Toronto, his home-base for the past two and a half years. He had not seen it in three months, and for a time had been certain he would never see it again. It was the image of Beth and her plea that he survive and return to her that had propelled him through the maelstrom of battle and its squalid aftermath.

Now here it was: a city spread out before him with its snow-capped chimney-pots, its soaring church spires, its cozy homes tucked into rumpled drifts, and its audacious public buildings proclaiming a fragile dominion over the engulfing forest and the vast frozen lake at its feet. Welcome aromas from the lakeshore brewery and the nearby distillery wafted his way as Marc and his companions slipped into the city proper, and the familiar façades of the King Street thoroughfare rose up on either side.

Marc thanked his travelling companions when they let him out at the post office on George Street. They would be happy to inform Colonel Margison at the garrison of his safe arrival, recovering health, and a promise to report by tomorrow afternoon. They also agreed to take the bulk of his luggage to the fort. Marc sucked in lungfuls of Toronto air and strode, with the merest trace of a limp, into the post office. There was a substantial bundle of letters waiting for him. He sat inside on a bench and read steadily for almost an hour. It was three o'clock when he finished.

He had learned a number of things: Beth's aunt was doing well and was wishing her away to Toronto where she belonged. Beth finally agreeing. Beth announcing her departure. Beth in Pittsburgh, but no sightings of the Hatches or Goodalls, whose departures she had learned of from Durfee. Beth on her way and predicting her arrival by January 26—tomorrow! Beth urging him to stay in the apartment over the shop. Beth grateful for his miraculous recovery. Beth.

Also, word from Uncle Frederick, via New York and the military post, that Uncle Jabez had left Marc a lifetime annuity of a thousand pounds a year. He was now a wealthy man. There was also news and earnest enquiry from Major Jenkin in Montreal, who hoped to be back in Toronto in time for any wedding. And finally a long, heartfelt letter from a lady in New York that made him at once happy and sad. The woman who had revealed herself to him as his mother was necessarily in the country to the south, and their tentative relationship was more surprise than familial comfort. Marc reflected that with Uncle Jabez's death, his links to the old country were frayed, if not severed. It had taken some time and not a little resistance on his part, but he realized with a pleasant shock that Canada was now truly his home.

The sun was still shining when he left the post office. He walked down to Front Street so he could take in the vista of the snow-bound lake and the distant horizon. Moving westward, he passed the Parliament buildings, where so much had been said to so little effect. Their cut-stone and brick façade gleamed in the southerly sun. He turned north on Peter Street, crossed Market, now called Wellington, and stopped before his former boarding-house. The Widow Standish, never far from sentry duty, came bustling out onto the porch in her slippers to greet him.

Marc put the simple belongings from his valise in his old room, then sat down and had tea with Mrs. Standish and her maid, Maisie. The women were agog at his war stories (well sanitized) and urged him to stay on until supper. But Marc managed to excuse himself, explaining that his dear friend, Horatio Cobb, would be expecting him. Well, then, he must go: duty was duty.

Marc walked east along King Street, where all the elegant shops were located. Just past Bay, he came upon Beth's millinery shop, which had once been part of Joshua Smallman's dry-goods emporium. While braced for the worst, he was still saddened and angered to see the display-windows boarded up. Mr. Ormsby spotted him from the adjacent shop and came out. He apologized profusely for not having been able to protect Beth's place from being vandalized. But for several weeks after the failed revolt, the city fathers—without regular troops—had been unable or unwilling to safeguard the property of perceived traitors or their sympathizers. Certainly Constable Cobb had done his best to help, but even he had not been successful. Things were quieter now, but the public hanging of Matthews and Lount, scheduled for Saturday morning, was likely to stir up passions yet again.

Marc thanked him, then walked slowly and disconsolately along King to Toronto Street, where the entire block from there to Church was taken up by the twin edifices of the Court House and jail. Constable Cobb was just leaving the police quarters and spied Marc in his distinctive uniform before Marc saw him.

"Well, now, Major, ain't you a sight fer soarin' eyes!"

"I'm glad to see you, too," Marc said, laughing for the first time in a long while.

After a hearty supper prepared by Dora and served by the children, Marc sat spellbound as Delia and Fabian recited duet scenes from Shakespeare, after which they were applauded and cheerfully ordered to bed—or rather as far as the bedroom, for the door thereof squeaked open and shut several times during the next two hours, whenever young ears pressed too eagerly up against it. While Dora sat by the fire knitting, Marc and Cobb exchanged war stories, one set distinguished by understatement, the other by forgivable hyperbole and dramatic heightening. Cobb was particularly dramatic when narrating, with appropriate sound effects and mimicry, his day at Government House before the *"infan-try in-sult"* on the unguarded capital, the highlight of which was the near-capture, not of a would-be political assassin, but a failed piglet thief.

"It wasn't exactly the *gun-power* plot," Cobb chuckled.

"It's the pig I feel sorry for," Dora chimed in, "not the governor."

"So you and two dozen armed citizens actually saved the city from falling?" Marc asked, amazed to hear that previous versions of the encounter relayed about Montreal were very near the truth.

"I was a regular Horatio at the bridge," Cobb said with a twinkle. More seriously, he added, "But you know, Major, I pointed my musket at the man in the moon and fired. I'd be damned if I'd shoot some poor dumb bugger just to save the skinny neck of Francis Bone Head."

"And one of them dumb buggers was my nephew, Jimmy Madden," Dora said. "What was Mister Cobb supposed to do, shoot his own kin?"

"Luckily fer everybody, both sides skedaddlled like jackrabbits," Cobb said.

"Don't *scourge-ilize* yerself, Mister Cobb."

"Well, it weren't no *Watered-loo,* Missus Cobb."

"But the militia arrived and completed the job properly two days later?" Marc asked.

"Yup. But that turned out even worse." Cobb looked to his wife. "Can I tell him?"

"Marc's a friend, ain't he?"

With much relish Cobb proceeded to recite a tale that would in time become a family legend, to be told and retold down the Cobbian generations. It seems that foolish young Jimmy Madden had run away and joined Mackenzie's rebels. He was present during that first unhappy encounter below Bloor Street, and had scampered away with his frightened cohorts. Scared to death but determined to remain steadfast in the cause, he stuck with Mackenzie and Lount at Montgomery's tavern until the militia arrived on December 7 to scatter the rebel force and send its remnants into flight. Jimmy had been spotted and identified. And pursued. Cobb returned from work that evening to find Jimmy cowering beside the fireplace and Dora wringing her hands.

What could be done? If Cobb were found to be harbouring a rebel fugitive, he could lose his job and his sole livelihood. He had taken an oath to uphold the law and already was feeling guilty for taking a pot-shot at the moon. But blood was blood.

This was Dora's sister's boy, foolish or not. No decision had yet been taken, however, when Fabian rushed in to say that a squad of militiamen was a block away and headed towards the house.

It was Dora, apparently, who devised the plan. She took Jimmy, a skinny and beardless youth, into her bedroom. The children were sent off to the neighbours out the back door, while Cobb waited alone for the troop to arrive. To his astonishment and dismay, it was led by the infamous Colonel MacNab himself. The colonel was polite but determined. The fugitive was known to be his wife's relative and had been seen earlier in the afternoon in the eastern part of town. He asked if the lad was present and, if not, whether Cobb had seen him. Cobb gave a curt no to each question. Was Mrs. Cobb at home? Yes, but she was seriously ill and could not be disturbed. A young female cousin, her nurse, was sleeping with her.

This reply seemed to deepen MacNab's suspicion, and he demanded to be allowed to examine every room in the house, including the mistress's bedchamber. Each room was duly searched while Cobb continued to plead with the colonel that his wife was far too ill to be disturbed. MacNab announced that he himself would enter the sick-room and check it out: Cobb's pleas had only fuelled his resolve. While his nervous underlings looked on, MacNab jerked open the door of the forbidden bower and strode manfully in.

"Well, sir, he come scuttlin' outta there backwards, faster than a crawfish with the heebie jeebies. All his medals was a-janglin', and his eyes were bulgin' like a throttled cock's. And he's tossin' out a string of the foulest curses you ever heard, all the while steerin' his bum towards the front door with his troop all a-goggle and a-gawk. He finally stops retreatin' when his arse hits the door-latch, then he turns to me and—wonder of wonders—makes a humble apology. He ain't been seen east of Parliament Street since!"

Both Cobbs roared with laughter and were soon joined by a filial echo from behind one of the bedroom doors. What Colonel MacNab—commander of the Yonge Street counterattack and instigator of the burning of the *Caroline* off Navy Island— saw when he violated the privy chamber of Dora Cobb was this: two women lying comatose and only partly covered by an eiderdown—one of them Rubenesque and bare-bosomed, the other skinny-framed but discreetly gowned and bonneted. The sight of Dora's promethean breasts, all but the nipples in vigorous view under the moonlight streaming through the window, would of itself have been shock enough for even the most battle-bitten officer, but the red splotches thereupon and those on her neck and cheeks were as terrifying as the plague itself. Dora kept her "pox" in place for the five days, until the city settled somewhat and Jimmy Madden could slip away undetected into the anonymity of the countryside.

"And we ain't seen hide nor hare of the lad since," Cobb said.

"Mister Cobb kept sayin' it was the best use of my face-paint he'd yet seen!" Dora chuckled. "I looked like a *hip-an'-pot-moose* with the measles!"

"The whole thing give us quite a fright," Cobb said, suddenly serious. "But what else could we do, Major?"

That was a question Marc had been compelled to ask himself on more than one occasion in the past few months.

* * *

Marc slept in once again. He took a late breakfast with the widow and Maisie. They both mentioned that today was the day the gibbets would be completed in the Court House square, in time for the hangings scheduled for the next morning. It was clear from their faces that neither approved of hanging in general or the hanging of Matthews and Lount in particular. Marc decided to walk along King Street to Beth's shop, for that was where she had indicated she would go as soon as she arrived by coach from Niagara. He turned south at Bay and entered the service lane that ran behind the shops on the south side of King. The entrance to Beth's apartment was off the lane, and he was certain he would see wood-smoke coming from the rear chimney if she were home. But the back windows were all dark, and the chimney-pot cold and ugly.

Marc felt he could no longer delay his return to the regiment and the difficult interview he must have with Colonel Margison. He walked somewhat aimlessly along the lane towards Yonge Street at the far end. He thought he could hear the pounding of hammers from the direction of the Court House a block farther east. Before reaching Yonge he turned into an alley between two of the King Street shops, a regular shortcut. He heard footsteps behind him but paid them little heed. It was not until the hand struck his shoulder and tried to hurl him against the nearest brick wall that he realized he was in danger. In a purely reflex action, he lurched away from the pressuring hand and, luckily, avoided the blow that would have knocked his shako silly and him unconscious.

Marc heard the "ooof" of the assailant's breath and the crack of the weapon against the brick as it grazed his forehead and spun him partly around. His cap went flying. Marc threw one arm up to ward off the next blow, but it did not come immediately. Instead, a powerful set of fingers gripped him by the neck and began to lift him off the ground. He gagged and lashed out with his boots, hitting nothing but air. He still could not see the attacker, who must somehow be twisted to one side of him. Hot, angered breath was striking him behind the left ear.

"I been waitin' a long time fer this! You're a bitch of a man to corner, but I got you now, ain't I?"

Marc tried to respond, but the fingers on his throat refused to ease their murderous grip.

"Got nothin' to say, eh? After what you done to my brother!"

Marc could not breathe. The bare, callused fingers were pressing deeply into his throat, and a thumb was squeezing his larynx with enough force to shatter it. One more ounce of pressure and it would burst, killing him instantly. But he had no strength to wriggle free or fight back, even with the adrenaline-rush surging through him. He was not the man he had once been.

"I can throttle you like a pullet, or I can beat yer brains out with this club. You got any preference?"

For a moment Marc found his throat free from those deadly fingers, but he was unable to utter a word, even as he heard the homicidal whisper of the assailant's sleeve being raised for the final, fatal strike.

It never arrived. The villain gasped, then released a long, simmering sigh. His weight slowly collapsed against Marc's left side. Reluctantly, the fingers relaxed their death-grip. He felt the assailant's body slither downward past his own. Marc himself was saved from falling into the snow by a pair of bracing hands: different hands, kinder hands. He blanked out.

When he opened his eyes moments later, someone was splashing snow gently against his face.

"Jesus, Major. You ain't been in town a day and already you got someone riled up enough to knock yer noggin inta next week!"

"Cobb?" The word came out as a raw whisper from Marc's aching throat.

"Well, you're on my patrol, ain't ya? I hope ya wasn't expectin' Wilkie?"

The assailant let out a wheezy groan next to Marc.

Cobb turned to the villain, rolled him over, and attached manacles to his wrists. "Head as hollow as a coconut—" Cobb interrupted himself. "Jesus, I know who you are!"

Dazed and still seeing a colourful array of stars, Marc leaned over to have a look at the man so determined to kill him.

"You been callin' yerself McGinty, ain't ya?" Cobb shouted at the unconscious man. Then he turned to Marc. "This is the fella I was tellin' you about, Major—the one I caught stealin' a pig at Government House. His real name's Calvin Rumsey, from Buffalo."

Marc stared. His vision was starting to clear. Yes, this definitely could be the brother of Philo Rumsey, the man who had been involved in the death of Councillor Moncreiff a year ago last June. A man who might have good reason to hate him.

Cobb picked up Marc's shako cap. His eyes lit up as a new thought struck him. "Say, this must be the guy that tried to kill you on yer way home. I wondered why he ain't been seen around here since December. We just figured he'd scuttled back to Buffalo."

"Thanks, Cobb. You've saved my life—again."

"Part of the service, Major." Cobb prodded Rumsey with his right boot. "And this fella's got a date with the magistrate. So I guess you won't haveta keep a watch on yer back no more, will ya?"

But Marc didn't answer: he had toppled against the wall.

"Say, Major, are you okay?"

Marc was in the midst of answering, "I'm just fine," when he leaned over and retched.

SEVENTEEN

Marc spent the next six hours being swaddled, coddled, and otherwise overcared-for by Mrs. Standish and young Maisie, the former having an undue reverence for the authority of a uniform and the latter an equally undue reverence for its particular occupant. The blow to the head had been absorbed partly by the shako cap and the brick wall next to it, so that beyond an unsightly bump and a short-lived headache, no real damage had been done. The strangulation marks on the throat, however, proved least susceptible to treatment, though a warm bath and soothing poultices went a ways towards easing much of the pain and some of the indignity. That the perpetrator should be hanged, drawn, and quartered was proclaimed to the walls of every room of the boarding-house, their previous conviction against hanging notwithstanding.

There was considerable consternation among the distaff members of the establishment when the patient rose from his near-death bed, donned that reverence-inducing uniform, and asked Maisie ever so nicely if she would mind walking over to the livery stables at Government House and engaging a one-horse cutter to take him to the garrison. Maisie did not mind in the least.

Half an hour later the transportation arrived in front of the widow's porch. Marc was feeling so wonderfully recovered that he dismissed the driver with a shilling and took the reins himself. He wanted to be entirely alone as he drove the cutter south to Front Street and swung west until he reached the snow-packed path that wound its way through pretty stands of ever-green and wide stretches of marsh-ice towards Fort York. There was still an hour of brilliant light left before the sun would sink southwesterly over the vast lake.

When Marc had first arrived here, like most newcomers he had found that the brooding, primeval forests seemed to push all thought inward on itself while the freshwater seas without horizons sucked it outward to endless emptiness. But now, feeling almost native, he found a lonely drive like this—under va-cant skies and over blank tundra, where snow alone defined the landscape—most conducive to serious meditation. And he had much to think about. Relieved at last of the burden of being stalked, Mark was free to reflect on what it was he was going to say to Colonel Margison.

* * *

"This is a decision, Lieutenant, that should not be taken hastily, especially so soon after your first engagement and an injury such as you received in the line of duty."

They were closeted in Colonel George Margison's study. Whiskey and cigars having been aborted by mutual consent, the two men, who knew each other well, sat down opposite each other and without ceremony began to talk seriously about the matter at hand.

"I agree, sir. But during the many weeks of my convalescence in Montreal, I had nothing else to do but think."

"Very true. And I have also known you to be a very thoughtful, highly intelligent and supremely rational officer. But that is precisely my point: you have the potential to be a true leader in Her Majesty's army. Your ability, diligence, and devotion to duty have already won you one promotion, and I have little doubt that your heroic actions at St. Denis will see you made captain. Courage and presence of mind under fire and impeccable judgement—that is a rare combination. I am simply asking you, Marc, not to throw away the nearly five years of your life that you have dedicated to a military career, a career for which, in my humble opinion, God appears to have moulded you."

"I do appreciate the confidence you have shown in me, sir. But it is precisely because I have doubts that I can live up to the demands of being an officer that I am giving serious consideration to leaving this profession."

"You are referring to the grim business of ordering soldiers into situations where they are likely to be killed or maimed in front of you or beside you. But that is a common reaction during any first engagement. If you didn't have doubts, you wouldn't be human—or an effective officer."

"I believe I can cope with that aspect of warfare, sir, especially if I am willing to expose myself to the same dangers."

"As you amply demonstrated at St. Denis."

Marc hesitated, searching for the right words to continue. "At first I had great difficulty convincing myself that a ragtag collection of farmers and tradesmen was actually an enemy army like the French regulars. But when they started pointing muskets at us and one of our gunners collapsed beside me with a hole in his chest, then I had no qualms about what I was expected to do at St. Denis."

"What continues to trouble you, then?" The colonel seemed genuinely puzzled.

"It was the next week, when we returned and found no opposition. I presumed we would be asked to occupy the town, secure it, and re-establish the Queen's law."

"And you were not?"

"We were. But in addition we were ordered to raze the homes and destroy or confiscate all the property of any known rebels. As we knew little about any of them, beyond their leaders, Nelson and Papineau, we had to rely on vengeance-seeking loyalists pointing the finger at anyone they might have a grudge against."

"Yes, that is standard procedure after a victory, though in most cases we are looking at military stores and potential fortifications. In a civil conflict, it is more likely to be houses and barns."

"I found it deeply disturbing to burn the barns and seize the cattle of starving citizens, many of them women and children."

"Nevertheless, you did execute your duty, son. Remember that. You were gravely wounded while preparing to clear a rebel residence prior to torching it. And even though you found your orders to be morally distasteful and perhaps inherently unjust, you were, in fact, carrying them out, to the letter."

Marc had no reply because, as he had confessed to James Durfee, only his being shot had forestalled his having to make the decision to obey or ignore those orders. He did not know, then or now, what he would have done if Sergeant Ogletree had raised the torch and prepared to burn down that cabin.

"Hear me out on this, Marc. Please. You are still a long way from recovery from your injuries and subsequent illness. Decisions made immediately after a battle or the trauma of a wound are rarely sound ones. I am ordering you to take at least another month's leave before returning to active duty. Get yourself married. Invite me to the wedding. Discuss your future with Beth and with an old hand like Major Jenkin, who will be back here in a week. Then come and see me, and we'll have this talk again."

"You are very kind, sir."

"And should you then choose to leave, I can arrange for you to be invalided out at half pay."

"No, sir. That's generous of you—considering the bit of a limp I have—but I would feel right about it only if I were simply to resign my commission. I have recently come into some money, so I don't really need a pension."

"Having money doesn't mean you have to give it away," the colonel said with a wry smile.

"But I feel I must do the honourable thing."

"Why does that not surprise me?" The colonel rose and shook Marc's hand.

At the door he smiled and said, "And try to stay out of alleys, Lieutenant."

The sun was just going down as Marc approached the western outskirts of the city. A garish vermilion light was washing across the wind-sculpted drifts that rolled pleasingly down to the lakeshore. Marc had the sensation of gliding weightless in a benign dream: for a few blissful moments he was without thought of any kind.

Then the cutter hit a rut, and Marc had to pull the horse sharply to the left to avoid tipping over. It was this sudden movement that allowed him to spot the rumpled outline of something in the snow beside the path, nearly obscured by a pair of drifts hemming it in. Marc stopped the cutter, got out, and walked back a few yards.

At first he thought it might be a dead deer, trapped in the snow and starving. A brief afternoon flurry had obscured the edges of whatever it was, leaving only the brown oblong of an animal's belly—or was it a cloth coat? He hurried up to it and began brushing the loose snow away. Animal or human, it was not moving. He ran his ungloved fingers across the exposed surface. It was cloth. Someone had crawled under a large woollen overcoat, or been left there. With a single thrust Marc pulled the coat up and tossed it aside. Below, encased in snow except where the coat had provided cover, lay a tiny human figure in homespun trousers, macintosh, and tuque, curled or clenched in the fetal position.

Gently, Marc rolled the body face up. It was a young woman. Her eyes were closed, and the skin on her cheeks cold. Marc placed two fingers to her throat. Nothing. He tried another spot and found a faint pulse. She was alive, barely.

To her credit the Widow Standish, as curious as any cat, asked no questions when Marc carried the half-frozen body of a young woman into her parlour and begged her to do whatever she could for her while he went in search of a doctor. However, by the time Dr. Angus Withers arrived an hour later, there was nothing for him to diagnose or treat. A series of increasingly warm baths had revived the patient and restored a healthy heartbeat. She had even taken a few tablespoons of chicken broth before falling into a recuperative sleep on the sofa near the fireplace in the parlour. Miraculously, the only frostbite was on each of her exposed cheeks and the tip of her nose. A pair of mukluks, fur mittens, and the tuque had protected the other extremities. Maisie had already administered the appropriate ointment.

"I don't think she could have been in that snowbank for more than three or four hours," the doctor opined at the door. "But contrary to popular opinion, snow can be a kind of insulation. They tell me the Esquimaux live comfortably in snowhouses."

Marc thanked Angus and went into the living-room. There was something familiar about the woman, and he wanted to be present when she woke up. "I'll keep watch, Mrs. Standish. You and Maisie have had enough nursing for one day."

"Very well, sir," the widow replied, not quite sure if she ought to leave a man as handsome as Marc alone in a room with a female creature of unknown pedigree. But her reverence for the tunic won out. "Maisie and me'll just be next door."

"She'll need to be moved to one of your guest-rooms, ma'am. I'll pay for her board."

"You're the only guest we got at the moment. There's plenty of space."

"Thank you. By the way, did she say anything to you while you were helping bring her back?"

"Oh, yes, sir. Mind you, her voice was pretty weak, but she did talk."

"And?"

"We didn't catch a word of it. It was pure gibberish!"

Marc had dozed off. Supper had come and gone, and still the stranger slept, breathing deeply, her youthful body very much concerned to restore itself whatever the rest of her might wish. Mrs. Standish and Maisie had gone to bed. When Marc awoke from his pleasant cat-nap, the clock in the corner said 9:35. The fire had died down, but its embers still radiated a glowing heat. Three candle-lamps provided ample illumination. Marc pulled his chair up beside the sofa and examined the countenance of the sleeper.

She had thick black hair that, when fluffed out, would cascade in waves about her diminutive, heart-shaped face and caress her shoulders. Her facial features were similarly tiny, but beautifully proportioned. Even with the paleness that must have been the consequence of her brush with death, her complexion was dark. Her eyes, when they chose to reveal themselves, would be dark as well.

What on earth had she been doing out there at the edge of town? Had he passed her unknowingly on his way out to the fort? From her clothing, now tucked safely away, it was clear she was not impoverished. Two shillings had been discovered in her coat pocket. She was well fed and healthy looking: a young female in her prime. Yet she had not accidentally tumbled into those drifts. Her coat had been deliberately removed—by her or someone else—and she had curled herself up under it. To rest? Or to die?

Without warning the eyelids fluttered up, and a pair of black eyes peeped out—surprised, puzzled, wary—but very much alive. Marc stared. The eyes he was scrutinizing, and beginning to recognize, likewise began to focus in on the face before them.

"Isabelle LaCroix, *n'est-ce pas?*" he asked, hoping that his English-accented continental French would be understood.

Fear and astonishment contended in the look she gave him. "How do you know my name?" she asked in her own *joual.*

"Now we know each other's name. It's time, don't you think?"

She hardly dared to take her gaze off him, but did manage to glance about once or twice. "How did I get in this place?"

"I found you in a snowbank."

Tears overwhelmed her for several minutes. Marc offered

her his handkerchief, which she refused with a curt nod. "What right had you to save me from what I wished to do?"

"I had no idea who you were when I put you into my sleigh and brought you here to my landlady's house. It was Mrs. Standish and Maisie who brought you back to the living, not me."

She looked down at Maisie's flowered bathrobe. "I have no need to live."

"I thought it was God's prerogative to decide that sort of thing."

She peered up through her tear-filled eyes and said, coldly, "There is no God."

"I'll make us some tea," Marc said, starting to get up.

A small white hand shot out and grasped his wrist. "What do you intend to do with me?" she asked, suddenly afraid.

"You and I have unfinished business to discuss, haven't we?"

As quickly as it had come, the fear vanished and was instantly replaced by a glint of the fire and the undiluted hatred she had flashed across the cabin just before the bullet struck his thigh.

"For example, why have you been trying to kill me?" he asked.

"You murdered my lover," she said, spitting out the words.

"For that, I am truly sorry. I have been sorry every day since. But you know, as I do, that your lover had two pistols trained on me, one of which he fired while preparing to finish me off with the other."

"You were going to burn down—" She didn't complete the sentence. Her face crumpled. She dropped her head into her hands and wept.

Marc went to the kitchen, where Mrs. Standish had left a big kettle simmering on the wood-stove, and made tea. He filled two mugs and went back into the parlour.

Isabelle LaCroix had drawn her knees up and was resting her chin on them, with a woollen afghan wrapped around her legs. She had stopped crying. She took the mug of tea from Marc without looking at him, and sipped at it.

"I think it would be good for you if you just told me about it," he said gently.

For a minute he thought she had decided to say nothing more, simply curl up inside herself as she had tried to do with her body in the snowbank. But after a while she started to talk, slowly and hesitantly at first, but soon with vigour and purpose. "My Pierre is dead, and I have ruined what was left of my life. In the cabin, I thought you were dead, too. If not, I would have done something terrible then and there. But his mama and I rushed over to him. You shot his voice away. He was trying to tell me he loved me, but you shot all the words away."

"Tell me, please: did they burn down the house?"

The question seemed to startle her, interrupting the necessary flow of her own memories. "No," she said. "They didn't. I don't know why. It's still there. At least it was the day I left."

Perhaps I was never meant to burn down houses, Marc thought.

"After they put Pierre into the ground, I went up to Sorel. I heard the stories of the hero of St. Denis. I found out who he was."

"And you came, on your own, to Montreal? To find him and—?"

She looked over at Marc as if to say there was nothing unusual or surprising about what she had set out to do. "It was easy to get a job as an aide at the hospital. They paid us almost nothing, because we were French. At first they didn't think you would live. Then you woke up. I tried to keep out of your sight until—"

"Until you got your chance. Then one night while I was still helpless, you tried to drive a bayonet through my chest."

She looked at him again, but there was no hatred in her eyes now, just bewilderment, as if she had been living a nightmare and unexpectedly been awakened from it.

"Yes, but it was dark, and I was very afraid. The knife stuck in the wood. I couldn't get it out right away. When I did, I dropped it and then just turned and ran. I never came back. I told the big nurse I was sick. After a couple of days she sent me away, without my pay."

"And you need to tell me all this now."

"What does it matter? My life is over. What was left after Pierre died is now gone." She gave him a look that was half pleading and half rueful. "You should've left me to freeze."

"But how did you get all the way to Toronto, all these weeks later? You could not have been the one who shot at me near the river at Cornwall."

"I went back home. I took my dowry, and I came back to Montreal. My parents begged me not to go. The priest railed against me. Pierre's mama got down on her knees. But I had no life except to kill the one who killed my lover, then join him."

"In purgatory?"

"In Hell," she hissed, and the effort caused her to slump

back against the embroidered pillows. Marc held the mug for her, and she drank.

"So you got a pistol?"

"No. I hooked up with a group of *patriotes* from Lachine. After that awful day up at St. Eustache, that was their only way of fighting back. We knew all about you. When you left the city, we were right behind you."

"So it was they who set up the barricade, hoping I might wander a few steps too far from safety?"

"And you did, didn't you? But it was snowing. The men were afraid of that officer in the fancy uniform. When the first shot missed, they ran straight back to the river."

"But you didn't." It wasn't a question.

"They would not go farther into English territory. I thanked them and went on alone."

"But you are a woman and French-speaking. How could you survive and keep track of my movements?"

"I had money. And in the back concessions along the big river all the way to Gananoque, there are many French farms and woodlots. We have no difficulty recognizing one another."

"But how could you explain being there on your own, an unmarried young woman?"

"I gave a story about cousins in Belle Rivière."

"But you had no idea where I'd be."

"I kept ahead—walking, hiring rides, keeping away from the main road. I got to Prescott, found a Quebec family about half a mile away from the inn, and waited. When the coach came, I hid in the woods behind and watched for you. I saw you in the room on the end. I borrowed a knife from the people who put me up, and after dark I climbed up there—I used to walk the ridgepole on our barn when I was twelve—and I went in and killed you."

"And immediately killed yourself."

She was not certain how she should take this remark. "When I thought you were dead, I did not feel as I expected to."

"Elated, you mean. Fulfilled. Righteous."

"No, I felt hollow inside. Sad. Ashamed. I'd spent half my dowry, and I was alone among strangers."

"You must have seen me alive afterwards?"

"Not really. I went back to the place where I'd been staying. I had to return the knife. They were very poor. One of the boys there delivered meat to the hotel kitchen. He came home that afternoon to tell us a soldier had been shot behind the inn. 'You mean stabbed,' I said. 'No,' he said, 'shot with a pistol. An older fellow in the Glengarry militia.' 'You mean the army lieutenant,' I said. 'Oh, no,' he said, 'that fellow wasn't in his tunic, but he was alive and helping the doctor with the body.'"

"But if you felt so badly after you thought you'd killed me, why did you continue to follow me?"

She looked up at him as if he might be the one to answer that bewildering question. "I don't know. I knew I had no more heart to kill. But I couldn't go home, could I? And I felt connected to you somehow. But I did promise myself that if I saw you come home here and be happy, with—"

"With my own beloved?"

"Yes," she whispered. "I thought then the courage to avenge Pierre might come back to me."

"When did you get here?"

"Yesterday. But I only had a little money left. I suddenly realized I had nowhere to go and nothing to go back to. I was feeling sick, a deep pain in my stomach. I'd forgotten to eat for two days. I took a room for the night in some shanty on the edge of town. But I went out in the cold yesterday afternoon, and I waited by the road to the fort. You didn't come with the other two soldiers. I walked back into town. I saw you go into this house with the lady who looked after me earlier."

"Where you are safe."

She began to weep again, the soft, persistent, purgative weeping of women everywhere.

"You followed me from here this morning?"

"Yes. I saw you looking up at that empty apartment, and I thought 'Your woman is dead or gone.' I tried to be glad."

"Then you must have seen that fellow try to kill me in the alley?"

"I saw him turn in there waving a big club. A policeman was passing by the end of the lane. I went up to him and motioned for him to go into the alley. Then I left, and ran."

Cobb had not informed Marc of this interesting coincidence.

"You ran all the way out of the city?" he asked.

"Yes. Into the lovely, soft snow. I had nothing left now. Not even my hating."

"We seem to have saved each other today," Marc said.

Isabelle LaCroix gathered what little strength she had left, and said, "I heard the landlady tell her maid the reason for the pain in my belly—they didn't know I understand a little English."

"You're with child?"

She looked down, more in resignation than embarrassment.

"Then you must live. You must go home to your own kind. I will give you enough money to travel back to St. Denis, comfortably. You may repay me, if you feel you must, when you get rich someday."

She did not cry. For the moment she had no more tears. "But why are you doing this for someone who tried to kill you?"

Marc took her hand. "Because I killed your beloved," he said.

EIGHTEEN

Marc dressed carefully in the solitude of his room, avoiding the mirror. He left money and instructions with Mrs. Standish for the care of Isabelle LaCroix, who was still sleeping in the widow's premier bedchamber. Then he walked out into the cold Saturday sunshine as if this were just any other winter's day in the province. Cobb must have been lying in wait for him, for Marc had just passed Simcoe Street, going east along the south side of King, when he heard the familiar and confident stride of the constable coming up behind him.

"I wasn't sure you'd want to come this mornin', Major," he said, without comment on Marc's attire.

"I wasn't sure myself."

"You must've seen plenty of these things in London in yer day."

"I had lots of opportunities, but I didn't take them up."

They walked side by side in silence across Bay Street, nearing Yonge. The streets ahead were rapidly filling with people, on foot, in sleds, and mounted, all funnelling into King and surging eastward towards the Court House. Marc and Cobb passed Beth's shop.

"Don't worry, Major. She'll be here."

"I know."

"The stage from Hamilton's not in yet."

On the other side of Yonge they were slowed by the crowds ahead of them. The boardwalks on either side were overflowing, and all the traffic on the road itself had ground to a halt in a tangle of horses, cutters, toboggans, and impatient sightseers.

"So, are ya really thinkin' of gettin' outta the army business?" Cobb enquired, nudging his way forward with the tip of his truncheon.

"I have been thinking of little else lately."

"But what in the world would ya do?"

Marc smiled. "Why would I have to do anything? I've got a thousand a year for life from Uncle Jabez. I could simply be an English gentleman abroad."

Cobb snorted and said, "It's too late fer that now."

"Oh? And why is that?"

"You been mixin' too long with the locals. It takes some of the shine off yer *softa-fi-cation*."

"You may be right."

There was a shout somewhere in the crowd ahead of them.

"I could always go back to lawyering."

"Shufflin' paper and *coun-soling* widows and orphans all day? I can't see it."

"Neither can I. But I might try for the Bar. Don't you think I'd look smart in a periwig and gown?"

"Well, you could talk the plaster off the walls, that's fer sure."

They were having to step off the boardwalk and onto the ice-runnelled street itself to make any progress, while dodging hooves and errant horsewhips. An even louder roar shook the morning air, part cheer and part dismay.

"A hurrah fer *My-dame Gullet-keen,*" Cobb said with disgust.

"I never imagined it would be like this."

They found a quiet space in the doorway of the chemist's shop.

"You could always help Beth run the hattery."

Marc smiled as best he could, knowing that this curious, curmudgeonly man, who had against all odds become his friend, was attempting to keep him distracted from the grim events about to unfold a few hundred yards from where they stood.

"I'm afraid politics have ruined our chances there."

"It's ruined pretty near everythin'."

A drum-roll rippled and shuddered up by the jail: the troops arriving.

"You could always try bein' a policeman," Cobb suggested.

"I haven't got the stomach for it."

Cobb glanced down at the wheel of flesh that circumnavigated his middle and was kept sturdy by a steady feeding of warm beer and pub-grub. "I can't see you bustin' heads and manhandlin' drunks, but Sarge tells me over in England the bobbies hire a body they call an investigator to come in and help them find a murderer. And that's all he does. If he catches the culprit, he gets ten pounds or so. If he don't, he hasta go home and live off the *a-veils.*"

"At that fee there would have to be a lot of murders and he'd have to solve most of them just to keep bread on the table and his kiddies in shoes."

Cobb feigned surprise: "But I heard you English are a particularly murdersome people."

"I'm going to try to get closer," Marc said, edging back out into the surging throng.

"I'll see ya later, then, Major."

"Where're you going?"

"Over to the station, if I can get that far. There's a felon in our cell I'd like to *purr-sway* inta confessin' his sins."

The Cobbs had told Marc about the trial of Samuel Lount and Peter Matthews. Both men had been lieutenants in Mackenzie's rebel "army," and had conducted themselves during the two encounters on Yonge Street in December with courage and dedication. Neither denied his involvement. Neither recanted his actions nor forsook the cause they had willingly taken up. Attempts were made to have the prisoners, particularly Lount, incriminate their fellow rebels in return for leniency. Each refused, and was sentenced to hang as the first and foremost example of the fate awaiting all traitors in Upper Canada. The Tories, by and large, cheered. However, moderate Reformers like Robert Baldwin and Francis Hincks, who had stood aloof from actual insurrection, now stepped forward to plead for clemency. A petition with eight thousand names on it was presented to the new lieutenant-governor, Sir George Arthur. But like his predecessor, Arthur had already succumbed to the vengeful demands of the Family Compact, despite the fact that Lord Glenelg, the colonial secretary in London, had been advocating a policy of conciliation and tolerance for almost three years. On a more personal note, Matthews and Lount, if hanged, would between them leave a total of twenty-two destitute children. All such pleas, however, were obdurately rejected.

At six feet, Marc was tall enough to see over the heads of the two hundred or so people who had come out to witness the hangings. He stood on the south-side boardwalk of King Street and looked north across the road and over the public square in front of the adjacent Court House and jail. A pair of gallows had been erected in the space between the two buildings, and the grisly procedure had already begun.

It turned out that Cobb had been wrong. This was not the French peasantry gathered here and baying for blood. The shout Marc had heard had apparently been a supportive cheer at the first appearance of the rebel-martyrs, tempered by dismay at the sight of them bound and stepping forthrightly towards the gallows. The second roar—of universal disapprobation—had been directed at the arrival of a squad of regulars and three mounted officers. But there was no need for a troop of soldiers to keep the crowd from disrupting the awful ceremony. Those gathered in the square had now become eerily silent, as if the reality of what they were about to witness had struck home all at once.

Each of the condemned men was accompanied by a clergyman. The hangman appeared without warning behind one of the gallows and mounted the platform linking them. The crowd began to murmur morosely, but Lount held up his hand as if to say It's not the hangman who's to blame, and the murmuring ceased. The prayers of the clergymen were audible as Sheriff Jarvis, with tears streaming down his face, led the prisoners up to their respective gibbets and to the nooses swaying patiently in the breeze. Matthews and Lount knelt over the trap, praying, as the hangman slipped the rope about their necks.

Beth's gloveless hand eased into Marc's. Without taking his eyes off the scene before him, he gave it a welcoming squeeze. He felt her head wisp against his shoulder.

"You're not in uniform," she said.

"No, I am not."

She curled his fingers lovingly in hers "It's time to go," she said. "We've had enough of sadness."

Still holding hands, they turned sedately and began walking away from the despair of the Court House square. They walked slowly down Church Street, as the Lord's Prayer drifted away behind them, growing fainter and fainter. They crossed Market Street, bereft of people, just as the communal groan and the snap of the trap and the plunging rope sickened the air and the innocent morning. A tiny shudder disturbed the linking of the lovers' hands, but they carried on to Front Street, where the snows had blurred the borders of land and lake, so that they scarcely heard the second cry of bereavement, the anguish consequent upon the doing of what can never be undone. Still, the lovers walked westward along the shoreline, letting the slate-and-stone edifice of the city slide away unregretted. Past the bulwark of the provincial bank, past the contentious benches of Parliament, past the last outpost of civility.

Without forethought or premeditation their feet found the meandering path westward across the ice to the frozen spit of the island, the waters between it and the shore sculpted and flumed by an arctic wind that cared only for the law and beauty of its own instigation. They let the circle of the island and its echoing emptiness take them up, and paired in their circumambulation they spoke of many things that lay between them—matters past and matters future—and were content to have silence subsume the things that could not yet be uttered. They found themselves thus at the far edge of the island at the far edge of the land at the far edge of everything. For the time being, the only allegiance they owed was to the love they bore for each other.

EPILOGUE

April, 1838
Iowa Territory

Dear Mr. and Mrs. Edwards:

*This is not my writing, but these are my words. Winn is
copying them down as they come out. We got your letter,
and we are glad you got married and bought a cottage
in the city. Things out here are swell. Thomas and me are
starting a big farm of our own. There's hardly any trees
to chop down (so don't worry, Beth). The ground is black
and easy to turn, I could do it with a spoon! Mr. Hatch
is using the money you sent to start up a little mill. He's
gonna let me work the floodgate! Winn and Mary are
having more babies this summer. The first boy baby will*

be named Aaron. Our Susie's got herself a beau. Some Indians come down from the hills a while back and sold us ponies. Mine is called Silky. That's all for now. I hope you're feeling as happy and free as we are.

Your loving brother,
Aaron

Look for
Bloody Relations
by Don Gutteridge

Coming from Touchstone
in 2013